DARE GAME

MELINDA COLT

Dare Game
Copyright© 2019 by Melinda Colt
ISBN: 9798875686702
Crime consultant: Detective Simon McLean, author of *The Ten Percent*

www.MelindaColt.com
Cover Design: www.CoveredByMelinda.com

This is a fictional work. All characters and events in this publication, other than those clearly in the public domain, are solely the concepts and products of the author's imagination or are used to create a fictitious story and should not be construed as real. Any resemblance to real persons, living or dead, is purely coincidental.

All rights reserved. No part of this book may be used or reproduced, stored in a retrieval system, or transmitted, in any form by any means, without the prior permission in writing, except in the case of brief quotations, reviews, and articles.

For any other permission, please visit www.MelindaColt.com for contact links.

Dare Game
An Irish Garda Squad Novel
Melinda Colt

"Justice doesn't always balance the scales, but it's the best we have." — J.D. Robb, *Survivor in Death*

1

There were shades to murder only a seasoned cop would catch — a skill not easily learned and impossible for the faint of heart to deal with.

Detective Inspector John O'Sullivan examined the crime scene with dispassionate eyes. During the twenty years he'd been working his way up the command ladder of An Garda Síochána, Ireland's police force, he'd disciplined himself to give that impression. Nothing could be further from the truth. In John's opinion, the moment you stopped caring, you should surrender your badge.

"The victim is Maureen McKenna, age forty-eight. She was a doctor." The young Garda who'd first responded to the crime looked quite green, literally and figuratively. It was probably the first murder the young officer was attending up close. For some cops, looking at dead bodies didn't become any easier with time.

O'Sullivan nodded.

"Her husband found her when he arrived home from work," the rookie guard continued his report. "He called the ambulance first, and they contacted us. They claim the man was incoherent and in shock, but he managed to tell them his wife had been shot."

"Bloody hell," John cursed. It was never easy when a family member found the victim. "Did he touch the body? Where is he now?"

"He's outside in the ambulance. The poor fella was downright banjaxed, sir. They've sedated him. He admitted to touching her face, taking her hand ... Her blood's all over him, so he probably pulled her into his arms. As I said, he's in shock and doesn't remember the sequence of events too clearly."

"Thanks. I'll talk to him soon. Did you call the Technical Bureau?" John asked, referring to the team of crime scene forensic officers.

"Yes, sir."

"Good lad. Go and tell the ambulance to stand by."

With a soft rustle of his disposable protective gear, John knelt beside the body, struggling to bottle up his emotions. Pity and sadness wouldn't do Maureen any good now. Of course, her husband had touched her, hugged her, tried to lift her up into his arms — it's what any man would do if he found the woman he loved with a hole in the middle of her forehead and another between her breasts, her clothing and the floor around her drenched in blood.

Maureen had been a pretty woman, but the blue eyes that stared unseeingly up at him were already milky. For a second, John had a flashback of another pair of beautiful eyes. There hadn't been any blood on Shanna's face, yet her eyes had remained lifeless nonetheless, no matter how much he'd screamed and cried. All he'd wanted was to kill the son of a bitch who'd taken her from him, and he was denied even that.

He blinked several times, shaking off the memories, putting them aside for now. He had a job to do. Maybe this time, he would be able to find closure for the man who'd lost his wife so tragically.

Refocusing his attention, he returned to studying the crime scene.

It wasn't fear he saw on Maureen's face but surprise. No one expected to be killed coming home from work on what could've been just an ordinary day. The blood splatter on the bookshelf behind her indicated she'd been shot in this room, collapsed onto her back, and probably died instantly.

John leaned closer to inspect her body. Other than the gunshot wounds, he saw no signs of violence or a struggle, no defensive wounds. Her clothes were intact, and there were no obvious signs of sexual assault, although the pathologist would have to verify that. It was as if the killer had just walked in and shot her — twice, to make sure she was dead.

But who? Why? Those were the million-dollar questions. In John's experience, the most common motives for this kind of murder were passion, money, and revenge. Crimes of passion usually involved rape and/or rage. There were no visible signs of either here, but he had to keep the possibility in mind and pursue it. Either Maureen or her husband could have had an affair that had somehow led to this tragic ending.

Or had money been the motive? This didn't seem to be the case either. Maureen wore a gold wedding set with an impressive diamond and an expensive-looking watch on her left wrist. If a burglar or thief had come to steal something, even if it was just a specific piece of art, he wouldn't have left Maureen's jewelry behind. Besides, thieves were rarely killers. In fact, they usually avoided weapons because if they were caught and convicted, being armed would add to their penalty.

On the other hand, her husband could have arranged this, especially if there were financial issues and a hefty life insurance policy. He'd need to check that out. So far, he had a lot of questions and no answers yet.

John paused in his musings when he noticed something

partially hidden under the body's left shoulder. "What the hell is that?"

He bent to take a closer look. A playing card — an Ace of Spades. Puzzled, he turned it over, barely touching it with his gloved hand. Although it was stained with fresh blood that had congealed, he saw a symbol handwritten in dark-blue ink on the back of the card. It looked like a capital G or a crooked C, crossed by two horizontal lines instead of one.

He turned to the Garda, who'd returned and stood silently next to the front door.

John showed him the card. "Any idea what this is?"

"No, sir. The husband said it was lying on his wife's chest when he found her. I assume it fell off the body as he moved her."

John studied it again. An unmistakable sense of dread knotted his stomach. This reminded him of a signature or calling card. If that was the case, this murder was personal, and Maureen McKenna was the specific target.

So what was this about then? Envy? Jealousy? Revenge?

"You said she was a doctor?" John asked the Garda.

"That's what her husband said."

"Did he mention what kind?"

"No, sir."

Could this be the work of a deranged patient? Someone with psychological issues who blamed the doctor for everything that had gone wrong in his or her life? It looked too tidy to be a crime of passion.

John put the card down again for the forensic team to analyze, then stood and walked carefully throughout the house. Everything was neat and well-kept — except for the body on the bloody floor in the living room. The bookshelves were loaded with books, knick-knacks, and memorabilia. Several painting-sized framed photos adorned the walls, portraying a happy Maureen, a smiling man John assumed was her husband, and two boys, who had inherited their mother's red hair. The photos spanned the years from the time the boys were babies until the most recent ones, indicating they were now in their late teens or early twenties. Telling those two young men their mother had been murdered was going to be heartbreaking. When they demanded to know who had committed this atrocity and why, John would have no answers. Not yet, but by God, he would get them.

Flexing his fingers, he turned to the officer once more. "Any signs of forced entry?"

"No, sir. I checked all the doors and windows. There's no alarm system or security camera. This is supposed to be one of Dublin's safest neighborhoods. It appears she opened the door and invited the killer in."

John nodded thoughtfully. "Have ye spoken to any of the neighbors? Did anyone see anything suspicious or hear gunshots?"

"No, sir. Most were just arriving home from work. I've only talked to the family next door, but they said they didn't hear anything unusual prior to the arrival of the ambulance. When they saw the lights, they ran over to see what the fuss was. They were close friends. They're with the victim's husband now."

"Okay, thanks. Either the killer knew no one would be around, or he used a silencer."

John turned toward the entrance as his partner, Detective Inspector Aidan Connor, rushed in.

"Sorry I'm late," Aidan said, sliding on a pair of disposable gloves. "I got stuck in the effin' traffic. What do we have here?"

"I figured as much. We've got a real puzzle." John briefed him, omitting his speculations about the playing card for now.

While they were talking, the door opened again, and several forensic officers came in.

"Hey, Nóirín, how ya doing?" John greeted the leader of the group.

"Hey yourself." Not one to waste time, Nóirín stooped to examine the body.

"We'll give you guys some space. We'll be outside if you need us," John said, following Aidan out the front door.

A while later, Nóirín joined John and Aidan on the front stoop. "Ye got a nasty one here."

Nóirín Dempsey was a pretty woman in her forties who resembled a plump little housewife rather than the sharpest crime scene investigator and forensic expert in Dublin. Her blond hair and rosy cheeks gave her a deceptively harmless appearance, but her keen observation skills were priceless to the Garda and had helped close dozens of cases. Experts in the field were hard to find, so she was a renowned detective within the Garda Technical Bureau.

"So, what do you think?" John asked, ignoring the gawkers who had gathered on the sidewalk.

Nóirín took off her goggles, pursed her lips. "Detective O'Sullivan, we have a murder."

"Wow. *Revelation* — the new edition. Give this woman an award." Voice dripping sarcasm, John glanced at his partner.

Aidan's eyes crinkled with humor. Droplets of rainwater gleamed in his dark hair. "You can't help but love a woman with a sense of humor," he said, putting a hand around Nóirín's shoulders. "You should see her when we assist an autopsy, and she starts making cracks about the body."

"I've seen her at it." John turned back to Nóirín. "The playing card was partially hidden under the body. The husband said it was left on her chest, but it probably slipped off when he tried to lift his wife into his arms."

"We've bagged and tagged it for you. We'll take a closer look at the lab, but I can tell you this is something new — and rather disturbing. Ye might want to show it to Jenna before I get my hands on it. Maybe she's seen this before or knows where to start looking for answers." She handed him the evidence bag.

Detective Jenna Darcy was the Garda's secret weapon, a cybercrime expert who could work miracles at a computer. In this day and age, officers like her had become priceless for mostly all police work.

"Complete haymes." John shook his head. "I need you to tell me everything you can about this. What do you have so far?"

"Not much. It's one of the cleanest crime scenes I've ever seen, even though it was compromised by the victim's husband. We'll see what the autopsy shows, but I didn't see any bruising or defensive wounds. No traces of assault either. I've collected her electronic devices — phone and laptop — and placed them into evidence. Jenna and her team can have a go at them to see if the victim was active on social media, see if someone had threatened or bothered her that way. So far, that playing card is the only unusual piece of evidence we have. Ace of Spades," she mused. "The most powerful card in the deck — or so they say. My people are still looking. We'll gather everything we can for ye."

Huffing out a breath, John squared his shoulders. "Thanks, Nóirín. I'll go and see what the husband has to say."

He walked to the ambulance. Its lights flashed intermittently, red as Maureen's blood, blue as her eyes. Mr. McKenna sat just inside the doors at the back of the vehicle, his bloodstained hands clenched in his lap, his shirt more red than white.

"Brian McKenna?"

The man's head lifted automatically, but it took a few seconds before his vacant eyes focused on John. "Yes."

"I'm Detective John O'Sullivan. I'm very sorry for your loss. I know it's a terrible time for you, but I need to ask you a few questions."

Brian covered his face with bloodstained hands and started

to weep. "Jesus, is she really — who did this to her? Who killed my wife?"

"That's what we're trying to find out, sir. Can you tell me what happened when you came home today?"

Brian spoke slowly, his voice distant as if he were trying to remember events from the long-forgotten past. "I got home at about five-thirty *iarnóin,* the way I do most days if I'm not stuck at work. I walked in and called out for Maureen to see if she was home. There was no answer, so I assumed she was still at work. Then, I went into the living room, and I saw her lying on the floor ... There was blood everywhere ..."

He started crying again, his uncontrollable sobs causing his shoulders to shake.

John's jaw tightened. He understood the man's pain, knew what he was going through. Reaching out, he squeezed Brian's arm. It was hard, but for Maureen's sake, he had to dig and push for information.

"Mr. McKenna, did Maureen have any enemies? Was there anyone who might want to harm her?"

Brian shook his head, lowering his hands from his face. There was a bloodstain on his cheek, another on his forehead, but John didn't wipe them away. He didn't want to distract the man from the questions. The poor fellow was sedated, shocked by grief, struggling to concentrate.

"Everyone likes Maureen," Brian said, his voice raspy with tears. "She's a grand doctor. She always takes a keen interest in all her patients, and she volunteers at the clinic for people who can't afford health insurance. She's ... she was ... an amazing person."

He pressed his fist to his mouth to suppress another sob.

John's heart ached for him, but he had to continue his questioning. The only thing he could do to help this man was to find the person who'd made him a widower and had left two boys without a mother. When he heard footsteps behind him, he turned to see Aidan walking toward them.

"Mr. McKenna, this is my partner, Detective Aidan Connor. We'll do everything we can to find out what happened to your wife. Now, are you sure all of her patients were happy with her? What kind of doctor was she?"

"A cardiologist."

John glanced at a sober-faced Aidan standing beside him. When he cocked an eyebrow, John knew they were thinking the same thing.

"That's a job with a lot of responsibility. Has she ever lost a patient?" John asked.

Brian looked at him, his eyes half-glazed. It took a few moments for him to reply. "I don't know ... All doctors lose patients, don't they? Maureen wasn't a surgeon. She was a consulting physician. If she suspected a serious problem in a patient, she would recommend careful tests and always a second opinion."

"Did she ever receive any threats, have trouble with anyone, either recently or in the past?" Aidan asked.

Brian shook his head again. "No, she never mentioned anything like that. And she would've told me ... She told me everything."

John shifted his weight from one foot to the other. Rain wasn't doing his rheumatism-tinged knees any good, but he couldn't afford to think about them now. He continued with his questions, "What about her life outside of work? What did she like to do in her free time? Did she have any hobbies?"

Brian shrugged slightly. "She didn't have a lot of free time. Between her job and the hours she spent at the clinic, she was pretty busy. We both are." He didn't seem to realize he was alternating past and present tense. "I'm a telecommunications engineer, so my job is just as demanding, but whenever we have a bit of free time, we spend it together. We love just sitting on the couch and watching movies or cooking together. Since both our sons left for college, it's been just the two of us ..." His voice trailed off, drowned in memories.

A door slammed, and an ambulance attendant appeared next to them. "Excuse me, but I want to take Mr. McKenna's blood pressure again," she said, proceeding to do just that. "'Tis a very bad shock he had. I believe he blacked out earlier."

"We'll leave you to it," John said, stepping aside to make room for the woman. "One last question ... for now, Mr. McKenna. Were you at work today, all day?"

"I was."

"Okay." He would check out McKenna's alibi, but at the moment, he didn't want to upset the man any further. Every gut instinct he had told him Brian hadn't killed his wife. "We're very sorry for your loss," John repeated, meaning it. "We'll be in touch as soon as we find out more about your wife's murder. I promise you we'll find the killer and make sure he pays."

Brian's brown eyes overflowed with tears as he looked up at the two men. "How will that bring her back?"

John lowered his gaze. It was an all-too-common question. The platitudes he could offer seemed phony and empty. The truth was that most of the time, he had trouble finding a good answer himself.

Always by his side, Aidan answered for him. "Unfortunately, it won't. All we can do is find and punish the people who did this terrible thing. While it might be enough in the eyes of the law, we know it's never enough for those who've lost a loved one. But when criminals are brought to justice, it gives the survivors a sense of closure. We're very sorry, Mr. McKenna." Aidan looked at the house and property surrounded by yellow police tape. "Is there anywhere you can stay for a few days?"

Brian didn't seem to understand the question, so John clarified, "Your house is a crime scene, and the forensics will be there for a while, looking for evidence. You won't be able to stay there until we've cleared it. Do you have any friends or family you can stay with for a few days?"

Brian wet his dry lips, then shrugged slightly. "I suppose I can stay with Eughan and Tara. They're our next-door neighbors," he said, weakly lifting a hand to point out the couple who stood a few yards away, giving them privacy.

"That's good. You'll be hearing from us as soon as possible," John promised.

He and Aidan turned and started walking toward their police cars. It was still drizzling, but the clouds had parted a little to let a frail ray of evening sunlight peek through. Since most people had returned from work, more gawkers had gathered on the sidewalk, talking in whispers. John watched them, making mental notes of what he saw in each person's eyes — curiosity, uneasiness, pity, even fear. He saw a man in a black robe and slippers sliding an arm around his wife's shoulders and pulling her close to him. His gaze reflected gratitude because he wasn't the one sitting in an ambulance, covered in his dead wife's blood.

"What do you think?" Aidan jarred him out of his musings, leaning against the car and lighting a cigarette.

"Looks bad."

"Don't they all?"

"Yeah, but I have a feeling about this one, mate, and it's not good." John described the playing card to his partner and shared the suspicions he had.

Aidan frowned — something he often did, but he also smiled a lot, the deep indents in his cheeks balancing his expressive face. Most women would call those lines wrinkles, but in Aidan's case, they seemed to make him even more attractive to the opposite sex. At forty-three, he was two years older than John but looked almost a decade younger.

"What the hell could it mean, John?" Aidan asked.

"If I'm not mistaken, it's the killer's business card," John said thoughtfully. "Come on. The Gardaí only spoke to the people next door. Let's ditch these suits and start the door-to-door questioning ourselves."

Talking to the victim's neighbors was a monotonous job but often useful, with the potential of producing a lead that could help solve the case. It was something that had to be done asap, and Maureen McKenna's murder demanded a thorough investigation.

"You take the left side of the street; I'll take the other," John said. "If we're incredibly lucky, maybe someone saw or heard something."

"Right." Aidan exhaled smoke, narrowing his eyes when a wisp of wind blew it back in his face. "That kind of luck comes only when you sell your soul to the Devil."

2

Hayley Jones threw herself on the bed and stared out at the raindrops that slid down the windowpane. *Does it ever do anything other than rain in this country?* She'd been in Ireland only two days, and she already hated it and her mother for dragging her away from everything that mattered and bringing her to this God-forsaken place.

The sound of an ambulance and police cars caught her attention briefly, but she ignored it. Probably an accident. They happened everywhere.

Returning to her sulking, she wondered why *she* should be the one to suffer because her mother and father got divorced. It wasn't fair. Okay, so she hadn't paid a lot of attention to their relationship — what kid did? They'd seemed happy enough. They were Mom and Dad, parents just like everyone had and took for granted — until her father had moved out and left her with her mother. She'd hoped it was a temporary thing, that they would get back together, but there was no going back now. Her mother had insisted they move here, hoping she would accept the situation. Hayley couldn't hate it more. This dreary place was going to drag the life right out of her.

Even in this day and age, as hokey as it sounded, there hadn't been anyone in her class at the school she'd attended in New York City whose parents were divorced. One girl's parents had been living together for twenty years, and they weren't even legally married, but no one talked about that. The minute word got out that her parents were divorcing, that was all her classmates could gossip about. They stared at her as if she'd suddenly grown two heads. One by one, they began to avoid her, even the girls who used to be her best friends. During breaks, she sat alone. At lunch, she ate alone, like a pariah. She'd never been so lonely, so embarrassed.

Then, a miracle happened. She met Amy. Amy was a bad girl, the kind of girl who had green highlights in her hair and lots of piercings, the kind of girl everyone avoided but secretly wanted to be like.

Amy didn't give a shit about anyone. She smoked, drank, cursed, wore only black, listened to punk rock and metal music, and she was never without black eyeliner highlighting her green eyes. She looked like one of the witches from *The Craft* — Hayley's favorite old movie — a girl who did what she wanted, when she wanted, and screw the consequences.

When Amy spoke to her for the first time, Hayley was flattered. She'd been sitting on a bench in the schoolyard, watching her classmates play basketball. It had been one of *those* days, so she'd asked the teacher to be excused. She hated sports, and whenever she could, she lied about her periods, but the old creep actually kept a calendar with his students' menstrual cycles. How perverted was that? In any case, she couldn't get away with that excuse too often.

She'd been silently cursing the teacher when Amy had strolled over to her. In black leather pants, black boots, and a Black Sabbath T-shirt, she looked out of place among all the other girls dressed in pink, blue, or white.

"Want one?" she'd asked her, turning her hand discretely to show the cigarette she'd palmed.

And so it had begun, the best friendship Hayley had ever had. If her mother had taken just one look at Amy, she would have forbidden her from having anything to do with *that girl*. That was why Hayley had never invited Amy home and had never mentioned her to her mother. Amy was fun, a little crazy, totally reckless — definitely a forbidden-fruit kind of friend. But Amy knew how to listen when Hayley bitched about her problems and always seemed to understand her.

Amy's mother was a druggie, and her dad had left them before Amy was born. Unlike Hayley, Amy didn't dwell on it. She'd learned to be tough, which was what Hayley liked most about her. What would happen to their friendship now that she was stuck in Ireland?

Jesus, she was going to die here! In New York, there'd always been something to do, something to see, places to go and hang out. What would she do here? Watch the grass grow and the rain fall? And try to guess what people were saying?

Feeling more depressed than ever, she stretched out on the bed. It was only eight pm, but she was tired as hell. She fished out her phone from her pocket and started writing a message to Amy. At least her mother had had the decency and commonsense to arrange for cellphone service and internet for this place.

Hey, girlfriend. How are you doing? Hope you miss me already, just a little. I know I miss you. I'd give anything for us to hang out at your place now. I'd kill for a smoke! You have to be eighteen to buy cigarettes here, and you get carded, so it'll be hard for me to get any, especially with my mom on my back all the time, sniffing at me like a bloodhound.

She hesitated a bit on the last phrase. Actually, she really didn't like smoking, but Amy did, so she'd pretended to enjoy it just as much. Maybe it wasn't such a bad thing that she couldn't smoke anymore. Amy also smoked pot now and again, but Hayley had never tried it. She didn't know what had stopped her, but something in her subconscious always drew the line at experimenting with drugs.

It's cloudy and rainy here — what a fucking surprise! The house we rented is ancient and has two bedrooms. I picked the one closest to the bathroom. LOL. I like the double bed, and there's a large dresser — not that I have much to put in it anymore. There's a TV, too, and we can pick up some American channels, which I hope will make the time I spend here more bearable. It's incredibly cold for June, it's like March in NY, but my mom says we'll get used to it. She tries to be cheerful like this whole stupid thing is an adventure or something. I'm so sick of her treating me like a kid! I'd give anything to have your mom instead. At least she really is cheerful all the time, and she never nags you to do your homework, do your chores, clean your room, blah, blah, blah ...

Anyway, let me know how you are. I'm sorry we couldn't hang out last week, but things were crazy. The realtor and the new owners came to see the house twice, then after they closed the deal, we had to sort out every little thing, pack what we wanted to take, then give the rest away. I can't believe my home isn't my home anymore. My life has gone to shit. I wonder what will happen next. Sometimes ... Sometimes, I wish I could just die.

She pressed *send* without rereading the email.

Yawning, she stood and undressed, digging out a pair of pajamas from the dresser drawer. At least she'd unpacked — who cared if she'd just shoved everything away? Looking outside, she saw a police car and ambulance across the street. Someone had probably had a heart attack or something. Tough luck for them.

Pulling down the comforter, she curled up in bed and gave a satisfied groan. This bed was bigger than her old one. It might even be more comfortable, but she missed her own bed and sheets and blankets. Everything in this house had either been rented with the place or purchased yesterday during the shopping trip from hell.

How could her mother be so clueless? It had taken nearly two hours to find all the things on their list — no small feat since chicken scratch was easier to read than her mother's writing. Hayley couldn't understand why her mother insisted on using pen and paper instead of typing the list on her phone. The woman lived in another century.

As it had turned out, Hayley had to get a second cart to hold the bulkier items, like pillows, blankets, towels, glasses, dishes, and silverware. By the time they'd reached the checkout, people were checking them out, either amused or baffled.

Despite her defiant smirk, Hayley was flooded by mortification, which made her want to shrink. She didn't like drawing attention to herself, and that was exactly what they'd done. Mom had ignored the mutters behind them about: *some people buying the entire store.* She was actually grateful when they'd escaped to the parking lot and managed to stuff everything into their tiny red rental.

Hayley hadn't recognized the make — probably some European model — but the damn thing resembled a toy compared to their old car — a sleek black SUV she'd expected to be able to drive by the end of the summer. Something else that would never happen because her mother couldn't even dream of affording such a car now. Besides, one would have to be seventeen to get a driver's license here, so Hayley had one more year to wait. How stupid was that?

Eyelids drooping, she reached for her phone to check her messages — not that she expected any. Her heart jumped with joy when she saw an email from Amy. She tapped the screen and read it:

Hi, Hal! I'm so glad you wrote me. Sorry you're bummed out. I didn't know if I should call you last week since you had to spend so much time with your mom. I wish I could've said goodbye properly, but hey, life sucks, right? Anyway, I've got something SUPER COOL to show you, something that will chase all your blues away. I'm going to let you in on an online game, but you have to swear to keep it a secret. It's, like, super important that you don't tell anyone and that your mom doesn't find out. EVER! I'm going to give you the link, but make sure you use a Tor browser to access it.

All at once, Hayley was wide awake. People used Tor browsers to surf the Dark Web, which was the most dangerous side of the internet. She'd never visited the Dark Web, but she'd heard stories about it. Everything she saw on the news and much worse went on there — drug trafficking, contract killers, prostitution, child pornography, gun trade, and other stuff she didn't even want to know about. She'd heard some of the kids talk about it at school, but she'd assumed they were just bragging. Could she really check out this dark, secret side of the World Wide Web for herself? A twinge of excitement filled her as she finished reading Amy's message.

Here's the link to The Game. You'll have to create an account and wait for approval. Once you get it, let me know. Hayley, this is the most awesome game ever! Trust me, there's no way you'll be bored anymore once you're in. Give me a call when you manage to get rid of your mom for five fucking minutes. Miss you! Amy

The message ended with a line of a URL Hayley had never seen. She stared at her phone screen, chewing one of her short nails. What was this game Amy was so excited about? If she had asked her to use a Tor browser, it meant whatever links she accessed would be untraceable, and there would be no browsing history in her laptop of the websites she visited.

Slowly, she placed the phone back on her nightstand and switched off the bedside lamp. Yawning, she plopped back onto the pillow. She was still smiling when she fell asleep. For the first time in a long while, she went to bed, looking forward to waking up in the morning. She couldn't wait to learn what The Game was all about!

JOHN HAD KNOCKED on doors for the better part of an hour and had interviewed all the homeowners. This was his last hope. The house was almost directly across from the murder scene. Aidan had started from the other side and hadn't gotten to this one yet, so John took the lead. If anyone had seen anything, it would be whoever lived here. He rapped on the door and waited.

While he did, his cop's eye took in every detail of the small brick house with its tidy yard sporting beds of blooming roses. The compact red car parked in front of the house bore rental plates, so it was possible whoever lived inside was renting the house as well.

After a few moments, a woman opened the door cautiously, holding a dishcloth in one hand.

She was tall and slim, dressed in a T-shirt and a pair of baggy track pants. Her hair was short, an unruly mix of blond and brown, cut in a way that framed her face. She had rather spectacular gold-brown eyes, currently filled with suspicion and surprise as she gazed at him from under raised eyebrows.

"Yes? Can I help you?" Her accent was clearly American.

John held up his badge to her.

"Sorry to bother you, ma'am. I'm D.I. John O'Sullivan from An Garda Síochána. I'm investigating the murder of one of your neighbors, Maureen McKenna. Can you answer a few questions for me?"

Stunned by his words, her knuckles went white as she clutched the dishcloth, unconsciously lifting it to her chest.

"Murder? Here?" she breathed the words, worry suffusing her face.

"Yes. We believe it happened a few hours ago, maybe late this afternoon." He wouldn't know for sure until he had the time of death from the pathologist, but the woman hadn't gone into rigor, so it was as good a guess as any.

Her lips parted in shock as she seemed to notice for the first time the neighbors gathered in front of the McKenna house.

"Can I have your name, please?" John asked, notebook at the ready.

"Amber ... Amber Reed Jones, but I only use Reed now." Her voice and expression were filled with distress.

John noted the name change. That was interesting.

"Ms. Reed, did you know Maureen McKenna?"

"Who?" Her forehead creased.

"The victim. She lived right across the street from you."

Amber shook her head, shifting her gaze to him.

"No, I'm sorry ... We — my daughter and I — just moved in yesterday. I ... I rented this house online. I don't know anyone here. But ... What happened, officer —"

"Detective Inspector John O'Sullivan. I can't tell you much at this time, except that Mrs. McKenna's husband found her dead a few hours ago. Have you been home all day today?"

"Yes, I have. We've been unpacking and ... My daughter's in her room. She's gone to bed. Jet lag's a bitch at any age. You can either sleep, or you can't." She glanced nervously over her shoulder and lowered her voice a notch. "I don't want her to learn about this. She's sixteen and already upset enough because of our moving ..." She didn't finish her sentence.

John observed her, taking in the dark circles under her eyes and the white band on her tanned finger, where she should've had a wedding ring. That would explain the name change. She had the look of a single mom, either recently widowed or divorced. Given that he still wore his ring, he would guess the latter.

"Where did you live before you moved to Dublin, Ms. Reed?"

"New York City. I'm a web designer. I was recently hired by a firm here. I have all my documents and visas if you want to see them."

"That won't be necessary." He could get all that for himself later when he ran a check on her, as he would do for all the neighbors. "Did you hear anything suspicious today, like a car backfiring, any shouting, or anything like that?"

She shook her head again, shrugging helplessly.

"No, but even if there'd been any noise on the street, I wouldn't have heard it. Hayley, my daughter, loves music; she kept the volume up while we unpacked and arranged our things. Kind of hard to hear your own thoughts with that blasting in your ears all day."

John stopped himself from reciprocating her faint, nervous smile.

"I can imagine. I don't suppose you saw anyone entering the McKenna house or noticed anyone shady lurking about?"

"I haven't seen anyone, but even if I did, I wouldn't know they didn't belong. I didn't have time to look out the window today, except when I opened all of them this morning, and there was no one on the street then." She bit her lower lip. "Can you tell me what happened? How was she murdered?"

"I'm afraid I can't comment on an ongoing investigation."

"Of course not." She lowered her gaze to her bare feet, looking embarrassed for some reason.

John noticed her rather enchanting toenails tipped in a pale pink polish.

She pressed a palm to her forehead, her gaze taking in the neighborhood. Fear and worry darted from her dilated pupils.

"Good God," she groaned. "I thought New York was dangerous. Ireland is supposed to be safe. What have I done, bringing my daughter here?"

An unfamiliar emotion grew in John's chest as he watched helpless tears flooding those beautiful golden eyes. He wanted to reach out, take her hand, offer comfort, but that would be unprofessional. It took a lot of guts to leave everything behind and start over in a strange country with a teenager in tow, but if she thought she'd made a mistake ... He tried to reassure her with words instead.

"Ms. Reed, there's crime everywhere in the world. I can assure you Dublin is far below New York City in its crime rate. This is an unusual incident, definitely not the natural order of things around here. I don't think you have anything to worry about. This is one of the city's safer neighborhoods. Just be cautious. Don't open the door to strangers — although I suppose we all are strangers to ye." His suppressed smile surfaced at last. "Avoid isolated streets, and take the time to research the neighborhoods you and your lass should avoid. I'm sure you'll be fine."

The woman's gaze held an almost palpable need to believe what he was saying. When she nodded, a strand of hair slipped off her forehead, and she tucked it behind her ear.

"We will. Thank you, Detective. I'm sorry I couldn't be of any help. Do you have any clues, any idea as to who killed this poor woman, and why?"

"That's also confidential. Thank you for your time, Ms. Reed." He handed her his card. "If you remember anything at all, please call."

She reached for the card, nodded, and closed the door slowly.

After he heard the lock turn, John moved away. He'd only taken a couple of steps before he saw Aidan coming toward him.

"Anything?" John asked, hoping his partner had had more luck than him.

Aidan shook his head. "Not a single fucking lead. It seems this killer just materialized inside the house — bang, bang — and then, poof! He's gone."

John snorted at his partner's colorful description of the

murder. He'd long admired Aidan the ability to keep his sense of humor even in the most macabre situations. Sometimes, that ability was all that kept you sane in this line of work.

"I doubt it's a bloody illusionist we're searching for, but given the card ... Why did the killer choose that particular one, do you think? And what did he do with the rest of the deck?"

"God only knows. Did he write that symbol at home? And what the bloody hell do you think that scribbling means?"

John rubbed the back of his neck. "Only the killer knows that."

Aidan scratched his chin meditatively. "I don't think this guy's the full shilling, you know?"

John narrowed his eyes, and the dread in his stomach intensified. "He's not crazy, Aidan. Not by a long shot. He knows exactly what he's doing and why. It's up to us to catch up."

With one last glance at the small house, John turned and headed back to the crime scene.

At his side, Aidan continued his report. "No one saw or heard anything out of the ordinary, no strange vehicle near the house, nor any strange person. I asked about the victim's relationship with her husband, too, in case she had a lover or vice versa, but everyone says they were great together, never fought — the perfect couple."

John shook his head. "I don't think the husband had anything to do with it. He's devastated. Mind you, he could be a grand actor, but my gut tells me it wasn't him."

Aidan paused on the sidewalk to light a cigarette. His way of trying to quit was to light one cigarette after the other, hold it between his fingers and inhale the fumes while pretending to ignore it.

"I think so too, but it's part of the process. Have you got anything? Any lead from the hot MILF? You talked to her for quite a while."

John spared him a glance, but his mouth twitched into a smile. "How do you know she's a mom?"

"Well, she was wearing a Metallica T-shirt, wasn't she? It was sexy as hell but too small for her. Besides, I glimpsed a girl when she opened the window upstairs. She's either the MILF's daughter or her sister."

"Stop calling her that. It's disrespectful. The woman's name is Amber Reed, a transplanted American. Unfortunately, she couldn't tell me anything. She and her sixteen-year-old daughter moved in yesterday. They spent all day unpacking, with the music blasting. She didn't know Maureen or anyone else in the neighborhood."

Aidan took a short drag from the cigarette, his forehead creasing.

"Sixteen-year-old daughter?" He exhaled the smoke. "From the looks of her, she must've got up the pole in her teens." He chuckled. "So, what's her story?"

John gave him what little he'd learned.

"I'll run her credentials just as I'll do for everyone else on the street," he finished, "but I don't think she has any connection with this. In the morning, we'll visit the hospital and the clinic where Maureen worked. For now, you go home; get some sleep. I'll stick around here with the guys from the Technical Bureau."

Aidan nodded. "I'll see you in the morning."

John headed back toward the crime scene. The forensics team would be at it until the wee hours and then some. Hopefully, Nóirín would have something for them by tomorrow. Fingerprints on the mysterious card would certainly help.

3

Standing to the side of the window, Amber covertly watched the detective walk away and join another man.

Good Lord, a woman had been murdered only yards away, and she'd had no clue! A shiver raised her skin into goose bumps, and she squeezed her eyes shut, struggling to remember every minute of the day. Had she heard anything, seen anything? She did a mental recap of all they'd done today. They'd woken around nine, had sandwiches for breakfast, then began unpacking and putting things away. Soon, Hayley had turned on her laptop, connected her sound system, and drowned the house in Godsmack, Linkin Park, Three Days Grace, and all the other bands she liked, which sounded the same to Amber. Between the noise and the sheer physical exhaustion of putting the house together, her brain was mush.

For the life of her, she couldn't provide the police with any sort of information. She glanced down at the card she held. Detective O'Sullivan. John … While they'd talked, she couldn't help noticing how attractive he was, with his salt-and-pepper hair and intense, steely-gray eyes. She'd never met anyone with such unusual-colored eyes. His broad shoulders had nearly filled the doorframe. And he was tall — much taller than Dean, her two-timing scumbag of an ex-husband. She'd had to tilt her head back to look into John's face. She cursed herself for wearing Hayley's T-shirt and old, baggy track pants, then she felt foolish that such a trivial thought had even crossed her mind. He hadn't been there to hit on her. But what he'd said explained why his eyes looked so haunted. Being a cop seemed like one of the hardest jobs. One needed nerves of steel and strong motivation to deal with things most people didn't want to know existed. John must have a hell of a character.

Dean had been the only man she'd had a serious relationship with, so she was surprised by how long thoughts of John O'Sullivan lingered in her mind. It was a shame they hadn't met under different circumstances.

Shaking off the idea, she told herself it didn't matter. She was a single mom with a daughter to raise, not a desperate woman craving sex. Although she managed to believe that most days, some nights, she felt so lonely that she could hear the need rustling within her. It had been months since she had felt a man's touch, and even before the breakup, sex with Dean had been lukewarm at best for the last years of their marriage. But it wasn't only that. She missed basic human contact, the presence of a companion, someone to talk to, someone to ask for advice. She missed having someone to rely on when things got tough — like now.

Letting the curtain fall into place, she returned to the kitchen and the task at hand, but she couldn't concentrate. Doubt gnawed at her heart. Had she done the right thing? Less than forty-eight hours in their new home, and there'd been a murder practically on her doorstep. Damn! If Dean ever learned of this, she would never hear the end of it. Should she call him and tell him about it? Like hell. Their divorce had been finalized months ago, and she didn't owe him anything, especially not a news report. She doubted he cared anyway. If he had, he would have held on tighter to his family.

As it was, he hadn't even objected when she'd told him about receiving a job offer from a well-known company in Dublin, informing him she and Hayley would be moving to Ireland. But when she'd shared the wonderful news with Hayley, her daughter's reaction had been anger, not joy. She didn't want to leave her father and friends to move halfway around the world to a place where she didn't know anyone.

Already an introvert, Hayley had withdrawn deeper into her shell since the divorce, yet her fury over the move had surprised Amber. Why had she been so adamant? Had she had a secret boyfriend she'd been forced to leave behind? When Amber had tried to discuss the matter with her, Hayley had stomped out of the room glassy-eyed with tears and slammed her bedroom door behind her. That had been that.

Amber hadn't brought it up again since Hayley had appeared resigned to the move — especially once she realized Dean wouldn't interfere in the decision. Instead, she used her behavior, attitude, and sullenness to make it clear how martyred she felt and how unfair it was for her mother to rule her life.

Amber truly understood Hayley's frustration. She remembered being sixteen herself, and like Hayley, she'd been a quiet girl who'd resented her parents every time they'd moved. The *army brat* — as some kids had called her — never got to stay in one school long enough to make real friends and never truly settled anywhere. It wasn't until she went to Columbia that things had changed.

She'd been studying computer science, and Dean Jones had specialized in economics. The first time she'd seen him playing tennis on campus, she'd been bewitched by his tousled blond hair and dazzling blue eyes. Add to that the tanned, athletic body and killer smile, and she was a goner.

She'd been surprised when he'd reciprocated her interest. She considered herself plain, so when this gorgeous guy became her boyfriend, then her lover, she couldn't believe her luck. When he'd asked her to marry him, she'd said yes, not caring they were both almost too young to take that step. Now, she realized she'd accepted because of an innate, desperate need to settle down, as much — maybe even more — than because of her love for him.

Life with Dean had been pleasant — great even — during the first months of marriage. She'd gotten pregnant, they'd bought a house in the suburbs ... Theirs was the American dream.

Dean's career as a stockbroker allowed her the luxury of being a stay-at-home mom, but when Hayley was four, Amber decided she wanted more. Her first job with a small IT firm allowed her to work her way up to web designer. She'd done her best to divide her time between her career and being a good wife and mother.

"Obviously, I've done a crappy job at that," she mumbled, drying the last of the new dishware and putting the cups, plates, bowls, and glasses in the cupboard. She'd left everything that had been part of her life with Dean behind. If she and Hayley were going to start a new life, it was best to do it with the least baggage — both physical and emotional. Closing the cupboard door, she leaned against the table, deciding whether to tackle another chore or give in to her exhaustion and go to bed.

She stared down at her hands, dry and reddened from all the washing. God, they looked terrible! At thirty-eight, she was a stylish woman and loved taking care of herself, but since the divorce, she hadn't had the time or energy to pamper her body like she used to. That was about to change. She needed a polished appearance for her new job — and for herself. She always felt better when she looked good, and one of her favorite things in the beauty process was coloring her nails as the mood struck. Wincing at the dull, polish-free tips of her fingers, she decided tonight she'd treat herself to a manicure and a hand moisturizing treatment.

DESPITE HER BEST EFFORTS, Hayley couldn't sleep. She was hungry and too keyed up after reading Amy's email. The room seemed stuffy, so she flung the sheets aside and got up to open the window. Down on the street, the ambulance was gone, but the police cars were still there, the house across from hers ablaze with lights. A man wearing a yellow vest walked along the sidewalk across the street, dropped a cigarette, and crushed the butt under his foot.

What the hell had happened over there?

Debating whether or not to go down for a snack, she heard someone knock on the front door. Hayley cracked open her bedroom door, but she was too far down the hall to see anything. She could hear her mother's muted conversation with a man. By the time she grabbed her robe and found her slippers, the front door was closed. Curious, she went down to the kitchen, where her mother had been doing something. She was always doing something and expected everyone around her to be busy, too. The woman didn't know how to relax.

"Who was that?" Hayley asked, stepping into the room.

Her mom stood leaning against the table. Hearing Hayley's voice, she jumped, a deer-in-the-headlights look on her face, which was paler than usual. Maybe it just seemed that way because of the black T-shirt she'd borrowed from Hayley since she hadn't yet unpacked any of her casual clothes. Dressed like this, she looked vulnerable and young — young for a mom anyway.

She straightened, clearing her throat. "Who was who?" Her gaze didn't meet Hayley's.

"I heard the door, Mom."

"Oh, just a neighbor wanting to welcome us to the neighborhood."

"At almost nine o'clock at night?" Anger filled Hayley. "Don't lie to me. I'm not a stupid little kid. I saw the ambulance and the police cars across the street. I know something's going on. What is it? Is someone sick?"

Amber's lips parted, closed, then opened again. She seemed taken aback by Hayley's annoyance. Tough luck. She wasn't some green kindergartener who needed to be shielded from the ugliness of life. Besides, the divorce had taken care of that.

"There's been some trouble," her mother said. She sat down at the table and motioned Hayley to sit in the chair across from her. "The woman who lived across the street was murdered this afternoon. But don't worry, baby, the inspector assured me we're in no danger. It was probably someone who had a grudge against her, or ..." she trailed off, her hands dropping to the tabletop.

A cold chill crept up Hayley's spine as she sat, folding her legs under her. Murder? Here? How could it have happened without them hearing anything?

"How was she ... killed?" She tried to control the tremor in her voice.

Her mother looked up, shoulders slumping as if she bore the weight of the entire world.

"I don't know, honey. Her name was Maureen McKenna. I told the detective we'd just moved in and hadn't met anyone yet."

"You said he was an inspector," Hayley reminded her.

"Right. The terminology is probably related to rank, but what matters is that he's an investigator, a detective. He asked if we'd heard anything or seen anything suspicious. I told him that we were busy all day, that the music was loud, so we didn't hear anything."

Hayley was more than a little freaked out. Someone had been killed practically next door to them. Since she'd lived all her life in a large city like New York, violence of any kind wasn't a foreign concept. But her parents had always protected her, making sure she wasn't exposed to that side of reality. Not directly, anyway. Amy had probably seen some of the seedier sides of the city. She never talked about it, though.

"Well ... I hope they catch the killer fast. I'm going back to bed." Hayley walked to the fridge and poured herself a glass of milk. "Goodnight."

"Sleep tight," her mom said, glancing at her watch. "I have a couple loads of laundry to do, but I'm beat. Besides, I have to figure out how to program the washing machine first. It doesn't look anything like ours. I'll have to search for the operating instructions on the net. I'll just check the doors and go up to bed too."

"Okay. Night."

Hayley jogged up the stairs and into her room, closing the door behind her. Sitting cross-legged on the bed, she switched on her laptop. While it booted, she downed the glass of milk. Then she opened Amy's email.

She wasn't all that good with computers — not when she compared herself to some geeks at school. Some claimed they could hack the shit out of anything, but she wasn't sure she believed them. She might not know a lot, but she knew her way around the internet.

After she downloaded and installed the Tor browser, she pasted the link Amy had sent into it. Her heart pounded a little faster as the Underweb page loaded and displayed the website's home page. THE GAME. It was really plain, only a start-up interface — red writing on a black background — where she was required to confirm that she was at least fifteen years old.

Once she did, she was asked if she wanted to create an account. She clicked on YES, then followed a link to another page, where she began filling in the blank fields.

She typed @hal666 as a username, and as her password, she set the one she used for all her online accounts. Technically, it wasn't smart to use the same password every time, but come on! Who would want to hack her account, and why? No one was interested in boring, plain Hayley Jones.

By the time she clicked on *CREATE ACCOUNT*, her feet had twitched impatiently. It grew worse when she received a message to wait while her data was being verified. She hoped the game would be exciting enough to be worth all this trouble.

As she waited and watched the red circle work around and around on her monitor, she reached out for the TV remote on her nightstand. She flicked through channels, disinterested. It seemed there was nothing to watch, or maybe she simply was too bored. Finally, she stumbled over a dark comedy she remembered seeing once with her mom — *Vampire in Brooklyn*. The movie was way old, like from the nineties, but it was better than nothing.

It was almost over when her peripheral vision detected a change on the screen of her laptop. She grinned, seeing the bold red letters on the black background. WELCOME @hal666

"Yes!" She settled herself against the headboard and her fluffy new pillow. "So, what do I do now?"

A smaller button under the red welcome said START. She clicked it, and a new page opened, displaying a simple message. Whoever had designed the site hadn't spent a lot of time on bells and whistles.

Dare #1: Introduce yourself, @hal666. Post a selfie.

Hayley pouted, already starting to lose interest. Damn! So this was just another of the many stupid dare games out there. Why did Amy think it was such a big deal? She'd expected something more exciting than being asked to talk about herself and take a selfie. Hopefully, the dares would get more interesting as they escalated.

Taking her phone from the nightstand, she sat up, not bothering to fix her hair or even smile, and stared straight into the camera. Click!

She despised the girls at school who always felt the need to purse their lips and widen their eyes as they posted selfies after selfies on social media. Some of the cheerleaders were the worst. They fed on attention like a vampire feeds on blood. Most boys had to be idiots since they fell over themselves, struck by admiration for those pouty Barbie dolls.

Would there be cheerleaders at her new high school? Probably. That type infested the world. Maybe going to school here wouldn't be so bad.

Who was she kidding? She wouldn't fit in here any more than she had in NY. She wasn't good at sports — not that she knew a damn thing about cricket and field hockey. She could play soccer, but they didn't even call it that here.

She wasn't beautiful, didn't attract people the way others did, and didn't have a single talent. In her spare time, she loved to sit at home and read about everything. Mom had bought books on the history and geography of Ireland, and while she wanted to read them, she didn't want Mom to know she did. Unlike Amy, who was super cool, Hayley was a geek at heart, and that had to be the most uncool thing a teenager could be.

Turning the phone over, she studied her photo. Her long brown hair framed her face, making it look thinner and paler than it really was. She wished she'd inherited her mother's coloring, but her own eyes were darker, big enough to draw attention away from her other features. Although she and Amy always made fun of pretty girls, she secretly wanted to be beautiful, popular, admired. She craved attention just as badly as the fat-lipped bimbos she despised. But since she hadn't been blessed with natural blond hair, round blue eyes, or even noticeable boobs, it was pointless to dream of what-ifs.

She downloaded the selfie on her laptop, then uploaded it to THE GAME's website. She didn't expect any reaction, but within a couple of minutes, a message popped up on her screen,

DARE COMPLETE.

She shrugged, unimpressed, then clicked NEXT.

DARE #2: Do something you've never done before and post the video. No limits or rules — just show your creativity.

She cocked an eyebrow. What was this stuff about doing something she'd never done before? She'd never been to Ireland. Walking down the street was something she'd never done before. But it was hardly creative.

What was she supposed to do? Put a bag of dog shit in front of a neighbor's door, then wait until someone left the house and stepped in it? That might be funny, but she hadn't seen a dog in the neighborhood.

She snorted at the thought, thinking this was too much of a cliché and too gross. She had to be original. Maybe the more creative you were, the faster you moved through the levels. If she wanted to have fun with this game and finish it in style, she had to beat out the competition. What would Amy do?

She got out of bed and walked to the window. Across the street, the house was cordoned off with yellow police tape. Her heart tightened, filled with emotion. Was it pity for the person who'd been murdered or fear that the killer could strike again?

The police cars were gone, and the door was sealed with yellow crime scene tape. That was the term she'd heard used in numerous police procedural TV series. She loved those, but she never understood why people, other than the police or the pathologist, always threw up or fainted when they saw a dead body.

It couldn't be that bad. She'd been to a couple of funerals

with open caskets — okay, those had been creepy. But she'd seen horror movies with much scarier special effects than a little blood. Maybe it was different when it was fresh, and you knew the person. Maureen McKenna, that was the name Mom had used when referring to the murdered woman. What had she looked like before and after she was dead?

God, was she sick! Where had this morbid curiosity come from? Had she sucked up the doom and gloom of this place? Could she be a burgeoning psychopath?

Maybe it was just natural. There'd been a crowd on the street, trying to see what was going on, and when there was an accident, people often stopped to get a look. Many people were drawn to death and curious about the dead. Why else would they make so many movies about ghosts and hauntings? Why would so many debate things like life after death?

Hayley didn't believe in ghosts, but without empirical proof, she couldn't say they didn't exist. Ireland was renowned worldwide for all its haunted castles and the paranormal stuff that went on here. Who knew if any of it was true?

Shifting her feet, she pushed the curtain aside to open the window a bit wider. Propping her elbows on the ledge, she stared out in the night at the house outlined in the diffused glow of the streetlights. Was Maureen's spirit in there, next to the chalk outline of her body and the bloodstains it had left behind? She'd read somewhere that when people died violently, sometimes they didn't even realize they were dead. Another book claimed that, after death, the soul wandered for forty days and forty nights, visiting all the places they'd been to when they were alive.

Could she actually be living near a haunted house? What would it be like to sneak in there before the clean-up crew came and took everything away? What would it be like to see a real murder scene, not a posed one like in the movies?

She smiled, feeling her heart rate accelerate. Now *that* was an awesome dare! And definitely something she'd never done before. Most likely, no other player had the chance — or the guts — to do anything like that.

She must be insane to even consider it. Amy wouldn't think twice about doing something like this. Amy had guts. She wasn't a pussy. She liked danger and challenges. In fact, this wouldn't really be a challenge for Amy.

Hayley bit her lower lip as she sat back on the bed again. She would do this and prove she was no pussy either. It was too risky now because her mother would probably sleep with one eye open, tossing and worrying. Hayley vowed that tomorrow night, she'd sneak out of the house and perform her second dare.

4

John woke up only a few hours after he'd gone to sleep. He vaguely remembered arriving home last night, long after midnight, unlocking the door to his apartment with weary fingers and wiping his muddy shoes on the doormat. It was bright orange, a big green WELCOME printed on it. Shanna had chosen it when they'd bought their house and moved in together, only two months before they were married. The house had been too big for one person and held too many memories, so when she'd died, he'd sold it. But he'd kept a few things, like this doormat she'd loved so much.

He'd hung his jacket on the peg, taken off his shoes, then walked into the small living room and switched on the telly, the way he did every night. He rarely watched it, but it filled the silence since, once he was home, he always tried not to think, not to feel, not to remember. But of course, every night was the same.

Well, maybe not last night. Yesterday had been a particularly long, hard day. He'd imagined Brian McKenna calling his boys to tell them their mother had been murdered. Their reactions must have been heartbreaking.

It was never easy to tell people that a loved one was dead. He knew firsthand what it was like to receive that call. He'd gotten his five years, one month, and fourteen days ago, from a fellow officer who'd informed him his beloved Shanna had been killed. That was the day his soul had died along with hers.

Trying to shake off the memories, he rolled out of bed and went into the bathroom to shower. He let the scalding water run over his body, aware of every nerve ending that screamed with fatigue. He dried off with a towel, noticing it needed washing. When he caught his reflection in the mirror, he averted his gaze quickly. What was there to see? More gray hairs than dark, more lines than a year ago. Salt-and-pepper stubble darkened his sharp, angular features. Even his eyes were more gray than blue. When had he become a gray person?

Back in the living room, he stood for a moment, trying to decide whether he was hungry or not. He wasn't, but he had to eat. Shanna had always insisted he eat three meals a day, choose healthy food, and exercise, just as she'd cautioned against smoking and drinking excessively. She'd said she wanted him to live and see their great-grandchildren. As it turned out, they hadn't had any children in the three years they had been married. Busy with their careers, busy with securing their financial future, often too busy to enjoy one another, and postponing it for the weekends, for the holidays, for next year ... Until they ran out of time.

At least hers had been a quick death, not the living hell he was forced to face every single moment of his life without his soulmate. He understood Brian McKenna's pain. He'd been just as devastated when he'd become a widower. How many times had he wished he'd been the one to die?

His first thought had been to follow Shanna into the Great Beyond, but with the smidgeon of reasoning he retained, he'd stopped himself. He didn't know exactly why. Maybe because he believed in Karma and was afraid that, by killing himself, he wouldn't find Shanna in the next life and would lose her for all eternity. That fear had been the only thing that kept him alive — and the hope that one day he would be reunited with the love of his life.

Tearing himself out of the dark abyss, he walked to the kitchen and opened the fridge. He stared inside, then half-heartedly picked up a package of sliced ham and another of cheese.

"I'm sorry, *mo ghrá*, but this will have to do for this morning," he murmured to the unseen presence of his wife.

Taking two slices of bread from the half-empty bag, John made himself a sandwich. He glanced longingly at the bottle of whiskey in the cabinet. He wasn't much of a drinker, but last night he'd needed the alcohol and had indulged a little too much. The result was a nagging headache that didn't help his thinking at all, so he decided to drown it in strong, black coffee.

Carrying a steaming mug and his makeshift breakfast, he went back into the living room, settling down to eat in front of the telly, flipping through the channels, all the while allowing his mind to figure out the puzzle that was Maureen McKenna's death. Unless Nóirín or Jenna came up with something, he had no idea what to do next.

A pair of whiskey-colored eyes flashed through his mind. Amber Reed, the American who'd just moved into the neighborhood, with a teenage daughter and no wedding ring. He'd met dozens of beautiful and sexy women since he'd started dating again, but none of the relationships lasted or went beyond more than mutual sexual release. None of the women he dated touched his heart, and they must have sensed that. John wondered if he had become one of those toxic people no one wanted to be around. He wondered if his pain and misery created a palpable halo around him, which kept other people at a distance, with him trapped inside.

Still, his physical needs hadn't died with Shanna, no matter how much he wished they had. Now and again, a woman would catch his eye and stir something in him — a primordial need, a mindless hunger. He only acted on his urges if the woman was single and wanted the same thing and nothing more.

So why was he thinking of Amber Reed, a woman with whom he'd barely exchanged a few words — a woman whose life was probably as troubled and complicated as his?

Shaking off the disturbing thoughts, he finished his breakfast quickly and chugged down the coffee, then he went into the bedroom to dress. Today he had to be sharp as a blade. By hook or by crook, he had to move forward in the investigation of Maureen McKenna's murder.

AMBER SAT at the table sipping her second cup of coffee while Hayley toyed listlessly with her omelet, an I-don't-give-a-fuck look on her face. When had that expression replaced the charming sparkle in her daughter's brown eyes, the spark she'd had ever since she was a baby?

Although she knew every teenager went through this sort of phase, Amber couldn't help worrying about her daughter. The poor kid had to deal with things that were hard even for adults to accept and understand, and now there had been a murder not a hundred feet from her new home. It was enough to make anybody cranky.

"Could you pass the salt, sweetie?" she asked, stifling a sigh when Hayley handed her the salt without looking up. She had taken her phone out of her jeans' pocket and was texting something — hopefully not a gory message to her father about last night.

Resigned, Amber turned to her own breakfast and gazed around the kitchen. It was smaller and darker than theirs had been, sporting oak cupboards, a matching kitchen set, and plain yellow curtains. It would probably be bright enough if the sun were shining, but as it was, the dim light added to the gloom. Did the sun ever come out in Ireland?

"What time do we have to leave?" Hayley's voice jarred her from her thoughts.

Amber glanced at her watch, then forced a smile. "In about an hour. I know you really don't want to go shopping again, but we need groceries. When we get back, I have to tackle the washing. From the looks of it, most people hang things out to dry."

"How can they? It's rained ever since we got here," Hayley lamented.

Amber laughed, hoping it didn't sound too phony, but inside she felt exactly the same way.

"We'll learn. Maybe after we get the groceries, we can stop somewhere for lunch."

It wouldn't kill her to spend an extra hour with her daughter. She had to start work tomorrow and still didn't know what to do about Hayley. Taking her to work with her wasn't an option. Hiring a babysitter sounded crazy, and she knew Hayley would have a fit if she even suggested it. What else could she do? Her only option was to trust her daughter and give her strict instructions not to open the door to anyone and not to leave the house, at least for the time being. She wasn't sure how Hayley would react to that, but what other choice was there? Safety was the number one priority.

Gulping down the last of her coffee, Amber stood.

"I'm going up to shower. I won't be long."

Within fifteen minutes, she was back downstairs. Hayley stood looking out the living room window, waiting for her. When she turned around, Amber smiled.

"Ready? Let's go." She picked up the rental car keys from the coffee table. She would have to return it tomorrow, and then they would have to rely on public transportation until she could afford to buy a car.

After locking the front door, Amber went to the driver's side and climbed inside the sedan. Driving on the left was definitely a challenge, one that required a great deal more concentration than when she'd driven at home, although the traffic was much lighter than in New York.

"What do you think of this car?" she asked as Hayley got into the passenger seat, trying to fit her long legs in the narrow space.

"It's too small," Hayley said. "I have to curl up like a pretzel in it."

"It's just for a few days. If we like it here, and if we decide to stay, we'll buy a new one."

"We will?" Hayley seemed to brighten. "What kind?"

"We'll have to see. When and if the time comes, we'll go to a dealership together and discuss our options."

Hayley gaped, her wide eyes filled with excitement and distrust at the same time. "Do you mean it?"

"I do. After all, you'll be driving it, too, eventually. We're a team, honey. We've got this. Now, what's the address of that market?"

She programmed the information into the car's GPS. Within minutes she was gaining speed in the traffic, her fingers clutching the wheel, her eyes darting between the wet road and the GPS. Adjusting to this new life wouldn't be easy, but they would do it — one day at a time.

The battered brick and stone buildings, so different from those back home, reflected Dublin's age and history. Most of the structures were beautifully maintained. Flowers adorned every windowsill, their colorful beauty withstanding rain and wind, spreading optimism.

The hypermarket was similar to any of the superstores found in America. As they browsed the aisles, Amber pushed the cart, adding items to it now and again. Hayley's job was to read the list and scratch off what they'd found with the red pen she'd given her.

"What's next?" Amber asked, placing two jars of tomato sauce in the cart.

Hayley consulted the list, frowning at it.

"Umm ... I think it says milk. Geez, Mom, you've got the worst handwriting in the world!"

Amber laughed lightly. "I know. I've been using a keyboard for too long; I think I've almost forgotten how to write. Next time I'll put the list in my phone." She leaned over Hayley's shoulder to check what she'd written. "Yep, it's milk."

"There's also frozen lasagna." Hayley looked around. "Okay, where are the freezers? There's no logic in the way things are arranged in this store."

Eventually, they managed to find everything on the list — or at least similar products. When they left the store laden down with bags, the clouds had given way to glorious sunshine.

"That's more like it!" Amber smiled, and to her delight, Hayley grinned back at her.

The earthy scent of grass was almost unfamiliar, and it took Amber a few moments to identify it. She paused from loading the bags into the trunk. "Do you smell that?"

Hayley took a deep breath.

"Better than summer in New York, right?" Amber said, winking.

"We had rain and grass there, too."

"But the air was considerably more polluted. Maybe if we give it a wholehearted try, we'll come to love it here."

She knew her patient tone probably drove Hayley nuts, but she had to try.

Back home, they unpacked and put away the groceries. They both had agreed to order some takeout and eat in front of the TV, rather than eating in a restaurant.

"I'll order pizza from that place we passed," Amber said, arranging some cans of tuna in the pantry. "Will that work for you?"

"Whatever you want, Mom."

If that was as agreeable as she was going to get, Amber would take it.

After gathering the bags and putting them in the plastic bin, Hayley washed her hands.

"Mom, I'm going up to my room. Call me when the pizza gets here."

Amber had just finished putting the first load in the washer when her phone rang. She swiped to answer the call.

"Hello?"

"Howdy, it's me." Patty's usual cheerfulness warmed her instantly. "Are y'all unpacked yet?"

"Yep." Amber glanced at the clock. It was barely noon. Given the time difference, it looked like Patty was up early today. "Unpacked and as settled in as we can be. You're up early this morning."

"Field trip. The kids had to be at school early to beat the rush of traffic out of the city. Gosh, I miss you, Amber. I almost walked over to your house with sweet tea yesterday and caught myself just in time."

"Have the new owners moved in?"

"Not yet, sugar." Even after living more than twenty years in the North, her friend's voice hadn't lost its comforting, down-home Virginia accent. "How's Hayley doing?"

"About as well as you would expect. She's up in her room. She's really upset about this, Patty. Every time I try to talk to her ... to make her see things aren't as bad as she thinks, it's like hitting a brick wall." She massaged the bridge of her nose. "I've made such a mess of things. I'm beginning to think I've been a crappy mom, as well as a crappy wife."

"I don't want you to ever say that again," Patty admonished, her voice rising, and Amber could picture her friend shaking a finger at her. "That's simply not true. I watched you raising that girl, taking care of that man of yours, while you worked eight or ten hours a day. And you did a damn fine job. Dean was just too much of a pig to appreciate you. Mark my words ... you're better off without him. So is Hayley, even though she doesn't realize it yet."

"That may be, but I'm convinced she still blames me for the divorce."

"That's because you're too much of a lady to tell her the details about what that conniving son of a bitch did." She inhaled heavily. "You've done as much as is humanly possible to keep your family happy. It's just that men simply can't control their gonads. Doesn't matter how hard you work, how much you love them, or how much you worship them. It only takes a couple of times of your being too tired to give them a decent blow job, and their peckers start twitching in another direction."

Amber giggled. Patty always managed to make her feel better. She was a born nurturer, and her four children could attest to that. She knew when to cuddle, when to be brisk, when to ask questions, and when to listen. No wonder her husband was besotted with her.

"You always could make me laugh. You're what I'll miss most about home," Amber said, her eyes filling with tears.

"I know you're fixin' to cry. I can hear it in your voice. Don't. You're going to be so busy building that new life of yours, you won't have time to miss me. Besides, we got phones, emails, and even video chats as soon as Adam sets me up on the computer. And I did tell you we're planning to visit Ireland again soon, so we'll be stopping by." Her voice took on a dreamy quality. "You're going to love it there, Amber. It's so green and beautiful. Even when it rains, it's like a fairy tale land, not bleak and depressing like here."

Amber wasn't quite so sure of that.

"The people are so friendly," Patty continued. "It's the perfect place for you and Hayley to start over. Why ... there's hardly any crime there at all."

Amber choked, then coughed to cover up her faux pas. *Hardly* was a relative term.

"Are you okay, sugar?"

"I'm fine. Something went down the wrong way," she stammered.

Like a murder within spitting distance, as Patty would put it. The sound of a horn coming over the line surprised her.

"Oh, dang, I've got to go," Patty said. "Take care of yourself. I'll message you soon and send whatever mail comes your way next week."

"Okay, Patty. Say hi to Adam and the kids for me."

Amber ended the call, holding the phone to her chest for a few moments. She wished she had Patty's strength, her optimism, her apparent ability to deal with anything life threw at her. Once, she thought she was that kind of woman too, but now she wasn't sure about that. She wasn't sure about anything. With a heartfelt sigh, she keyed in the number for the pizza place, ordering two small pies before heading back to the laundry area.

5

Hayley shut the bedroom door, thought better of it, and cracked it open an inch. The last thing she wanted was for her mother to sneak up on her unannounced.

Amber's cellphone rang. Maybe it was the pizza place, verifying she'd placed the order. Whoever or whatever it was didn't matter, as long as it kept her mother occupied for a few minutes.

When they'd returned from the store, out of habit, Haley had checked her email messages and had found one from Amy.

Call me — anytime, day or night.

Now that she was sure Amber wouldn't be coming up to eavesdrop, she grabbed her cellphone and tapped out Amy's number, including the country code. Nice of dear old Dad to arrange an international calling plan for her. But he hadn't called her once since she and her mother had moved here. Probably he was furious with Amber for taking his daughter away — at least that's what she wanted to believe.

"Hey, what's up?" she whispered as soon as Amy answered.

"Hey! I was hoping you'd call." Amy sounded sleepy and excited all at the same time. "I miss hearing your voice."

"Me too, but I only have a few minutes. Mom's doing laundry. We're waiting for pizza for lunch."

"That's funny. You're having lunch, and it's too fucking early even for breakfast here."

"I know. Weird, right? How are things?"

"Same shit, different day. Except the shit is more exciting now. Have you entered The Game?" Amy asked. There was something in her voice that didn't fit with Hayley's appreciation of the game.

"Yeah, but I don't see what's so freaking exciting," she muttered. "Looks like any other stupid dare game to me."

"Are you crazy?" Amy shrieked. "In what other dare game does the winner get a $50,000 prize?"

Hayley gasped, forgetting to whisper.

"Holy shit! Did you say fifty grand? I didn't see that anywhere. How do you know?"

"I know because the guy who told me about The Game in the first place is close to finishing it. When you get past the first level, which means you complete the first set of dares, you have access to the forum, where the Game Master posts the videos of the coolest dares. That's where the pros are. And you know what the best part is? There isn't just one winner in this game. *Anyone* who completes all the dares gets a $50,000 prize."

Hayley blinked, still shocked by this news.

"Come on! This is bullshit. Who gives all that money to some kids just to take selfies and stupid shit like that? What's the catch?"

Amy made a scoffing sound.

"There's no catch. And you don't just take selfies, you idiot. That was just the first dare. You saw what the second one is. Who knows what kids will post? Each dare is gutsier than the one before. Who cares if someone wants to pay a shitload of money to see some videos with teenagers doing all sorts of stuff? The net is full of people who make huge bucks off this kind of shit. If people get off watching this stuff and they're willing to pay for it, I'll damn well do it."

Hayley stared out the window at the dark house across the street. She supposed there were a lot of people out there who would get a kick out of seeing a fresh murder scene. But 50k? No way!

She still wasn't convinced when she heard the doorbell ring.

"Damn, I've got to go, Amy. We'll chat more online. Fifty grand, really?"

"Would I shit you? Message me later."

The line went dead.

"Hayley, pizza's here," her mother called.

"Coming!"

Hayley ran to open the front door. Her stomach grumbled at the tantalizing aroma, and she smiled shyly at the red-headed delivery boy holding out two boxes to her. She took them and carried them over to the kitchen table while her mother paid the boy.

"Thank you," Amber said, closing the door and locking it.

As soon as they sat down at the kitchen table, Hayley reached for a slice. The soft crust overflowed with ham and pepperoni, olives, and big chunks of mushrooms, all topped off with a thick layer of melted cheese.

"It's delicious," Mom said, but she didn't seem to have much of an appetite.

Between them, they'd barely managed to finish one pizza before each of them was full. Hayley figured both she and her mom were thinking the same thing. The possibility they might not be safe because there was a killer on the loose had a way of screwing with one's mind.

After she finished her third slice, Hayley pushed back her

chair. The scraping sound was absurdly loud in the tense silence.

"Do you need me for anything?" she asked.

Her mother raised her eyebrows. Hayley wondered if she had really been that big a bitch, that Amber was surprised at her obligatory question. Her mother's eyes were shadowed, and she looked not only tired but defeated. Hayley felt a twinge of guilt.

"No, honey, I'm fine," her mom said, dusting crumbs off her hands. "I'll finish the laundry and then organize my closet."

"Okay. If you need me, I'll be in my room."

Hurrying out of the kitchen, she returned to her room and stood in front of the window. The police car was back, but it was just sitting there as if the men inside were waiting for someone. No one was going in or out of the house yet.

Fifty grand! She still couldn't wrap her head around that idea. If she wanted a shot at that prize money, then she needed to grow a set of balls. Tonight was the night because the crime scene clean-up would probably start tomorrow. She didn't have much time left.

IT WAS JUST BEFORE 1:15 in the afternoon when John and Aidan entered the Garda headquarters, dragging their tired feet. They'd stopped to grab a quick bite, but the fish and chips felt like lead in John's gut.

Their visits to the hospital where Maureen worked and to the clinic where she volunteered hadn't unearthed a single lead. Apparently, everyone liked the victim, everyone was shocked to hear about her murder, and no one could think of any person who would want to harm Doctor McKenna.

"I still think we should take a closer look at the husband," Aidan said, pushing the door open.

"We will, but he didn't do it, and you know it. You're grasping at straws."

"Considering he's the only straw we've got ... Damn, my bones feel like I'm eighty."

"Then I must be a hundred and eighty." John shrugged out of his jacket, then dug into a pocket and took out the transparent plastic evidence bag. "The husband isn't the only straw we've got. Let's see if Jenna's here. I want to show her this playing card before I give it to Nóirín at the lab."

Units like CID and Cybercrime used to work separately, but since crime and corruption had become more varied and frequent in Ireland, a special unit had been formed, which encompassed detectives with various areas of expertise working together at the official Garda headquarters in Phoenix Park. This had required some adapting, but in the end, it proved effective, and cases were solved faster when detectives were able to join forces. John was grateful for the new and improved system. The special squad was a small but very powerful team.

Detective Sergeant Jenna Darcy was the best computer specialist in the cybercrime unit. When the six-foot redhead with an amazon's body and a porn star's mouth had started working for the Garda, there hadn't been a single cop who didn't want to shag her. Now, two years later, she was as respected as the superintendent. Her sharp mind and ruthlessness had earned her a fearless reputation, and even though she was only thirty years old, she had impressive experience in her field. She specialized in internet fraud but had also solved cases involving identity theft, child pornography, human trafficking, and many others. She could work more magic just by sitting on her sexy ass in front of a computer than anyone else in the whole of Ireland. If there was anything on the internet to help solve the McKenna case, Jenna would find it.

She'd been lucky — and probably sly — enough to get an

office all to herself, instead of the usual cubicle where most IT officers worked. Granted, the room was no bigger than a closet, but it ensured the privacy and silence a crime fighter needed in order to focus. John knocked, then entered without waiting for a reply. None was necessary here. Following protocol wasn't as important as doing the job well.

Jenna sat at her desk, green eyes focusing on the monitor in front of her. A pencil stuck out from behind one ear while she chewed absently on another.

She lifted her gaze to see who had entered. John noticed her pupils dilate and knew it was a reaction to Aidan's presence, not his. His partner remained propped against the half-opened door while John advanced into the small room.

"Hey, Jenna, do ye have a free minute?"

"For you, Detective, I have more than a few. What's up?" Her breathy voice was flirtatious even when she was deadly serious.

"We picked up a murder last evening. This was left at the scene, on the body's chest." He handed her the evidence bag. "I want you to take some photos and do a search, see if you can find anything similar, or if we can figure out what it signifies."

Jenna took the bloody card and studied it, turning the clear plastic bag over to get a good look at both sides. Reaching for her phone, she used it to photograph the card from several angles.

"I can't say I've seen this particular symbol before," she mused. "It isn't a hieroglyph or tarot card symbol, and it doesn't look like a letter in any alphabet I'm familiar with. I'll run it through the system and see if anything comes up. Obviously, it means something to the killer, and he — or she — had a reason to leave it behind."

She looked up at John, then past him at Aidan, addressing the question to him. "You don't have any leads?"

Aidan shrugged as though his jacket were too tight.

"None worth mentioning. John's afraid this is the killer's ... business card."

"And ye don't think this is the only business card he intends to plant on a dead body." Jenna finished his thought.

"Unfortunately, that's my fear." John reached out for the card. "So we desperately need your help. If this guy is just starting, he needs to be stopped, and if it isn't his first time, then ... Anything you can find is useful, any connection or hint as to its meaning."

Jenna returned his serious, worried gaze.

"I'll start working on this right away and notify you as soon as I find something — if I do."

"Thanks, Jenna. I owe you." John smiled at her. "There's a pint in it the next time we're at the pub."

Aidan opened the door, and John followed him out.

"How come you're the only one in the Garda, other than me, who hasn't asked Jenna out on a date?" John asked as they headed downstairs to the crime lab.

"Are you kidding?" Aidan snorted. "I'm old enough to be that lass's father."

John guffawed. "The hell you are. You're only thirteen years older, which isn't that big a difference in age. At least, she doesn't seem to think so. I've seen the sparkle in her eyes whenever she looks at you."

"You're delusional," Aidan mumbled, shoving open the door to the lab. "Get your mind out of the gutter. We've got more important stuff to do."

"Aye. Like pray for a miracle and hope Nóirín finds the killer's fingerprints on this card. And that he's in the system."

"Right. And maybe tomorrow morning, he'll come to surrender, riding a flying pig."

John laughed but sobered quickly when he spotted Nóirín.

"Afternoon," he said, flashing her a quick smile.

"Right back at ya. Murphy stopped by and left this for you. The autopsy report on your victim."

"Did you read it? Is there anything in there we can use?" John asked, cop mode full-on.

Nóirín gestured vaguely with the papers she held in one hand.

"Not much that you don't know already. Maureen McKenna was forty-eight, healthy, a non-smoker, didn't use drugs, and had a broken tibia, which healed more than ten years ago. There were no defensive wounds on her, no bruising, nothing under her fingernails. She was shot in the living room, once in the chest and once in the forehead. Ballistics are working to identify the type of gun. One bullet was still in her chest, and the other had gone through her skull and was stuck in the wall. We went through the house with a fine-toothed comb. The only prints belonged to her, her husband, and their sons. You'll read all that in my report as soon as it's ready," she finished, taking a gulp of air. "In the meantime, take this one."

John took the autopsy report from her, curbing his impatience to have all the evidence now, to have a thread he could use to start looking for this bastard.

"Here." He handed her the playing card. "We showed it to Jenna, and she's doing what she can to figure it out. Now it's time for you to work your magic."

"I'll do what I can." Nóirín reached for the evidence bag. "You need to catch this monster. That woman didn't deserve to die in such a way."

John nodded slowly. He shared Nóirín's feelings, which was one of the reasons he did this job and gave it his best. The thought that he wasn't the only one standing for the innocent urged him on, made him fight to find justice for the victims whose families counted on him.

Quietly, he thanked Nóirín, then followed Aidan back to the office they shared.

"BLOODY EFFIN' hell."

John turned away from the computer screen. He'd spent the afternoon running background checks on all of the neighbors, including Amber Reed. He'd also verified Brian McKenna. As he suspected, there hadn't been any hint of impropriety or anything that could point to guilt. The man's alibi had checked out, and now, thanks to that, they officially had no leads.

Nóirín shoved open the door to the small office, the playing card inside the evidence bag she held.

"Brought this back to ye," she said, dropping the small bag onto his desk.

"Any fingerprints on it?"

Nóirín shook her head.

"Nothing. I can tell you it came from a new, regular deck, one you can buy anywhere, from a gas station to a supermarket. The handwriting on it was quite neat, done with a regular pen. Again, nothing distinctive about it. The killer could have gotten it anywhere, even borrowed it at the post office. I'm sorry, John. I'm going to work as fast as I can on this. I've sent techs back to have a look outside and scout the rest of the neighborhood. Maybe we missed something, a shoe print, a cigarette butt … After seeing what was done to that poor woman, we all want justice for her."

John watched her close the door behind herself, brushing his knuckles against his lips.

Damn! What were they supposed to do now?

He glanced at his watch. It was after five. Standing, he turned to Aidan, who was going over the statements the Gardaí had gathered so far from the hospital and clinic staff.

"I'm going down to see Jenna."

His partner gave him a thumbs up without taking his eyes off his computer screen.

John lumbered down the hall, bone tired. He doubted Jenna would have anything for them, and if she didn't, he was all out of options. He knocked on her door and opened it.

"Afternoon, Jenna. I know it hasn't been long, but have you had a chance to —"

"I was just about to pick up the phone. Didn't know ye had the second sight," she said before he finished the question. "I have something, John. And it's bad. Really bad. Better get Aidan, so I don't have to repeat all of this."

His gut tightened as he stared at her pale face and the deep shadows under her eyes.

"I'll be right back."

He jogged down the hall to his office. Aidan was sipping steaming coffee and puffing away on an electronic cigarette.

"Get your arse in gear. Jenna has something for us."

He pivoted to retrace his steps, knowing his partner was right behind him. They closed the distance between their office and hers in seconds, closing the door behind them. John propped his hands against her desk, leaning slightly forward, while Aidan leaned against the wall.

"We're here, so what did you find that has you so *buartha*? What is it, Jenna?"

She looked at him, then at Aidan, her green eyes tired but sharp, her brow deeply creased.

"Get this. I found three more victims killed with the same MO as Maureen McKenna," she stated.

Although he was by no means a fainting damsel, John's knees went rubbery, and he dropped into one of the chairs facing the desk.

Aidan stepped forward, grabbed the other chair, and sat. "Go way outta that. A serial killer?"

Jenna moistened her lips, then nodded slowly. "Not just any old serial killer. An *international* one. There's a victim in the United States, Italy, and another in France. All shot in their homes. Same type and location of wounds, same Ace of Spades left on the bodies. All cases remain unsolved."

John sank deeper into the chair, feeling a cold sweat run down his back. Apprehension made his voice ragged.

"Effin' gobshite. This is worse than I'd thought. Much worse."

He absently traced the dent in his chin with the tip of his thumb. It was an unconscious gesture, one he made only when he was deep in thought. He caught himself doing it and put his hand down as Jenna continued her summary.

Her voice, slightly scratchy by nature, now sounded as if she desperately needed a drink, but although she held a water bottle in one hand, she went on without pausing.

"Victim number one is Frank Baxter, age fifty-five, lived in Boston, Massachusetts, in the United States. He was a banker, married, had one son, and was killed on January 17th of this year. The investigator was Detective Maggie Coldwell. The case remains unsolved. Victim number two is Paula Rossi, age thirty-seven, lived in Milan, Italy. She was single and worked as an editor for a high-class women's magazine. Her murder made quite a ruckus in Italy at the time of her death, which was March 10th this year, but since Comissario Matteo Ventura didn't have any leads, the case went cold. Victim number three is Sasha Leon, a forty-nine-year-old truck driver from Paris, France, who was killed on April 1st. Dispatch apparently thought it was an April Fool's hoax when a neighbor called to report him dead and described the crime scene. The man in charge is Lieutenant Hugo Gaspard, and although no further progress has been reported, it says here the investigation is still ongoing. And you both know who victim number four is."

When she finally paused to breathe, she raised the water bottle and downed half of its contents in a couple of gulps. During the briefing, she'd worked her fingers up and down the plastic bottle, nearly ripping off the label.

Thirst sated, she gazed at John, then Aidan, then back again.

John was silent. He drummed his fingers on his thigh, and part of his mind was obsessively trying to identify the tune in his head. Realizing his shocked brain was avoiding the subject at hand with these trivial thoughts, he stood abruptly. He paced the small office like a tiger in a cage, forcing his mind to work, to analyze, to solve, as he'd been trained to do.

This was no longer just a murder investigation. It was a crisis. One glance at Aidan told him his partner shared his opinion. He turned to Jenna.

"Do you have anything other than what you've already told us?"

She shook her head, a strand of red curly hair falling over her forehead. A halo of fatigue hovered around her as she propped her chin on her hands.

"Not much else, no. It took me all the time you gave me to get this much, but I'll keep digging."

"This is a lot," Aidan said, cracking his knuckles. "No one else has made the connection?"

"Not that I can see, but then, they don't have me working with them, do they?" Although tired, her smile was still cocky.

"You've done a grand job, lass, and we owe you big," John said.

"Once I started unearthing this haymes, I set all my other work aside. You guys need all the help you can get. This is some serious shit. I'll send you all the data I have so far. I suppose you'll have to contact Interpol?"

Squaring his shoulders, John nodded gravely.

"Yeah, that's the protocol. But Maureen McKenna is still our case, and *we* will find this son of a bitch."

"Damn right." Aidan got to his feet as well, dragging his fingers through his hair.

"Thanks a lot, Jenna," John said, reaching out across the desk to shake her hand. "You've done an amazing job."

"You're welcome. I just wish I didn't have such bad news."

"That makes two of us," Aidan muttered as he headed to the door, followed by John. "Go home and get some sleep, kid. You've earned it."

John noticed Jenna's annoyed frown when Aidan referred to her as *kid* — the way he usually did — but he was too preoccupied to give it more than a passing thought. They had more pressing matters to attend to.

6

In their office once more, John sat at his desk and switched on his computer. He rubbed his tired eyes and leaned back in his chair, taking in the narrow room with white walls gone almost as gray as the carpeted floor. The ceiling needed patching, especially around the naked light bulb, where it was as dark and sinister as this case. They could always request a better office, but they'd gotten used to this space, which felt as moody and cranky as the two of them in turn.

He was grateful for the large window they kept open in good weather. In the old days, before smoking indoors was prohibited, it had prevented him from choking to death on the smoke of Aidan's two-pack-a-day habit. The sad-looking plants on the windowsill had yet to recover from that abuse, but like him, they soldiered on, refusing to give up when doing so would've been easier.

The computer dinged, announcing the arrival of the files Jenna had sent him. John accessed the folder and read everything aloud. There wasn't much more than what she'd already told them, but every scrap of information mattered.

He focused on the monitor as if he were trying to reach beyond all those words that formed the puzzle to find the clue to solving it. The answers were in there, somewhere — they had to be — but digging them up might be the biggest challenge in his career until now. And he wouldn't be solving this fecking puzzle alone.

"What do a banker, an editor, a truck driver, and a doctor have in common? Four people, two male, two female, four different nationalities. Who killed them, and why?" he mused aloud.

Aidan paced the worn carpet. He cleared his throat before he attempted a reply.

"Well, for one thing, they have the same killer. You know we'll have to talk to the others, don't you? See what each of the investigators have to say, ask them to share their files, and hope they'll cooperate."

"As soon as we contact Interpol, they'll have no choice. It's common courtesy."

Aidan walked to his desk and switched on his own computer.

"Like hen's teeth have I seen such courtesy," he said dryly. "It's been a while since the murders. Trails have gone cold — if there were any trails to begin with. But ... let's start making calls. You take the one in America; I'll take the other two."

John glanced at his watch. It was after six his time, which made it roughly noon in Boston. The detective was probably out having lunch.

"I'll call Interpol first, then Italy. I'll wait a couple of hours before I deal with the Americans. You handle France."

AN HOUR and a dozen phone calls later, they compared notes over cold coffee.

John went first.

"Interpol has less data than we do, but they want us to share anything we have, as soon as we get it. It didn't sit well with them that we discovered it may be a serial killer before they did. The Italian was helpful, even if his English sucks, and we'll need a translator to understand whatever he sends us. He's promised to send me the electronic case file. He needs approval from his superiors, but he seemed confident he would get it. If we're lucky, we'll have something to work with by tomorrow. Paula Rossi's murder was big news, so they're open to whatever help they can get."

Aidan nodded thoughtfully, his chair swaying in the same rhythm as his chin.

"That's great news. I haven't had quite the same cooperation. Lieutenant Hugo Gaspard's English was decent, but he wasn't nearly as quick to cooperate, even when I mentioned Interpol's involvement. He said he would consult with his captain and get back to me."

John's jaw tightened, and his eyes became angry slits. Furious, he slammed his hands against the desk.

"Pompous bugger! What the hell's wrong with that arsehole? Doesn't he understand the gravity of the situation? Does he not see the killer can strike again, at any time, in any country? Any delay might result in another victim."

"I don't know. That's procedure, mate — at least that's what he called it. If you ask me, bureaucracy kills more people than any disease or criminal," Aidan said.

John stared gloomily out the window. The sun was setting, bathing the sky in beautiful shades of pink, but it did nothing to lift his spirits. Maureen would never see a beautiful sunset again, nor would the other three this bastard had killed. He massaged the spot between his eyebrows, where a headache stalked from behind his tired eyes.

"You know what bugs me about this whole deal?" Aidan's

question was rhetorical. "Why didn't any of the other jurisdictions suspect this was a serial killer? I admit I didn't think of it either, but you nailed it from the first." He gave John a chagrinned half-smile.

John shook his head. "It was gut instinct, but there really was nothing to indicate a serial killer. If it weren't for Jenna, we'd be as flummoxed as the rest."

"You and your gut. You've got a bloodhound's nose when it comes to these things. Left to my own devices, I would still be looking at the husband."

John smiled faintly, giving his partner a skeptical look.

"No, you wouldn't. You've sensed there was something more to this, but like me, you didn't want to believe it." He took a sip of coffee and winced. It tasted like cold, bitter tar. "But you have a point. Brian McKenna is our best lead right now. Even the sickest killer has a motive, even if it's a different one for each victim. Brian might be the key to helping us find out why Maureen was killed. Let's try to talk to him again tomorrow. Maybe now that the shock's worn off, he'll be more coherent."

He turned off his computer monitor, pushed back his chair, and stood, stuffing a slip of paper into his pocket. "I'll call the detective in Boston from home. I'm too knackered to stay here any longer."

"How are you dealing with this, John?" Aidan's face creased with concern. "I know it can't be easy for you."

John looked at his friend, appreciating his understanding. In the ten years since they'd been partners, a special bond had taken root between them. Even though he'd blocked everyone out when Shanna had died, he knew Aidan would've done anything to help him. Maybe he understood his suffering better than anyone else. Being a bachelor didn't mean Aidan hadn't loved and lost someone special. Who knew? Men didn't talk about such things.

Shaking his head, he grabbed his jacket.

"I'm okay. I'll manage. For the sake of Brian McKenna and all the others. I'll see you in the morning."

IT WAS a little after ten that night when John dialed the number he'd been given for the Boston Police Department. It should be midafternoon there. Hopefully, the detective he wanted wasn't away on vacation.

"Good afternoon, Boston Police Department. How may I direct your call?"

"I'm calling from Ireland. This is John O' Sullivan from the Garda Síochána."

"I'm sorry?" the woman asked, her tone implying she thought him addle-minded.

"The Irish police services. I would like to speak to Detective Maggie Coldwell concerning a murder case."

"One moment, please."

He waited while his call was transferred to what he hoped would be the right detective.

"Detective Coldwell here. What can I do for you? I hear you're calling from frigging Ireland."

Lucky for her, John wasn't one to take umbrage at things too easily. Obviously, he'd caught Detective Coldwell at a bad time. If this was her usual attitude, then he hoped she didn't do a lot of public relations work. Diplomacy and courtesy didn't appear to be her strong suit.

"Yes, I'm Detective Inspector O'Sullivan from the Garda Síochána."

"Garda, what?"

John took a deep breath. He was hanging on to his patience by a thread. "The Irish Police. Listen, Detective, I have a difficult situation on my hands here, and I need your help. Do you recall the murder of a man named Frank Baxter? Shot in his home, one bullet in the head, the second in the chest, a playing card left on the body ... Ring any bells?"

"Maybe." Her voice was filled with caution, all belligerence gone. "Why?"

"Because I have an identical murder here in Dublin, and I've found two more — one in Italy, another in France — same Modus Operandi. Apparently, we're dealing with an international serial killer."

"Son of a bitch. I didn't see that coming. Go on, Inspector. What have you got, and what do you need from me?"

Ten minutes later, John was convinced of both her professionalism and skills as a detective. He ended the call, leaning heavily back on the sofa. This effin' case had more tentacles than a damn octopus.

Coldwell had agreed to forward the electronic file as soon as she was back at her desk. John hoped they would have the French and Italian files soon. In the meantime, he would analyze what he had so far and try to find the missing pieces to this puzzle. Something connected the victims. It had to.

With a supreme effort of will, he stood and headed to the bathroom to shower. Tomorrow was going to be another long day.

HAYLEY FAKED a yawn when the sitcom she'd been watching with her mother ended. She stretched, dragging a hand down her face.

"I'm going to take a shower, then try to get some sleep," she said.

"So early? It's barely nine."

Hayley shrugged, the movement jerky and defensive.

"I'm tired. I've been stuck inside for, like, ages. It's boring. Maybe it's jetlag still. How long before that crap passes?"

Her mother smiled. "Some people get over it sooner than others. I'm tired too, and since tomorrow's my first day at work, I'll go to bed as well. Goodnight, honey."

"Night."

Hayley led the way upstairs and waited until she heard her mother close the door to her room. Then she undressed and went to shower. There was no way she could leave the house yet, so she might as well get on with business.

The bathroom was roomy and even had a bidet. Hayley had never used one but knew what it was for. She opted to take a bath instead of a shower, and while soaking in the hot, sudsy water, fleshed out her plan.

Her bedroom was on the second floor. She could make a dramatic escape using her bedsheets — she could've climbed down a tree if there'd been one — but it would be simpler to use the front door to sneak in and out of the house. As long as she was very quiet, she should be safe. If Mom caught her downstairs, she could say she got up for a glass of milk or a bottle of water.

Back in her room, she dried her hair, impatiently counting the minutes. At 9:53, she looked out the window once more. The cop car was gone, which was a good thing, and the crime scene tape was still there, which was even better. It was going to look awesome in a video! There was still too much traffic, though — cars, bicycles, and people walking. Didn't they know there was a killer in the area? She would definitely have to wait a little longer.

Crawling back into bed, she used the time to research The Game. She searched *The Game* on the regular web, which of course, proved to be useless. There were millions of games out there. How unimaginative was this game creator if he couldn't find a more exciting name for it?

Half an hour later, eyelids drooping, Hayley still hadn't found anything of interest. Since Amy wasn't active on chat and there was nothing else to do, she opted to sleep for a couple of hours — just until it would be safe to cross the street and break into the McKenna house. God, if she thought about it like that, she would never have the nerve to do it. Breaking and entering was a crime — but she wasn't there to take anything. She was just completing a dare. Goofy kid stuff. No biggie. She just had to complete that second dare and prove to herself and to Amy how awesome she was. That's all there was to it. She couldn't think of it any other way.

She set her phone alarm for three in the morning. When they'd gone shopping earlier, she'd heard a tourist whining that it was impossible to get a drink after 11:30 at night. By three, all the drunks should be sound asleep, too. After turning down the alarm's volume to be certain her mother wouldn't hear it, she switched off the bedside lamp and nestled into bed.

She was tired, but the adrenaline pumping through her veins kept her awake. Amy's words echoed in her ears. Fifty grand for any player who completed all the dares. Wow! It sounded too good to be true. Still, what if it wasn't? It wasn't a lot of money when you thought about it, but it might make her more popular at her new school. She had to find out. She needed to do this, not just for The Game, but to prove to herself that she wasn't a weak-hearted coward. Just once, she wanted to be one of the cool kids.

It seemed only minutes had passed when the soft ring of the alarm jolted Hayley from a restless sleep. Instantly, she was wide-awake and ready. She slipped out of bed, walked to the window, and glanced outside. The street was dark, not a soul in sight.

Time to go. Cracking open her bedroom door, she listened closely, but there was no noise coming from her mom's bedroom. Quickly, she donned her jeans and a hoodie, grabbed the pair of gloves she'd found in her suitcase, her pencil flashlight, and her phone. Her sneakers were down by the front door. She would put them on once she was outside. With one last, calming breath, she eased open her bedroom door once more.

Moving as cautiously as she could, she made her way out of the house. She took it as a good omen when none of the floorboards or the wooden steps creaked as she descended the stairs. Even the front door cooperated, uttering barely any noise when she pushed it open. Mom had mentioned oiling the hinges. How providential was that?

The night was chilly; the air filled with the ozone scent of another rainy day. Hayley crossed the street, darting anxious glances back and forth, but every window she could see was dark. It was quiet — too quiet. There'd always been some sound of one kind or another back home — sirens, cars, dogs barking. This silence was eerie.

Would the McKennas have an alarm system? There wasn't one in the house Mom had rented, but if the neighbors had one, that would certainly change things.

With each step she took toward the crime scene, her heartbeat quickened. She stopped, staring at the yellow police tape blocking the front door, careful to stay in the shadows, away from the glare of the streetlight one house over.

The McKenna house, like half the houses on the block, was similar to the one she and her mom occupied, which meant it had a back door, too. That might be a better way inside since she had no clue how to remove the tape and put it back the same way. She uttered a curse when she found the kitchen door locked.

"Smart move, genius. Did you really think the police would leave it open for you?" she mumbled to herself, her voice loud in the silence.

She stared at the yellow crime scene tape that spanned the doorframe rather than the door, her great plans in shambles. After several minutes she had a brainstorm. She crept along the wall until she reached the kitchen window. It was an old-fashioned one, the kind you had to lift instead of pulling open. Propping both her gloved palms on it, Hayley pushed upward, holding her breath in case the shrill scream of an alarm split the night. A sigh of relief escaped her when the glass slid up without a sound.

"Oh, boy," she whispered, noticing her hands were shaking.

Careful to touch as little as possible, she eased herself inside, one limb at a time, and landed in a heap on the floor. Muttering a curse, she rubbed her throbbing tailbone, then turned on the slim pencil-styled flashlight. Switching on the camera of her phone, she started filming her adventure.

"Here we go," she said in a stage whisper, trying to make the video even more interesting for her future audience. She was going to make sure she filmed the yellow police tape when she left. "Welcome to a fresh crime scene. My neighbor was killed in this very house yesterday. Someone broke in and shot her in the head and in the chest. Let's see what traces we can find."

Standing in the kitchen, the only light from the penlight and her night camera, her flashlight splitting the darkness with shaky light, she wondered what the hell had possessed her to do this. The money? The thrill? Because if she was looking for an adrenalin rush, this was it.

She moved out of the kitchen into the hallway, absently whispering some running commentary. The narrow light crept over the pictures of the McKenna family, all covered in what she assumed was fingerprint powder. She held the phone close for the viewers to see. Within seconds, she wrinkled her nose. There was an unfamiliar metallic scent, maybe something the crime scene investigators had used. As she stepped into the living room, the stench reminded her of meat packages left in the trash can on warm summer days.

Stepping farther into the room was surreal. Every surface was covered in powder. There was no chalk outline as she'd expected, but she knew where Maureen had fallen and died. The space was marked by a huge maroon stain — she'd expected red, but since the carpet was deep blue, how could it be? The beige wall behind the stain was splattered with red spots — cast off, they called it on TV. She edged close to the wall. What was that near the tiny hole? Her stomach heaved at the possibilities. Brain matter? Hair? She turned her attention back to the floor once more, bending lower to get a close-up, but jerked back, gasping. Barely visible in the light were tiny maggots crawling through the dried blood. Gross! She'd learned in science class that fly eggs hatched into maggots within twelve to twenty-four hours. How long had it been? Thirty-six or more?

Her gut tightened with an apprehension she couldn't understand. Was it pity for the poor woman who'd died so violently? Was it fear that she'd gone too far? Committed a crime? Been deeply disrespectful to the dead?

The grandfather clock chimed the half-hour, and Hayley yelped.

What if Maureen's soul really was still here, and she'd disturbed her? Hayley wasn't a religious person and didn't spend much time thinking about God, but right now, if there was anything to the whole myth about Heaven and Hell, she hoped God and Maureen's spirit would forgive her.

Backing out of the room, careful not to disturb anything else, she slipped out the kitchen window and lowered it back down. She walked slowly around the house and filmed the front door marked by crime scene tape. When she was sure she'd caught all the interesting elements, she turned off the flashlight.

"Until next time," she whispered menacingly, staring right into the camera of her phone. Then she turned it off and ran out of the yard as if the hounds of Hell were after her.

Heart pounding so hard she was sure her mother would hear it, she removed her shoes on the stoop and stepped back into the house. Moving cautiously back to her room, she enabled the Wi-Fi connection on her phone. She downloaded the video on her laptop, then watched it a couple of times. Pleased with it, she accessed The Game and uploaded it on the *Dare* page. As she waited for the video to be processed, she threw herself onto the bed, fully clothed, trembling, both terrified and elated by what she'd done. She would definitely win this game!

7

John pried his eyes open at six, the same way he did each and every day. He hadn't gotten much sleep last night, tangled in as many dreams and memories as he'd been in the sweat-dampened sheets.

He rolled out of bed, stretched, and padded to the kitchen. He programmed the coffee maker; while it worked, he took a quick shower and shaved. Even though more than 80 percent of Irish people preferred tea to coffee, he'd found the latter more to his liking — not that he didn't enjoy a good cuppa now and again. But strong coffee kept him going during times like this when he needed all the sharpness and resistance he could muster.

Back in the bedroom, he donned a pair of dark-blue jeans and a matching shirt. He didn't miss the days when he had to wear a uniform, but as a crime detective, he was permitted to dress in civilian clothes. At first, that had meant a suit and tie, but he'd discovered people were just as intimidated by that get-up as they were by a uniformed officer and less likely to offer information or talk openly.

He rushed to the kitchen, his shirt and jeans still unbuttoned. He poured the coffee in a mug and set it in a pot of cold water — a trick he'd devised to cool it quickly enough to drink.

By the time he'd found a pair of socks and finished dressing, the coffee was perfect. He gulped down half of it like a shot of whiskey, holstered his gun on his right hip, grabbed his keys and jacket, then headed out the door.

His Range Rover was sometimes a bit too large for city traffic, but it was the only indulgence he'd allowed himself. In his rare free days, he liked taking long drives, especially along the coast or the beautiful Irish countryside, where there was nothing but green and gray vegetation and rocks, as far as the eye could see. When the pressure of work became too much, when the voices of his dreams and demons became too loud, he would jump into his car and hit the road, speeding away from what he could never be rid of.

Once he reached the station, he pulled the car into his spot, noticing Aidan's battered sedan was already there. Did the man never sleep?

John entered the office, took off his jacket, and draped it on the back of his chair. He unholstered his gun, put it in his bottom drawer, and let his skin breathe through the thin cotton of his shirt. It was going to be a hot one. It was barely eight, and already the heat was palpable — no help since they had a long day ahead of them. On his desk were both the autopsy and the forensic reports.

Aidan entered, carrying two cups of coffee.

"We have the electronic case file from Italy," he announced, handing John one of the cups.

"God bless that comissario," John said, meaning it.

"Yep. Unfortunately, the information's in Italian, and my Italian is as good as my Greek." Aidan chuckled. "But don't worry, I know how to take care of it."

"Don't use an online translation program. They're not very

accurate, and we need all the accuracy we can get to find something in those papers."

"No fret. I have a real person in mind to do it, and you can be sure it'll be an excellent translation. I'll be back shortly."

Picking up the phone, John called the Paris police department and asked to speak with Lieutenant Gaspard. Aidan hadn't had much luck, so he would give it a try.

By the time the series of operators he'd had to deal with connected him to Gaspard, John was tapping his fingers against the desk impatiently. His mood didn't improve when the French police officer barked in broken English that he'd passed the matter on to his superior, and there was nothing else he could do other than wait for orders.

John might have understood the situation better if he'd believed Gaspard's excuse to be valid. He didn't. He sensed the man was behaving evasively simply because he didn't want to cooperate. Whether it was a matter of politics or ego, John didn't know, but at the moment, he didn't care. After trying in vain to reason with the man, his temper got the best of him.

"Listen to me, you frog-eating, snail-sipping arrogant dosser! Four people are dead — four that we know of. Killed by the same fucking individual, who's most likely planning a fifth murder as we speak. I don't blame you for not figuring this one out — neither did the Yanks or the Italians — but if another person dies because of a pissing contest between cops, it will be on your conscience. So make yourself useful and send me that case file today before I get pissed off enough to fly over there and shove a baguette up your arse! And while I'm there, I might have a little chat with the media."

Knowing that was a complication Gaspard and his superiors wouldn't want on their hands, he ended the call and shoved the phone toward the corner of his desk. A reminiscence of yesterday's headache lurked around his temples, but he didn't have time to acknowledge the discomfort. He opened the report Nóirín had left for him and began reading, just as Aidan returned.

"I gave the Italian case file to Gina." Aidan sat at his desk and started to puff away on an electronic cigarette. "She said she'd have it translated in a couple of hours."

"Good. I'm looking at the forensic report." Seconds later, John began coughing. "For God's sake, open the window before the smoke alarm goes off," he snapped, glaring at the cherry-flavored vapor that quickly filled the room.

"Oh, for fuck's sake!" Holding the cigarette between his teeth, Aidan dragged a chair under the smoke alarm, climbed on it, unscrewed the sensor, then set it on his desk. "There, we can use it as a paperweight."

John burst out laughing. Aidan's gesture was irresponsible, but it had relieved the tension, if only for a moment. Living dangerously was part of a cop's job. There were a million things more likely to kill you than fire. Besides, the building was full of smoke detectors, so one disabled sensor wouldn't make that big a difference. He hoped.

"You're crazy, you know that? I thought you're quitting smoking."

"I'm working on it." Aidan pushed his chair back behind his desk and brushed away the dust prints left by his boots.

"You really think so, huh? Never mind." John bent his head over the report again. "Okay, evidence shows that Maureen McKenna was shot with a Remington 1911. One bullet went straight through her skull and was dug out from the wall behind her. The forensic pathologist extracted the other one from her sternum. She notes here that they found fragments of plastic with traces of gasoline on them on the floor. Most likely, the killer used a homemade silencer, made from the oil filter or a fuel filter of a car."

"That doesn't sound like a professional hitman to me," Aidan remarked. "I mean, you would think a person who kills four people in four different countries within six months, without leaving a trace, would have state-of-the-art equipment, wouldn't you?"

"Yeah ... You would think that." John reached for the mouse and opened his email. He grinned. "Detective Coldwell from Boston sent me her electronic case file on the murder of Frank Baxter. Let's compare notes, shall we?"

He waited as the old printer creaked and gagged, slowly spitting out the report sheets one by one. When it finished, he set them side by side next to the McKenna file. Aidan put his cigarette away, grabbed his chair, and moved to sit next to John. Shoulder to shoulder, they bent over the reports.

"The killer used a Glock 17 for Frank Baxter," John went on. "There's no mention of a silencer, but the pattern's the same: one bullet in the chest, the other in the head. And the same playing card left on the body — an Ace of Spades, the same symbol scribbled, this time in dark marker, on the back of it." He flicked the pages until he found the photos taken at the crime scene. "Detective Coldwell can't mail us the actual card since you know that, according to the chain of custody, I would have to go to them to see any physical evidence, and there's no time for that now. So we only have these."

He absently tapped his fingers on the desk, analyzing the close-up photos of the cards. "What the hell could this symbol mean?"

His question was rhetorical, but Aidan answered anyway. "Jenna didn't find any clue to its meaning."

"I know. I wonder if he writes on the cards after he kills the victims, or if he comes prepared, the symbol already written."

"It would make more sense to come prepared. He can't afford to waste any time after he shoots his victims."

"Yeah ... But see here?" John pulled two of the photos closer, putting his index fingers on each one to illustrate his point. "In Baxter's case, the symbol is drawn neatly, as if the killer took his time and was careful about his calligraphy. In Maureen's case, it's scribbled, as if the killer was in a hurry."

"You're right. I did notice that, but I haven't given it too much thought since I can't sign my own name the same way twice. A lot of people are inconsistent in their handwriting."

"True. Perhaps I'll consult a graphologist to see what he can tell me about this person from what little handwriting we have. Maybe he can give us a clue on age ... if he's left-handed, right-handed ... Any information at this point will be useful. I'll also ask Chelsea Campbell to assist and see if she can give us a psychological profile. We should've called her to the crime scene," John mused.

"I know," Aidan agreed. "In our defense, who would've guessed we were dealing with a serial killer?"

John nodded. "The best I can do is copy her on all the reports, see what she can tell us from that."

"I can tell you one thing. He's a sick fuck," Aidan grumbled, his eyes on the photos of the dead people. "I just can't understand how this bastard chooses his victims. Does he have a system? Is there a motive? Is it just a lottery invented by a twisted mind?"

John wished he knew the answer. Did it lie here among the notes and photos in front of him? For the first time in his career, he was afraid he might not solve this murder. He'd dealt with a serial killer once before, but the man had killed in Dublin alone, and John had found him quickly. This case was as far from that one as were the poles. Without a doubt, this was the most challenging and frightening case he'd ever encountered.

He glanced at the clock.

"We'd better get going. I told Mrs. Green we'd be by to see Brian McKenna this morning. Let's hope he can help us."

∾

AMBER STARED GLOOMILY at Maureen's pretty face smiling down from the newspaper's front page. Her coffee had gone cold next to it while she read the sketchy article over and over and looked at the photos of the murdered woman. She'd been so lovely, a good doctor. And apparently had a perfect family — a wonderful husband and two beautiful sons left grieving her. Who would want to kill this nice woman, and why? Not even the press dared speculate.

Although the day had started quite warm, Amber's skin was taut with goose bumps. She was supposed to go to work in less than half an hour and leave her daughter alone in a new neighborhood, where a murder had just taken place.

"Lord, what the hell am I going to do?"

She lowered her face to her palms, her mind working desperately to find a solution. Would it help if they moved to a new neighborhood? Would Hayley be safer in another place? But this *was* a safe neighborhood, according to her research. Respectable families lived here. She'd been very specific when she'd spoken with the realtor, insisting safety had to be the first criteria.

Maureen had probably felt safe too, but now she was dead. She'd probably opened the door to her killer without a second thought. The most frustrating thing was that the police — Garda, she corrected herself — didn't have a clue as to why she'd been killed. At least, that was what the newspaper claimed. How could she keep her daughter safe with a murderer on the loose?

Hearing soft footsteps, Amber looked up to see Hayley descending the stairs.

"Morning, sweetie. You're up early."

Hayley rubbed her eyes. "I didn't get much sleep last night," she said around a yawn.

"How come?"

A wary look tinged her daughter's brown eyes, and she

shrugged defensively. "Don't know. It's a new place; I'm not used to it."

Amber saw her gaze dart to the newspaper and Maureen's picture.

When she sat, Amber could've sworn her daughter paled. Although she was almost out of time, she leaned forward and looked straight into Hayley's eyes, signaling this was a serious conversation.

"Honey, I need you to be very careful. Do not, under any circumstances, open the door to anyone. And don't go out of the house for now, okay?"

Hayley's face darkened. "You want me to stay locked up in here all day long?"

"It's just for a few days until I find a better solution, or the police find the ... murderer. This is serious, Hayley." Amber gripped her daughter's hand. "I don't want you to be scared, but I do want you to be very careful. If you stay at home and don't open the door to anyone, you should be safe."

Hayley bit her lip, then glanced at the newspaper once more. "The person who killed that woman had a reason, right? I mean, people don't just kill for the hell of it. That woman must have pissed off the killer somehow. What did the policeman say?"

"Detective O'Sullivan didn't tell me anything. He couldn't have, even if he'd known something, because this kind of information is confidential. It's a police matter, but we have to do all that we can to protect ourselves until they catch this criminal. So, please, *please* do as I say, okay?"

Her eyes begged Hayley to obey just this once without an argument.

As Hayley gave a grudging nod, Amber exhaled, grateful her daughter had understood the seriousness of the situation.

"Good. When I come back from work, we'll go for a walk or something," she said, forcing a smile. "I have to go now. If I'm late on my first day, that won't look good. Oh, I made French toast," she added over her shoulder, rushing up the stairs.

Since she'd showered earlier, all she had to do now was toss aside her robe and select an outfit that looked professional but not tight-assed. She chose a pair of black slacks and a beige shirt, with rolled-up sleeves decorated by oversized buttons, which made it look casual and chic.

After applying her basic cosmetics, she brushed her hair, then grabbed her bag and car keys. When she got downstairs, Hayley was curled up on the living room sofa, nibbling a slice of French toast and flipping through TV channels.

Amber stood in the doorway, watching her daughter. After a moment, Hayley looked up.

"I'm sorry you have to stay inside, honey," Amber said. "But it's just for a little while. Your safety is the most important thing to me." She paused, trying not to get too emotional and show Hayley how scared she was. "We'll sort this out, I promise. If the police don't find this guy, we'll move to another neighborhood. Take care, please. I'll call you on my lunch break."

"Okay."

"I love you."

As expected, Hayley mumbled an obligatory "You too," but Amber was already resigned to that. All teenagers were the same at this age. They scorned any display of affection — especially from their parents.

Giving her daughter a quick smile and a wave, she rushed out the door.

Her spirits lifted as she drove along the sunny streets. Traffic was a pleasure compared to New York. She'd programmed the address of her new workplace into the GPS, pleased to see she would be there in another twenty minutes. With a bit of luck, she would be right on time. Pretty amazing for a stranger in town.

Her thoughts flew back to Hayley again, trying to find a

solution to ensure her daughter's safety. She wondered if the Garda were any closer to catching the killer, even though it had been less than three days since the murder.

Her mind rested briefly on the memory of Detective O'Sullivan. Could she call him to ask about their progress? The newspaper had been vague on details. She shook her head. Hadn't he said he couldn't comment on an ongoing investigation? Maybe she could ask for advice on how to keep Hayley safe. Wasn't that part of his job — ensuring the safety of others?

Lost in her musings, she would've missed the entry into the company parking lot had the GPS's robotic voice not announced it. She picked a spot, parked the car, grabbed her purse, and climbed out, locking the vehicle behind her.

As she stared up at the brick-and-glass building, her stomach fluttered. She was more nervous than she'd expected. What if no one liked her? What if her coworkers treated her like the American outsider she was? Too late for doubts now. She entered the building, feeling a lot like a lamb being led to slaughter.

Amanda, her new boss, was an intimidating forty-something blonde wearing a red power suit and killer heels. She led Amber to the office she would share with seven others and introduced her to everybody. As she shook hands, Amber struggled to remember names and faces — one of her weak points and the reason she'd chosen this behind-the-scenes type of job. The trick she'd taught herself was to associate a name with a distinctive feature. Molly had red-framed glasses, Jeff wore a silver stud earring in his left ear, Sean had reddish hair and a red nose — probably allergies, a cold, or maybe too much whiskey.

The four men and three women, most of them in their thirties and forties, greeted her warmly. Amber was used to having her own office and was apprehensive about the lack of privacy implied by the cubicles.

"I was quite impressed by your resume," Amanda said, tapping one red nail against Amber's desk. "I like the diversity in your work. You've created and maintained websites for coffee shops, wedding planners, lingerie stores, software companies, and so on. You should feel right at home here." She handed Amber a file. "Here's a list of clients and their requirements. Take a look and cobble something together for me. At the end of the day, we'll take half an hour to discuss your ideas."

With no more preamble than that, she left Amber to her work.

"Welcome to L & L," Kathy said. The pretty brunette with short, spiky hair and magenta lips. "Hope you'll like it here."

Amber returned her smile, appreciating the other woman's dimples as she winked at her. Inhaling deeply, she fished in her purse and extracted the glasses she was too vain to wear in public. Then, pleased to see the area was quiet and everyone focused on their own work, she reached for the folder and dove in.

8

Once her mother locked the door behind her, Hayley felt better — or so she thought until she glanced at the newspaper featuring Maureen's picture. The house's silence took on a grave-like quality. Pangs of fear and guilt ate at her as she looked down at the woman she hadn't known but whose house she'd broken into last night.

In daylight, the whole thing seemed impossible, but she had a video to prove that it hadn't been a dream.

Shaking off the eerie nocturnal memories, she grabbed her unfinished piece of toast and went upstairs. After switching on her TV to drown out the silence, she opened her laptop and accessed The Game's now-familiar website.

Stunned, she sat up straight. She'd done it. The screen flashed a new message.

DARE COMPLETE.

Expecting a new dare at this level, she was surprised by the next message.

CONGRATULATIONS, @hal666. You have been promoted to LEVEL TWO.

Gaping, she saw a new button on her screen — FORUM. As

she accessed it, she saw her video had been posted for people to see, among the most popular videos. The impressive number of hits left for the post she'd titled Fresh Murder Scene by @hal666 included comments like "Fucking awesome!" and "You go, girl!" and "OMG, you have serious balls, @hal666!"

Reading them, Hayley grinned. Pride filled her with confidence. For the first time in her life, she, Hayley Jones, was part of the cool ones.

She raised an eyebrow and frowned. Why had she moved up so quickly? Did each level have some kind of point system? If it did, based on the views and comments, she'd kicked ass. Go big or don't go at all. If Amy were here, she'd give her a high five for sure.

She sighed, wondering if she'd ever see Amy again. The screen flashed, pulling her out of her thoughts.

DARE #3: *Take something from a store. Don't pay for it. Don't forget to post the video.*

Whoa! What was it with this Game Master? Did he get off watching kids commit crimes and get away with it? Uneasiness filled her, but in truth, breaking the law had been her idea, not his. Dare #2 had been wide open. She could've done almost anything to satisfy the dare — dye her hair green, go skinny dipping, walk naked on the street — but maybe then she wouldn't have scored all the points.

She was one step closer to $50,000.

Hayley chewed her bottom lip. Still, this was shoplifting. Back home, lots of kids took things. It was a game to them. Amy was almost a pro. This would be easy for her. But if Hayley got caught, her mom would kill her — that was assuming she didn't die of embarrassment first. It wasn't as if she didn't get a generous allowance from her mother and father.

Gnawing the inside of her cheek, she looked at the screen, wishing it were a portal to another life. Her heart suddenly ached. Why couldn't Dad call instead of sending money? Was he really that busy? Too busy to call her?

She missed him, although she tried not to think of him too often. Sometimes at night, she couldn't help remembering how he used to tuck her in when she was little, read her bedtime stories, stroke her hair, and make sure she was always well covered by the duvet. She remembered the cozy feeling she used to have when she heard her parents talk or laugh together, a feeling forever lost to her now.

Not ready or able to deal with the third dare yet, she logged into her social media account, then clicked on her dad's profile. As always, regret filled her at the sight of his handsome face. She used to scroll through his photos or posts at least once a day, wondering if he ever thought of her, if he visited her profile, if he missed her face or if he'd already forgotten it.

She was chewing at a loose cuticle when she spotted something on his status. She froze, eyes glued to the screen, refusing to believe he could do this to her.

An hour ago, her father had posted an event that screamed at her. It couldn't have been louder had it been announced by megaphone.

GOT ENGAGED.

Heart emojis framed the words. Attached to the announcement was a photo of her dad, grinning broadly, and a red-headed, silicone-pumped bitch he'd tagged as Lena. Beyond the heavy make-up, she looked only slightly older than Hayley. When the hell had her dad met this woman, and what had possessed him to become engaged with such a creature?

Misery and fury flooded her as she stared at the photo of the happy couple, who looked as glamorous and carefree as movie stars. Lena's lips were so full of collagen or whatever she'd used to enhance them that her smile was more like a grimace. To Hayley, her exaggerated plastic-like features were grotesque, a monstrous excess of artificiality. How could her dad even think of marrying this woman, who looked so cheap and whorish, when he'd had her mom, a quiet, classy beauty? Was this what men wanted in women — fake lips, fake tits, fake eyelashes, fake hair, fake everything?

Unshed tears blurred her vision. She didn't know this man anymore. Probably never had. Her mom had done the best thing in divorcing him. But why did doing the right thing hurt so much?

Her jaw stiffened as she clenched her teeth, her eyes turning to slits. If doing the right thing sucked and doing the wrong thing would bring her popularity and money, she knew what she had to do.

JOHN PARKED the dark blue unmarked car in front of Amber Reed's house. The company hired to clean up the crime scene was already at work. By the time they finished, there would be no trace of the ghastly thing that had happened to Maureen McKenna in her own living room. Would Brian keep the house, or would he sell it like John had, unable to live with the grim memories?

"Brian McKenna should be waiting for us," he told Aidan, leading the way to the home next to the McKenna house.

Before he even knocked, a forty-something woman with a svelte figure and kind brown eyes opened the door.

"I'm Detective John O'Sullivan, and this is Detective Aidan Connor, Mrs. Green. We met the other night briefly."

"Come in, Detectives. We were expecting you. Brian's through here. I've taken a few days off so as not to leave the poor man alone," she said, tucking a strand of pale-brown hair back into her loose ponytail. "I've made him some valerian tea. Would you like some, too?"

"No, thank you," John replied. "We just want to talk with Mr. McKenna for a few minutes."

She led them through a narrow hallway into the sunny, roomy kitchen, where Brian McKenna sat at a round table, a steaming cup in front of him.

"I'll leave you to it then."

After Mrs. Green withdrew quietly, John approached the kitchen table, Aidan by his side. They pulled out chairs and sat across from Brian, studying the man. He looked as broken as he had the night of the murder. Someone had given him clean clothes, but he was unshaven, his brown hair disheveled. No longer sedated, his eyes were clear as he gazed back at them.

"Did you find the person who killed my wife?" His voice was rusty, as though he'd screamed — or sobbed — for days.

"Not yet, I'm afraid," John admitted. "We're working on it. Mr. McKenna, we have some leads, but we need your help. That's why we're here. We need you to answer a few more questions."

Brian didn't move, other than his eyes. "Okay."

John was anxious to get to business, but his heart urged him to take a moment. "How are you holding on?"

He realized how stupid the question was the moment the words were said, even if they were well-meant, so he tried again. "How are your sons? Will they come here?"

Brian nodded so slightly that John almost missed the movement. "Yes, they're flying from Edinburgh around noon. Tara and Eughan insist we all stay here until ... until we can go back home."

"We're sorry about that inconvenience," Aidan said diplomatically. "We're going to let you know soon when you can return home. It shouldn't be much longer."

Brian nodded slowly. "Tara and Eughan assured me we can stay here as long as we need to. The boys will be getting back to school after ... after the funeral. It's what their mother would've wanted." His haunted gaze lifted toward them. "When will you let me ... make the arrangements for the funeral?"

"I think tomorrow," John answered. "The day after that, at the latest." He linked his fingers, propped them on the round wooden table, and leaned toward the man. "Mr. McKenna, I've already talked to you, but when I did, you were in no shape to answer questions. It's critical that we establish a motive for your wife's murder. Please think again. Was there anyone — anyone at all — who would want to harm her? Take your time. Think hard, and tell me whatever comes to your mind, even if it doesn't seem relevant to you."

Brian buried his face in his hands, massaging his forehead as though to conjure up the essence of all his memories. The steam from the untouched cup of tea rose, fading against his fingers like a soft, ghostly caress.

Finally, he lifted his head and looked at John.

"I'm sorry, but I simply can't think of anyone who disliked her, much less hated her. We both lived simple lives, divided our time between home and work. We didn't have many close friends, but we did socialize occasionally. At the hospital, Maureen got along well with everyone. She worked hard and was dedicated to her patients. She knew most of them by their first name, and the majority of those who came to her remained faithful patients. If anyone had ever threatened her or started a dispute, she would've told me as soon as —"

He stopped abruptly, his eyes distant, his brow creasing.

John's muscles tensed. He didn't move for fear he might chase away the memories struggling to surface in Brian's mind.

After a few moments, Brian spoke again.

"There was one man, a few months ago, but ... I don't think —"

"Let us decide what's important or not," Aidan said, voicing John's thoughts. "What about that guy?"

Brian took a deep breath, then started talking, the words lucid and tumbling from his mouth.

"Around the end of last year, a woman came to Maureen for a consultation. The woman was in her sixties, and that was her first appointment with Maureen. She complained of chest and back pains, and after Maureen assessed her condition, she reached the conclusion it wasn't a heart problem but neuralgia in the woman's back that was causing the pain. She gave her something for it but urged her, in writing, to submit to a more thorough examination and testing, especially since she was overweight."

"What happened?" John asked when Brian paused for several moments.

Brian sighed, shaking his head sorrowfully. "The woman didn't take Maureen's advice and had a fatal heart attack a few weeks later. It turned out she had undiagnosed diabetes, which caused cardio-respiratory insufficiency and other complications ... I don't remember the details. What I do recall is that the woman's husband blamed Maureen. He went to her office, effin' and blindin', threatening to sue her for malpractice. Maureen was quite upset about it. She told me she felt guilty for not pushing harder for the tests, despite the fact that she'd done all she could for her patient."

"Then what happened?" Aidan prompted.

"Nothing. We never heard from him again. The medical counsel determined Maureen had followed procedure, her diagnosis was correct, and she couldn't be held accountable for the woman's death. The patient should have followed her instructions to take the blood tests and the endocrinology checkup Maureen had recommended. Failing to do so had proved fatal."

John took out his notepad. "Can you give me this man's name?"

Brian shook his head again. "No, I'm sorry. Maureen told

me about the case but never mentioned names — confidentiality, you see. She might've used a first name, but if she did, I don't remember it."

Aidan cursed, the sound barely audible, but John shared his partner's frustration. He returned the notebook to his jacket pocket.

"We'll try to find out more at the hospital. But this is good information, Mr. McKenna." John dug out his wallet, extracted a business card, and placed it on the table next to Brian. "Call me if you think of anything else, any sort of situation where someone might have wanted to harm Maureen." He stood. "I'll let you know when you can make the funeral arrangements."

Glancing over his shoulder before leaving, John looked Brian straight in the eyes.

"I want you to know we'll do everything we can to find the person who did this to Maureen, to you, and to your sons. I promise you that."

Brian nodded, then lowered his shattered gaze back to the cold tea.

As they walked out of the house, John squinted against the sun. Summer was finally getting serious. Instinctively, he glanced at the house across the road — Amber's house. Thinking of her had occupied more than a few minutes of his time the last couple of nights. As expected, there was no trace of her, and he refused to acknowledge the quick flash of disappointment.

"We should really take her to a car wash," Aidan remarked, crashing into his thoughts as they headed toward the battered, dark-blue sedan.

"Take who, where?"

"The car. What did you think I was talking about? I don't know how we're supposed to be inconspicuous driving around in a dusty old Flint-mobile."

John snuffled a laugh. "She's done her job these past years.

And don't worry about washing her. The weatherman said it'll rain this weekend."

"Of course it will," Aidan grumbled, opening the passenger door.

"Let's go over to the hospital first and see if we can get the name of the man who threatened Maureen. This could be a good lead." John got behind the wheel and started the engine.

"But what would an old guy like that have to do with an American banker, a young Italian journalist, or a French truck driver?"

"I don't know, mate, I just don't know. We have to pursue the leads we get and hope they take us somewhere. We'll take things one at a time." He rolled his tense shoulders. "This is the most fucked up case I've ever had in my life."

"I bet it has you re-thinking your decision to become a police officer," Aidan joked. "It's funny, but you never told me how you ended up in the Garda. In my case, I'm a fourth-generation guard." He used the general Irish term for a policeman. "I didn't have much choice. But what made you want to work with the police?"

John stared out the windshield, dredging up memories that were nearly three decades old.

"Well, I dinna have much of a family," he began. "Dad was a deadbeat alcoholic, and Mum rarely saw the inside of a church. They were always fighting about something or other. For as long as I could remember, all I wanted was to get the hell out of that house. Usually, they only battled with words, but one night he came home so fluthered, he could barely walk. Mum didn't have the good sense to shut up and stay out of his way. I was in the kitchen when he hit her. He shoved her back against the wall and hit her again, all the while calling her a whore, a bloody cunt, and words to that effect."

He paused, focusing on the slight traffic in order to distance himself from the pain of those faraway recollections.

Aidan stayed quiet, giving him the time he needed to collect himself.

After a few moments, John continued. "I was scared witless, afraid he would kill her. They'd taught us in school to call the emergency number when we thought someone was in danger, so I managed to sneak out of the kitchen and into the living room, where the phone was. I don't know what I babbled to the operator, but in less than ten minutes, there was a loud knock at the door. By then, Da had cooled off a bit, but Mum's mouth was bleeding, and she was crying. I feared that old dosser more than God, so when he opened the door and saw the two guards, I was sure he knew I'd called them and that he would kill me as soon as they left. But they didn't leave. They called an ambulance for my mum, then they tried to question both of them. She wouldn't say a word, of course, and he was too ossified to be coherent, so as was his nature, he became belligerent. When one guard restrained my big bad father in two moves, it was like watching a god strike down a demon. That was when I knew what I wanted to be when I grew up."

He smiled, half-bitterly, half-proudly. "Since that day, the two still shouted at one another now and again, but I didn't care. I had a goal. As soon as I finished school, I enrolled in the Garda College. The rest, you know."

Aidan made a scoffing sound. "Aye, that I do. I still remember the punch you popped me when we met in our second year at the Garda College."

John laughed out loud. He hadn't thought of that moment in ages. "Well, it was a pub fight, and you started it by hitting on my mot. You asked for it, mate."

"I rather did, didn't I? I've always been a sucker for a beautiful woman, and your girlfriend was quite a looker."

They both grinned.

"Those were the good old days," John said wistfully.

"Old, my ass. *These* are the old days, twenty years later,

when we both feel rheumatism hovering over us every cloudy day. People in other countries say we always complain about the weather, but we have bloody good reasons to."

John chuckled. "Not today."

Once they reached the hospital, John eased the car between a slick Mercedes and an Audi long enough to be a limousine.

"And to think some doctors complain they don't get paid enough," he muttered, jutting his chin toward the expensive cars. "Let's go straight to Maureen's office and see if her assistant remembers that guy who threatened her."

"I can't imagine why she and everyone else forgot about this incident. We questioned all of them the day after the murder, and no one has mentioned it."

"You know what it's like. News of Maureen's death shocked them all. Once time has passed, they remember stuff they'd thought insignificant."

They entered the clinic area. The nurse at the window was the same one they'd talked to before, and as soon as John mentioned the incident, she nodded.

"Yes, I remember now," she said, eyes slightly narrowed as if to conjure up the memory faster. "I don't know how I could've forgotten it. The man was a nasty one. 'Twas at the beginning of the year, early February, I think. Dr. McKenna was very upset, not so much about the man's accusations but about his wife's death. She felt a bit responsible, even though she wasn't in the slightest."

"Can you give us their names?" John asked.

The woman reached for the mouse and focused on the computer's monitor. "Of course. You'll have to give me a few minutes to access and search Dr. McKenna's files."

Her fingers moved swiftly across the keyboard, but within a few minutes, her blue eyes rose from the screen, and she gawked at the two men.

"Surely you wouldn't be thinking this man killed Dr. McKenna, would you?"

"At this time, all we're doing is gathering as much pertinent information as possible," Aidan gave her the standard police BS.

The nurse blinked, frowned, and then returned to her search.

"He couldn't have done it." She moved her eyes from the screen to Aidan, then back again. "The man was at least seventy years old. Besides, he may have behaved like a hooligan, but he was an educated man."

"If he's innocent, he has no reason to worry," John answered, knowing even educated men committed crimes.

He ran his finger under his collar. The window was open, but it wasn't offering much of a breeze. The heat was making him impatient and edgy. Had the French authorities sent him the case files yet? How close was Gina to translating those Italian files?

The facts gnawed at him. What reason would a man in his seventies have for becoming an international serial killer? The death of his wife could've sent him around the bend, but according to the nurse, the woman hadn't died until February, and the murder in the United States had taken place a month before that. He flexed his hand in frustration, stretching then clenching his fingers. How much time did he have before the killer struck again?

"There! I found it," the nurse said triumphantly.

John and Aidan moved forward eagerly.

"Mrs. Harriet Connelly, aged sixty-eight," she read from the screen. "We don't have her husband's name on file, but I have her address. Do you need it?"

"We would appreciate that very much," John said. This could be the break they needed. "Can you please make a copy of all the information you have on Mrs. Connelly?"

The nurse's lips parted, a wary expression clouding her features.

"Well ... This is confidential information. I don't think I should give it to you. Mr. Connelly has already threatened to sue the hospital —"

"Ms. Corrigan." John leaned against the desk, looking at the nurse intently. "Like I said before ... If this man has nothing to hide, he has nothing to worry about. We can get a warrant to obtain this information, but that will cost us time we don't have. Do you want Dr. McKenna's murderer found and punished?"

The woman's gaze flicked toward Aidan, where she encountered the same implacable expression. After a moment's hesitation, she relented.

"I'll print you a copy of Mrs. Connelly's file. Will that do?"

"It would be grand. Thank you," John replied, giving her a half-smile he didn't really mean.

Once in the car, a virtual sweatbox, John turned on the engine and cranked up the AC.

"It's fierce heat today," Aidan said. "Not that I'm complaining. According to the weather channel, this will be the hottest summer in the past decade."

"That's a fret. One more thing to look forward to — global warming."

"We did it to ourselves, you know." Aidan reached out and turned the AC up higher.

John took his police tablet and input the name Connelly and the address they'd been given. He handed the tablet to Aidan.

"Best to go see this man now," he suggested, backing out of the parking spot and heading toward one of the more expensive neighborhoods in Dublin.

9

Hayley glanced outside. The blue sedan parked in front of her house was gone. The only movement on the street was the cleaning crew going in and out of the McKenna house. Could they really clean that up so the place didn't smell and look like a crime scene? She seriously doubted it. Nevertheless, it made no difference to her. She would never be going in there again.

She switched off the laptop, donned her jeans and a loose, blue T-shirt. In the bathroom, she washed her face and brushed her teeth. After pulling her hair into a playful ponytail, she was satisfied with the fresh, innocent look it gave her. How could anyone believe she was anything but a nice, inoffensive teenager?

Grabbing her phone and house keys, she stuffed them into a fashionable, medium-sized bag. Her mother was bound to call, but hopefully, she would be back before she did — or in jail if she failed.

"Failure is not an option," she muttered, slipping on her sneakers.

Outside, the sun had chased away the gloomy clouds,

promising a summer day like she remembered from back home. After locking the door to the house, she stood for a moment on the sidewalk, thinking. Where should she try her luck? In a small shop or at the supermarket? There was a mall within half an hour's walking distance. Bigger shops were a better target since they would be more crowded. What should she snag? And how the hell was she supposed to film it without getting caught?

Inspired, she sat on the stoop, activated the internet connection on her phone, and called Amy via chat. Amy was a veteran shoplifter. While discovering this about her friend had shocked Hayley, she'd been even more surprised to learn some people earned their living that way.

"What's up?" Amy answered groggily. "I was sleeping. It's the middle of the night."

"You did say to call day or night."

"Yeah ... Hey, I saw the video," Amy remembered, sleep forgotten. "Was that real?"

"Uh-huh. But how can you and other people see my posts? I can't see anyone else's."

"That's because you're Level One, and I'm Level Two. When you get to Level Two and pass the first dare, you gain access to the forum, then you can comment and see other players' profiles and the truly amazing posts the Game Master selects of those one level below you. It's like a pyramid. The higher you get, the more you get to enjoy."

"That's weird," Hayley said, shifting the phone to her other ear.

"I think it's cool. Keeps you focused. You want to be the best. So, was the video real? Did you actually break into a house where a murder happened?"

"Yep. I never thought I could pull it off, but ... I did."

"You've got some serious balls, girlfriend."

Her cheeks grew warm at the admiration in Amy's voice. "It

was fucking creepy getting into her house, seeing the dried blood on the walls and the carpet ... Shit, Amy. I can't believe I did it."

Amy snorted. "This is why you play the game, Hal. It's not just for the money. It's to test your limits. No wimp could ever finish this kind of game. It's not like you've got anything better to do, right?"

"Maybe I could help dear old Dad organize his wedding." Hayley almost hissed the bitter-tasting words into the phone.

"His what? What the hell are you talking about?"

She described how she'd learned of her dad's engagement. By the time she finished, Amy was cursing him and that home-wrecker using words that made Hayley feel much better. She couldn't have spoken about her father that way, but she wasn't sad to hear Amy do it.

"I can't believe he's marrying that cock-sucking, cheap-looking whore," Amy said in the end. "I'm sure that's why your mom divorced him; he was probably slipping it to that bitch while he was still married to your mom. No one gets involved and in love so fast after a divorce. But don't worry, they deserve one another."

"I know." The thought that her father had cheated on her mother had already crossed Hayley's mind. Hearing it from Amy made all the sense in the world. She didn't understand why her mom never told her the truth.

"So why did you call so early?" Amy asked, yawning.

"Oh ... I need your help with something."

Hayley stood and walked in the direction of the mall. As she explained what she needed, she could hear the grin in Amy's voice on the other side of the Atlantic.

"You reached level two in just two moves?" she squealed. "Lucky you! As to what you want — piece of cake. Do exactly what I tell you. Remember, the more awesome the dare is, the more points it'll score."

"I hear you. So what do I do?"

With Amy keeping her company via the phone, coaching her on what to do and how to act, Hayley reached the mall within ten minutes. Thank God for unlimited internet plans and for social media calls services.

As instructed, she browsed the shops, genuinely awed by some of the merchandise. She wasn't a shopaholic, but like any girl, she loved clothes, makeup, jewelry, and glitter. She was about to head to the stairs leading to the next level when a top on a mannequin caught her eye. She stopped in front of the shop window, admiring the pink, snug number crossed by silver lines. It was gorgeous, not the style she'd worn of late, but maybe it was time for a change.

Entering the shop, she made sure not to rush, keeping her face neutral as she browsed the aisles. She saw the row of pink tops and slowly made her way over to them. She chose one in her size and lifted it up to examine it. The fabric was incredibly soft yet seemed durable. When she checked the price tag, she gulped but reminded herself that expensive was good since this was the top she was going to steal.

She draped it over her arm, then continued browsing as Amy had instructed, choosing a few more items before heading nonchalantly toward the fitting rooms. Since the area at the back of the store wasn't supervised, there was no one to check the number of items she had. Perfect.

Heart pounding, she went into one of the rooms and locked the door behind her. Her pulse raced as she took out her phone and started to film. It was a bit tricky to do with only one hand, so she propped the phone on the wall hanger and figured out a good angle for it to film her reflection in the mirror.

After filming the top's price tag, she searched for the bar code sensors that could set off the alarm at the exit. Some, if tampered with, would explode, spewing dye all over her, but those were usually on really expensive designer items. While this top wasn't cheap, it wasn't quite up there. She ripped off the tag and searched for other anti-theft gadgets. Finding none, she removed her own top, making sure the camera would not show her black bra.

She donned the pink top, then slid her own blue T-shirt over it. Shifting from side to side in front of the tridimensional mirrors, she made sure no part of the pink top was visible. Did the T-shirt fall naturally? God, if she got caught, she would die. Mom would never trust or forgive her, not even if she completed The Game and earned the fifty grand.

"Keep your eyes on the prize," Amy had said earlier when Hayley had expressed doubts about what she was doing. If this was the first dare of Level Two, what crazy stuff would she have to do next? Assuming she got away this time.

Straightening her back, she adjusted her bag on her shoulder. She stuck her phone carefully into her jeans pocket, making sure the camera lens was uncovered and still filming. Adjusting her features into a neutral expression once more, she exited the fitting room, hanging the clothes she didn't want on the nearby rack. Her heart pounded so hard she could feel it in the lobes of her burning ears.

It took tremendous self-control not to dash toward the exit, but she walked calmly, even made a small detour here and there to look at other items. Finally, pouting a little as if she was disappointed she hadn't found anything to her liking, she headed toward the doors.

She held her breath as they swished open and stepped through them, but there wasn't a single beep. Taking her time, she walked out of the mall, checking to make sure she wasn't being followed.

Once outside and halfway down the block, she took out her phone and couldn't hold back the wide grin she aimed at the camera before ending the video with a wink. She'd done it!

Walking home, she called Amy again to share her victory and maybe gloat a little.

"Way to go!" Amy exclaimed.

"Thanks so much for the tips. Hope this isn't cheating."

Amy giggled. "Nah ... And if it is, who cares? You can toss me 10 percent of the prize if it eases your guilt when you win. I doubt this is the last time you'll need my help. Just remember. Focus on the competition and the prize, and whatever you do, don't freak out."

Her stomach, still filled with knots of adrenalin, lurched at Amy's last remark. Hayley swallowed nervously.

"Why should I freak out?"

Amy's hesitation did nothing to alleviate her worries. "No reason, I was just saying ... Earning fifty grand isn't an easy job, you know. Bye."

Frowning, Hayley ended the call and glanced at her watch. If she wasn't so worried her mother would call her before she got home and realize she was out, she would be freaking out right now over Amy's words.

EVEN WITH THE AC turned up full blast, it was still hot in the car.

John stopped at a pedestrian crossing, took out a paper napkin from the map pocket in the door, and wiped the sweat on his forehead. "So, what have we got?"

"Possibly another dead end. Malcom Henry Connelly, aged seventy-two," Aidan said, reading the info off the tablet. "Four years ago, he retired from the bench. He's from a wealthy family, a third-generation law graduate from Oxford University. He was married to Harriet Connelly — maiden name, Duncan — for thirty-two years. She taught primary school until she died of a heart attack in February of this year. They have a daughter, Clarissa Cole, age twenty-eight."

"A judge from old money, huh? The nurse did say he was educated." John tapped his fingers thoughtfully on the steering wheel. "That's a class of powerful people who wield considerable influence and don't like to be crossed. That combination can make a man feel invincible."

"Invincible enough to get away with murder?"

"We'll find out, won't we? The downside is that surely he knows all of our tricks in the trade. If he did have something to do with this, he won't be easy to trap. But if he's involved, you can be damn sure we'll get him."

John drove through the crosswalk and continued to their destination. Twenty minutes later, he pulled the car to the curb in front of the Connelly mansion. Perhaps the description was a bit pompous, but the house was impressive enough to justify it.

John used the brass doorknocker to pound on the massive, ornate wooden door. Within a matter of minutes, it opened.

The man standing before him was still tall considering his age and quite distinguished-looking. His white hair, brushed back from his face, revealed a high forehead, and his entire demeanor suggested authority.

"Can I help you?" His hooded eyes watched them cautiously.

"Mr. Henry Connelly?" John asked.

"It's Judge Connelly, but yes. And you are?"

John and Aidan showed him their badges.

"Detectives O'Sullivan and Connor. May we have a few minutes of your time, sir?" John maintained the deference a man in Connelly's position would expect as his due. "We have a few questions for you."

"What questions?"

"We're investigating the murder of Dr. Maureen McKenna.

Have you heard about it?" John let the words sink in, studying the man's reaction.

Surprisingly, there was none. Body language was often a traitor in a guilty person, but Connelly remained almost too impassive. No dilation of the pupils, no nervous gestures, no dry gulping — nothing.

"I've read about it in the newspaper," Connelly admitted, his tone flat. "What does that have to do with me?" He made no move to invite them inside.

"We heard you and Dr. McKenna had a disagreement," Aidan said, drawing the judge's attention to him, giving John time to examine their suspect.

"There was no disagreement," he answered, raising his chin. "It was merely a misunderstanding."

"Begging your pardon, sir, but by all accounts, you considered her responsible for your wife's death and threatened her," John reminded him, folding his arms over his chest. "I would say that's more than a misunderstanding, Judge."

Connelly glared at him, his bushy eyebrows emphasizing the menace in his eyes. "I was extremely upset about my wife's death, Detective. When in such distress, any man can say things he doesn't mean, as it's human nature. Am I a suspect?"

John held his gaze with the same firmness.

"As I said, we simply want to talk to you." If he wanted to do this out on the stoop in front of the neighbors, so be it. "Where were you on Monday last between one and four in the afternoon?"

"I was at my daughter's house, visiting with my three grandchildren. We had a late lunch, then watched a movie together. Actually, the children watched it. Clarissa and I chatted most of the time."

John was sweating, tired of standing in the sun, looking up at this pompous arsehole, who stood in the shadow and talked down to them. Unfortunately, he didn't have any evidence to arrest the judge, and glancing at the man's bony, trembling hands, he doubted he could hold a gun, much less shoot it accurately. Connelly appeared in no shape to move quickly and inconspicuously. Besides, Maureen never would have opened the door to him, much less invited him into her home, considering their altercation.

Instead of voicing his thoughts, John nodded. "Would you give us your daughter's name so we can verify your alibi?"

He used the word *alibi* deliberately to see if it would shake the smug bastard. Connelly seemed only slightly taken aback but recovered quickly. John didn't expect the old man to be so cooperative, but he spelled his daughter's name and address for Aidan, who noted down the information. Ever the diplomat, Aidan thanked Connelly for his time before they left.

"That was weird," Aidan said once they were back in the car. "At first, the old bugger is antagonistic from the second he opens the door, then, just like that, he does an about-face, changes tactics, and hands us his daughter's information, so we can call and ask her whether her father was at her house, or off topping someone."

"It doesn't jibe, I agree, but we've got nothing on him." John pulled the keys out of his pocket and started the engine. "We'll keep him under observation. He's definitely a suspicious character. But is he an international serial killer?"

"Why not? He's rich enough to globetrot."

"True, but is he *healthy* enough? Did you see the way his hands trembled? I'm guessing he's got Parkinson's disease. Given his quick change of temper, he could have some mild dementia as well — I hear they're prone to mood swings. If we can get a court order for his medical files, we can check it out for ourselves. Capable or not, Aidan, I just don't see this guy pulling off four murders without leaving a trace; however, he stays on the list."

"He's the only one on the bloody list."

"Fuck, yeah, but we have to start somewhere. Would you call his daughter while I drive us back to the office?"

"Sure." Aidan reached for his cellphone and made the call.

"Connelly's daughter verified his story," he reported five minutes later. "I have the impression she has a few questions of her own she would like answered, but she didn't ask any — not even the ones I would've expected. She claimed she's never heard of Dr. McKenna." He chuckled. "I doubt she realizes I was calling because her father is a suspect in a murder case."

"She can't be that dimwitted," John said, parking the car.

"She isn't. I'm just good at interviewing people."

John reluctantly grinned back at him. Aidan was indeed good at talking to people, at getting them to trust him until they told him things they hadn't planned on revealing.

They walked toward the glass doors of police headquarters, which slid open, enveloping them in coolness. John never thought the day would come when he'd think this was a small corner of heaven.

"We'd best try and find something else," he said. "Let's see if the forensics found anything on the victim's computer or cellphone. With the way cybercrime is growing by the hour, maybe the killer stalked her on one of the social media websites. Maybe he stalked them all. Let's see if any of the other victims are connected in any way through social media. Hell, maybe they knew each other personally," John speculated, knowing this was a long shot.

"I'm still not sure we did the right thing leaving Connelly behind," Aidan said thoughtfully. "We should've brought him in for a formal interview. He and his daughter could well have cooked this up together."

"I think that's unlikely. Connelly had a reason to kill Maureen, we know that, but what's his connection to the other victims? We *will* bring him in for an interview because I'm not satisfied with our conversation either, but we need more info on all the murders first, or else we'll look like incompetent fools."

"I hear you." Aidan rubbed his stomach lightly. "Listen, I'm going to get a sandwich or something. I'm starving. Do you want anything?"

John shook his head. "No," he said automatically, then changed his mind, focusing on his partner. "Actually, yes, just get me whatever you're getting. Thanks."

Aidan opened the door and almost clashed with Gina, who was about to do the same.

"All done," she said in her sexy-accented English, smiling and waving a slender folder at him.

"Gina, I would ask ye to marry me if I didn't know your husband would shoot me dead." Aidan grabbed the papers with a triumphant grin.

"You're an angel for doing this," John said.

He was quite impressed with the Garda's newest member, Gina Raguzzi, a pretty brunette who'd recently arrived from sunny Italy. She'd followed her husband, a successful business consultant whose firm had transferred him to Dublin. Gina specialized in domestic abuse, but today she'd played translator for them, and John couldn't be happier.

After she and Aidan left the office, chatting and flirting, he anxiously focused on the newly arrived pages describing the murder of Paula Rossi.

10

Amber arrived home long after six. She was later than she'd hoped, but she'd had to return the car, which was an additional expense they could do without. Gas alone was more than double the price here compared to the US. She'd gotten temporary transportation passes for both herself and Hayley. All they had to do was figure out which bus to take to get home.

Kathy from the office had assured her that Dublin's public transportation system was excellent. Amber had managed to get the right bus but had to walk a couple of blocks. By the time she got home, she was as grateful as she was exhausted. She'd stopped by McDonald's, hoping the sight of something familiar would raise her daughter's spirits. The food choices weren't exactly the same as home, but they were close enough.

She felt guilty forcing her daughter to stay locked inside the house all day, but it was for her own safety. What else was she supposed to do? It was just for a short while, she reassured herself. Come the weekend, they could explore the city, figure out some routes where Hayley could walk safely. Maybe by then, the murder would be solved and the killer behind bars.

She knew that was an unrealistic thought, but as she dragged her tired feet up the front steps, it was all she could do not to burst into tears. She'd thought being a mom was the hardest job in the world, but she discovered that being a single mom beat it. Single moms deserved statues in museums and to have planets named after them.

Hayley was in the living room, watching TV and crunching potato chips. When her daughter looked over her shoulder, Amber swore she was glad to see her. But would she admit it? Never. Sadly, if something could make Hayley love and miss her, it was loneliness.

"Hi, sweetie." Amber worked her feet out of her flats and set her bag down on the hall stand. "How are you?"

"Great." Hayley dragged on the word, which was dripping sarcasm. "Why are you home so late?"

Moving over to the couch, Amber put the McDonald's bag down on the coffee table, happy to see her daughter perk up at the sight of it. At least that had been a good choice.

While Hayley dug the food out of the bag, Amber summarized her day and described her new co-workers.

"I promise we'll have loads of fun this weekend," she finished. "We just need time to adjust."

Happy to see Hayley was already munching on a double cheeseburger, she went upstairs to wash her hands, then undressed and donned summer-weight cotton pajamas.

Back in the living room, she sat next to her daughter and fished out a sandwich from the paper bag. It had gotten cold, but since she hadn't eaten anything all day, it was delicious. She was just reaching for some fries when she noticed Hayley's clothes.

"Have you been out?"

Hayley looked at her sideways, then gave her an innocent shake of the head. "No. I just didn't want to sit around in my pajamas all day," she said, her mouth full. "I'm not a toddler."

That was a new one. Given a choice, Hayley would opt for pajamas all day, any day. Suspicion speared Amber. She might've bought that explanation, but she'd never seen the pink-and-silver top before and certainly never washed it. Not only did her daughter prefer dark colors, but Hayley hadn't owned anything pink since she was seven years old.

"I don't recall that top," she remarked, hoping she sounded nonchalant rather than nosy. "Have I seen it before?"

"You must've. I got it last summer. I just haven't worn it until now."

Amber watched her a moment longer, dread replacing the happiness she'd felt minutes earlier. Hayley was lying. She'd disobeyed her instructions and had gone out, probably shopping — hence the new top.

That wasn't acceptable. But what the hell could she do? Hire a bodyguard? Chain her daughter to the toilet?

Trusting her to act like a responsible adult obviously wasn't working. But how to deal with this? If she accused her of lying, it would only alienate her more. Besides, she would never get a confession. She knew how stubborn Hayley could be because she'd inherited that trait from her. On the other hand, if she pretended she believed her, lying might become a habit for her daughter, the way it was for most teenagers.

Starting tomorrow, Amber would have to find a way to check up on her more often. She would call her every hour if necessary. She would also find a way to update and check the parental control program she'd installed on Hayley's laptop, which they'd bought for her before she'd discovered Dean was having an affair. But to do it, she needed to get her hands on the laptop without her daughter's knowledge, which was difficult at the moment.

God, she was as deceiving as she'd suspected Hayley to be. Deciding to give the impression she'd accepted her explanation about the top, Amber continued eating her sandwich.

"So, what did you do today?" she asked between bites.

Hayley shifted on the sofa beside her. "Nothing much. Watched TV, surfed the net ... Found out that Dad is getting married."

Amber stopped chewing. As she swallowed, the piece of sandwich landed like lead in her stomach. She hadn't seen this coming; she'd assumed Lena was only a temporary distraction for Dean. Apparently, he wasn't as classy as he'd once been. Maybe he was going through a midlife crisis and needed to make sure his twenty-something redheaded bimbo stuck by him by putting a ring on her finger.

"How do you know?" she asked.

"He posted it on social media."

Hayley had always been a girl of few words, but Amber knew her emotions ran deep. What a hell of a thing for that jerk to do. The least he could've done was tell her himself first. Her daughter had to be terribly hurt by this piece of news. Hell, she was angry and bitter herself, even though she had no love left for the cheating bastard.

But Hayley loved him. He was still her daddy, and this slight on his part must really hurt. The changes she'd had to go through these past months were tough, something no kid should experience. Amber was doing her best to make ends meet and rebuild their lives while Dean was moving on, flaunting his happiness and, by extension, humiliating his ex-wife and daughter.

Her appetite gone, Amber tossed the half-eaten sandwich into the paper bag.

"I'm sorry," she said quietly, not knowing what else to say.

Hayley turned her head to look at her. "Did you know about her? Was he cheating on you with that woman? Is that why you divorced him?"

Amber stared down at her hands. The light trace where her wedding band had been still marked her ring finger. All at once, she wanted to rip off that piece of her skin. She nodded, feeling guilty and not knowing why.

"Yes, Hayley. That's why I left your father ... because he was having an affair."

"Why didn't you tell me?"

"I don't know. I didn't want you to suffer. Maybe I was afraid you wouldn't believe me if I told you. I know your dad has always been your hero. I guess I was afraid you'd blame me for his cheating."

"That's crazy," Hayley snapped, staring at her. "I deserved to know. I'm not a kid, Mom. I know about life, and relationships, and cheating. How could it be your fault?"

Amber's shoulders slumped, and she shook her head in defeat. "I don't know, honey. I did my best to be a good wife, a good mom ... Finding out about Dean's infidelity broke me to pieces. I didn't want you to feel that kind of pain — ever. I just wanted to protect you; that's why I didn't tell you. I'm sorry."

Hayley pondered this for a while, chewing her bottom lip. When she finally spoke, she sounded more like an adult than she'd ever had.

"You have nothing to be sorry about, Mom. If he wants to marry that plastic woman, that's on him. He doesn't deserve you — or me."

Joy and gratitude filled Amber's heart. It was probably the most beautiful thing her daughter had said to her, and the first time she had acknowledged the divorce hadn't been Amber's fault.

Reaching out, she took Hayley's hand in hers, not caring if the gesture embarrassed her teenage daughter, who didn't like being touched in what she considered sappy ways.

"Thanks, baby." Amber's throat was tight, and she tried to pick her words carefully, struggling not to cry. "I appreciate what you said. I know Dean is your father, and I know you're probably angry and feel betrayed right now. He does have the right to do whatever he wants with his life, and ... well ... We're not supposed to judge anyone's decisions. But I want you to know that I will never, ever desert you. I'm always here for you, no matter what."

Hayley didn't say anything. But after a few moments, she moved closer, put the bag of food on the floor, and snuggled next to Amber, leaning into her.

Amber's chest constricted as she pressed her lips against her daughter's hair, hoping Hayley wouldn't feel the tear sliding down her cheek.

She'd forgotten how much she missed holding her baby like this, inhaling the fruity smell of her shampoo, feeling her body nestled next to hers. What a wonder that this beautiful young woman had grown inside of her, life of her life, blood of her blood.

From the day she'd learned of her pregnancy, Amber had showered her baby with love, stroking her belly protectively, talking to her, guarding her as if she were the most precious thing on earth. To her, she was and always would be.

They sat like that for a while, wordless, watching TV. After a few minutes, Amber gave up trying to figure out what show they were watching.

"What is this?"

Hayley gave her one of those shocked, annoyed looks, which almost spelled *Geez, Mom, under what rock have you lived?*

"How can you not recognize *Vampire Diaries*? It's one of the most popular shows ever. Everyone watches it."

"Everyone your age, maybe. I haven't had a chance to watch it." Amber feigned interest in whatever happened on the screen but couldn't follow the storyline.

She sighed. Despite her best efforts, she simply didn't enjoy the programs, movies, and music her daughter liked. Where were the good old days when they would spend hours watching classic cartoons like *Scooby-Doo* and the Disney princess movies?

She should be grateful that Hayley's rebellious side didn't include a nose or tongue stud or a tattoo — at least not where she could see it. Amber had smelled cigarette smoke on her a few times, but when she snooped in her room — as any mother had the God-given right to do — she hadn't found any incriminating evidence. Hayley must've picked up the smell at school, in a taxi, or on a bus.

Although all Amber wanted was to take a shower and crash into bed, she felt obliged to ask, "Do you want to go out for a walk or something?"

"Not really. Can we just sit outside and get some air? It was so hot in here today. I had to sit with the fan right in my face."

"Sorry. If it were our house, I would have had air conditioning installed. It never occurred to me we might need it here. But I doubt the heatwave will last too long. Let's get some air. Maybe we should buy some lawn chairs."

She glanced down at her pajamas and deemed them decent enough to wear outside. Leading the way, she and Hayley went out on the veranda and sat on the steps.

The neighborhood, strictly residential, was an attractive one sporting neat, almost identical two-story brick houses, with green postage-stamp-sized lawns, well-maintained sidewalks, and flower beds, many in full bloom. People took pride in their homes, and it showed.

Across the street, the crime tape was gone from the McKenna house, but there were still cleaners at work inside. Amber hoped they would finish soon, so the street resumed its false air of security.

A Range Rover pulled up in front of the McKenna house. When the driver got out of the vehicle, Amber recognized the tall, solid man. It was Detective O'Sullivan. His laser gray-blue eyes scrutinized the neighborhood. When he spotted

Amber and Hayley, his gaze seemed to soften a little. His smile was so faint Amber thought she might have imagined it, but he also gave them a nod of acknowledgment before going up the walkway to the house next door to the murder scene.

"Is that the detective who told you about the murder?" Hayley asked.

"Yes. His name's John O'Sullivan."

"Do you think he caught the killer yet?"

"I don't know."

Amber shuddered, a chill racing up her spine at the visual reminder of the crime. With the houses looking so similar, what if the killer had gotten the wrong one? The newspaper had maintained how well-liked Dr. McKenna had been. What if she hadn't been the intended victim?

Forcefully pushing away her grim thoughts, she shifted toward her daughter. "It's cooled down considerably. Have you had enough air?"

She was too tired and worried to feel guilty when Hayley nodded.

"Then let's go back inside. We'll open all the windows and see if we can create a cross breeze to let the hot air out and some of this cooler air inside. At night it's downright chilly."

Ten minutes later, hair fluttering in the current created by the open windows, Amber turned to Hayley.

"I'll close the windows when I go to bed. The upstairs ones can stay open. Have you had enough to eat?"

"Yeah." Hayley yawned, settling in front of the TV once more.

Amber reached for the leftovers of their meal. "I'll go take a bath. Maybe I'll find something to watch on TV."

She pretended not to see Hayley's eyebrows twitch, which suggested Amber's taste in television was so ancient it belonged in a museum. Slightly amused, she went to the kitchen, threw away the bag containing the leftovers, and then padded upstairs.

In the bathroom, she turned on the water, adding lavender oil to it. While the tub filled, she went to her bedroom and undressed, placing her pajamas on the armchair.

Although the furniture in the house wasn't new, she liked its arrangement, especially in this room, with the large bed and roomy nightstands. Dean had always complained about the useless stuff she kept on her nightstand — hand lotion, earplugs, lip balm, sleep mask, and so on. Contrary to what he said, none of those things were useless to her.

She no longer needed earplugs. Dean wasn't there to snore the house down, and since her bedroom window had shutters, the eye mask she used to put on every night had begun to gather dust.

"That's progress."

She placed the earplugs and mask inside one of the drawers. Then she sat on the edge of the bed, clad only in black lace panties.

With a cross breeze upstairs, the room was the perfect temperature, and she enjoyed that. Back home, she couldn't survive without air conditioning during summer, but they would seldom need it here.

The scent of lavender carried through the half-open bedroom door, luring her back to the bathroom. The tub was full. She turned off the tap, slipped off her underwear, and stepped into the warm water with an almost sensual sigh.

Making a conscious effort, she relaxed her muscles, breathing and focusing on each part of her body. She stretched her legs, then wiggled her toes, noticing the pink nail polish was beginning to fade. This was one of her small secret pleasures. She'd never gone to a salon but pampered them herself, using any color she was in the mood for.

She was thinking deep red when she remembered Hayley's

news, and her enthusiasm fell. So, Dean was actually marrying that bimbo. She tried hard not to badmouth him — or the slut — in front of anyone, especially Hayley, but now she let her resentment surface.

"The bitch and the beast. This should be an interesting match."

They wouldn't be together long. A relationship like that was doomed to fail simply because of the way it had begun. If Dean had cheated on one wife, what would stop him from doing the same to his second one?

On the other hand, a forty-year-old man might find it hard to satisfy a woman in her twenties, who probably had the sexual appetite of a rabbit in heat. No matter what went wrong — and she was sure something would — she was going to enjoy hearing about it. Yes, damn it, she was only human, not a saint.

What bothered her was how he'd treated Hayley. He'd hurt his daughter probably more than he'd hurt her, and she would never forgive him for that. The good thing about all this was that Hayley had started to see Amber's dedication toward her and the sacrifices she'd made. Maybe it would all work out for the best in the end.

Amber closed her eyes and let her mind wander.

She liked her new job, although it would be more demanding than she'd initially thought. The only problem was dividing her time between work and Hayley. Hopefully, once school started, her daughter would make some friends and have a chance to hang out with some nice young people. However, since the neighbor's murder had freaked out Hayley, she still wondered if she should find a new neighborhood to move into.

Where were the police in solving the case? It looked as though they were releasing the house. Maybe they had solid leads or even a suspect in custody. But how could she find out?

It wasn't as if she could go to the police station and ask. Damn! Why hadn't she called John O'Sullivan over when she'd seen him earlier?

The memory of his sexy eyes and athletic body brought on an unwanted stir of desire. Any woman with a pulse had to acknowledge he was a great-looking man. But since he was in his forties, no doubt he had a wife and kids, maybe even a mistress or two. Who knew?

Ever since it had happened to her, she'd begun to look cynically at every relationship, every man who smiled at her. Although John's direct gaze had exuded integrity and he'd been all business, could a woman ever be sure about a man's character?

"Not even after you've lived with the bastard for more than seventeen years," she mumbled, her calm destroyed once more.

Getting out of the water, she dried herself with one of the new, fluffy, beige towels she and Hayley had bought to match the bathroom.

Back in her pajamas, she settled cross-legged on her bed and opened her laptop, anxious to put a few finishing touches on the presentation she'd promised Amanda. She blinked hard a few times to clear her vision and chase away the fatigue. Between worrying about a killer on the loose, her daughter's safety, and her new job, she would be lucky to get any sleep tonight.

11

The next morning, after Mom had left for work, Hayley lay on her belly in bed, watching TV and browsing The Game website, excited now she had access to the forum. This was what Amy had meant about being able to see the best dares from the level below her. She was anxious to see if her shoplifting video had made it to the gallery, but her jaw dropped as she watched another video showing a grainy, poorly lit video of a teenaged boy stealing a car.

Holy shit! She giggled, but her stomach churned with uneasiness. Grand Theft Auto was just a game to her, but this guy had taken it to the next level.

The comments she could read — there were some in languages she didn't recognize — clearly showed the other players were impressed with this guy's nerve. He'd probably scored a gazillion points for that. She thought of leaving a comment, too, but wasn't sure what to say, so she scrolled down, whooping when she saw her shoplifting video. Was she fucking fabulous or what? The Game Master had obviously approved of her actions. Smug self-satisfaction grew in her as she read the comments praising her skills and her taste in clothes. She was on a roll!

Shoving aside the doubts she'd felt watching the car theft, she took a deep breath and clicked on the Next Dare button. Her eyes grew wide when she read the message.

DARE #4: *Get a tattoo and explain what you chose and why. Post the explanation and a picture of the fresh tattoo.*

Oh, boy!

While she'd broken laws to complete the previous dares, enjoying the thrill and ignoring the guilt, this was crossing a different set of limits. If her mother saw a tattoo on her, there would be hell to pay. Piercings and tattoos came under the "maiming your body" category — a hard limit for her mother. Mom could be a pushover at times, but when she got mad, Hayley swore even the devil feared her.

Rolling onto her back, she stared up at the white ceiling with its large, blue light fixture. Chewing her lower lip, she pondered the situation. Mom didn't have to see the tattoo. She could get one in a place always covered by clothes, like the small of her back, for instance — although a tattoo in that particular place was dubbed a tramp-stamp, and it might show in a bathing suit. But that was a far-fetched situation since the idea of a holiday in the sun was as far as the moon right now. Even if that possibility became a reality, she could wear a one-piece suit.

She'd always wanted a tattoo. Amy had a couple of them, really cool stuff — a naughty-looking angel with horns on her left shoulder blade and a pentagram on her right wrist. When Hayley had asked her if the pentagram meant anything, Amy had shrugged and said she just liked the way it looked.

Excitement parted Hayley's lips into a naughty smile. She could get away with this, just as she had with the navel piercing Amy had talked her into. She'd had it for months, and so far,

Mom had no clue. Grinning, she reached for her laptop again and started browsing the web for tattoo ideas.

She'd been at it the better part of an hour when she found it. This was the one. While she didn't know exactly why or what specific significance it had, to her, it screamed freedom, life, color — the very things she felt had been denied to her. It was the best way to explain it.

The image depicted a colorful feather, its upper-right half dispersing into small, flying birds, all done in a watercolor style that lacked any rough edges.

Lost in admiring her selection, she nearly jumped out of her skin when her cellphone rang with Mom's familiar tune. What was with her today? This was the second time her mother called this morning. Did she suspect that Hayley had lied about staying in yesterday? Damn it. She shouldn't have worn the pink top yet. She had underestimated her mother.

"Hey, Mom, what's up?" she asked as if having the warden check on the prisoner every hour was normal.

"Hi, honey. Just wondering what you would like for dinner. I can stop at that little market on the way home."

"Don't know. Whatever you decide will be fine. You know I love your cooking." Might as well stroke the ego while she was at it.

"Okay. That sounds good. So, what are you doing?"

There was too much curiosity in the question for it to be small talk. Hayley was positive her mom smelled a rat.

"Just watching TV and playing League of Legends." Each new lie came easier to her lips, but Hayley had no idea how much of them Amber believed. She cleared her throat. "It looks like they've finished across the street. The cleaners are gone."

"That's good. Well, I have to get back to work. I'll talk to you later."

Hayley put the phone away thoughtfully. Mom was going to call again; that was a given. She'd better get this dare done before she ran out of time. After dressing quickly, she Googled the closest tattoo parlor in the area, groaning when she saw it was half an hour away by bus. She'd thought of calling a cab, but that might be too expensive. Cursing, she transferred the image of the tattoo she wanted from her laptop to her phone, then took off like a marathon runner.

SHE WAS STILL BREATHING HARD a couple of hours later as the tattoo artist worked on her back. In a way, she was grateful she was in such a rush she hadn't had time to think about what she was doing, or else she might have lost her nerve.

When her mother called again, Hayley instantly forgot about the stinging pain.

"Can we take a break?" she asked the tattoo artist, fishing her phone out of her pocket.

She ran to the toilet in time to answer on the fourth ring.

"Why are you out of breath?" Mom asked, her voice filled with suspicion.

"I was in the bathroom," she said — truthfully enough. "My phone was in the bedroom. It's not like I carry it with me everywhere." Actually, she did, but she hoped she sounded annoyed enough for her mother to let it go.

"I'm sorry, sweetie. I just wondered if the house was uncomfortably warm."

Right ...

"It's okay, better than yesterday. Listen, Mom, I need to ... you know ... finish. Can we talk later?"

"Of course. Love you."

"Me, too."

Whooshing out a breath, Hayley supported herself against the door for a moment. This shit was getting exhausting. After all those crazy dares and this cat-and-mouse game she played with her mother, she damn well deserved the fifty grand.

Straightening herself, she tucked her phone in her pocket and went back to sit in front of the tattooist. The sooner he finished, the better.

Almost two hours later, back at home, Hayley couldn't stop admiring the tattoo artist's work. She stared over her shoulder in the mirror at the completed tattoo adorning her right shoulder blade. The guy had gotten a bit carried away and gone slightly beyond the area she'd outlined, spreading the tiny birds all over her right shoulder. Hell, she might not be able to wear a tank top in front of her mother all summer — or at least until she was eighteen and could do whatever the hell she wanted. But she didn't regret it one single second. The result was spectacular.

Like the previous dares she'd fulfilled, she couldn't believe she'd had the guts to do it. Truth be told, the reality of it hadn't sunk in yet. If her mother did see it, she could play the *I'm-a-poor-little-girl-hurt-by-my-father's-behavior* card to mitigate her anger.

Suddenly, she grinned. Adrenalin rushes could be addictive. She was playing with fire, and if she got caught, the shit would hit the fan big time, but somehow she couldn't stop herself. It wasn't only the prize that made her want to win this game. She'd discovered a sense of competition she didn't know she possessed. All those admiring comments she'd received on the earlier dares and the fact that the Game Master had found them worthy of posting filled her with a sense of accomplishment and intense satisfaction.

Finally, she, Hayley Jones, was popular, even though it was only in the virtual universe, among people she would never meet, people who would never know that she was actually a shy girl who would rather stay home with a good book than hang out with friends.

She jumped when a bolt of lightning split the sky, followed by a clap of thunder that shook the house and rattled the windows. As she was jogging back home from the bus station, she'd thought she'd imagined the menacing clouds gathering above, but apparently, the storm was real. Within seconds, her cellphone rang again. Slightly spooked, she swiped the screen to answer, noticing her fingers were trembling.

"Hey, Mom. Boy, your new job must be really boring if you can keep calling me like this," she said, trying to sound amused rather than exasperated.

"I'll always make time for you, sweetie, as often as I have to."

Hayley could swear her mother's tone carried traces of warning as well as sarcasm. She was worse than a frigging spy.

"I'm just worried about you," Mom said. "There's a storm on the way, and I know how much you dislike them."

"That was when I was a kid. I think they're cool now."

"Glad to know you've gotten so old. Have you had any lunch?"

Shit! She hadn't even thought about food.

"I wasn't really hungry. I ate breakfast late. Actually, I was on my way downstairs to see what I can find in the fridge. Hold on."

She deliberately held the phone next to the TV. A British daytime sitcom was running, and Hayley wanted her mother to hear the sound.

"So, how are you doing? Have you eaten?" she asked her mother as she jogged down the stairs, making as much noise as she could.

"I've had a club sandwich and a salad. There are a couple of nice, affordable little restaurants close to where I work. I'm actually at one now, finishing my coffee."

"Are you alone?"

"Yes."

"Haven't you made any friends at work?"

"Not really. I've only been here a couple of days, and we're all busy. I'm still getting a grip on my job and remembering names. You know how I suck at that."

"Yeah." Hayley opened the fridge and looked inside. "There's some leftover pasta in here from yesterday. I'll reheat it in the microwave. It looks cheesy enough," she said, managing to inject enthusiasm into her voice.

"I was thinking I would make shrimp tonight."

Hayley's stomach grumbled, and she perked up. Mom's shrimp was yummy.

"That sounds great. Do we have to go shopping for groceries? I could really use a stretch. I'm sick of sitting in the house, and the storm will be long gone by then," she muttered, knowing it was expected.

"I have frozen shrimp in the freezer, but I can come straight home and pick you up. We can take a cab from the supermarket afterward."

"Sure. I'll talk to you later."

"Bye, honey. Oh, make sure to close the windows if it rains."

"I will. Bye."

Finally! Hayley ended the call, took out the leftover pasta from the fridge, grabbed a fork, and dashed back up the stairs. Heating the food was optional, and she couldn't be bothered with that now. She couldn't wait to get upstairs, upload the picture of her new tattoo, and delete it from her phone, in case Mama Hari ever got her hands on it.

After placing the casserole on her nightstand, she went into the bathroom again and stood with her back to the mirror, admiring her tattoo. The shades of pink, yellow, purple, and aqua merged harmoniously in an artistic painting effect. God, it was well worth the pain and the considerable hole in her cash. The reddened skin still stung and would take a while to heal, but since she wasn't the type to wear skimpy clothes, Mom wouldn't notice.

She took several pictures before returning to the bedroom and pulling on a loose T-shirt. As she ate her pasta, she browsed the photos to see which ones were the most flattering. When she finally decided on the one she wanted to use, she cropped it so only her shoulder was visible. She was self-conscious of her body and was secretly worried she might never have decent-sized boobs. What she had now looked like a couple of mosquito bites. Her mother wasn't what you would call well-endowed either, so she could never hope to have big breasts. Not like Amy, who looked amazing in a bra and wasn't in the least bit shy about undressing in front of her.

Life wasn't fair, but Hayley had already learned that. Maybe she could get breast implants when she won the 50k prize. The thought made her giggle, and she coughed when she choked on her food. Mom would go berserk. But with fifty grand in her pocket, Hayley would have options. Maybe she wouldn't stick around here. Maybe she would go back to New York and find a place with Amy.

"Yeah, right," she snorted.

Her mom and dad would hunt her down, along with the FBI, CIA, and every other letter of the alphabet organization in the world.

But winning was still a long way away. She wouldn't count her chickens yet. Switching on her laptop, she logged into The Game. As she waited for the photo to upload, proving she'd completed the final dare for this level, her stomach quivered with excitement. She thought the explanation on why she'd chosen that particular tattoo was rather poetic. Freedom — that was a $50,000 word — either that or a myth.

She grinned when she saw the message that flashed on the screen. DARE COMPLETE. WELCOME TO LEVEL THREE.

She was so excited that it took her three tries to grasp the meaning of the next dare. When it finally sunk in, her jaw dropped.

"What the hell?" she whispered, her voice tinged with horror.

She leaned closer to the screen, not wanting to believe what she was reading. This was the first dare in the third level, but never in a million years would she have imagined something like this. Sure, the other dares had been open-ended, letting you make what you wanted of them, but this one was specific — too specific.

Slamming down the lid of her laptop, she rushed to the bathroom as the pasta revolted in her belly. The Game was no longer just an edgy means of getting thrills. It was sick, freaking sick!

THE SPASMS in Hayley's stomach seemed to go on forever, keeping time with the thunder and lightning filling the air around her through the open windows. Finally, after what seemed an eternity, they stopped.

She stood, shaking, and went through the house and closed the windows as the rain pelted against the panes. There was no way she could fulfill that dare — not for fifty grand, not for a million bucks!

Gradually, the storm within her calmed as the one outside ebbed. She returned to the bathroom and brushed her teeth to get the taste of vomit out of her mouth. It wasn't the words of the dare that had made her puke but the images they conjured in her mind.

Trembling, she made sure there was no sign that she'd been ill. If she thought her mother was hovering over her now, it would be far worse if she believed Hayley was sick.

She returned to her room and opened her computer. The webpage was still there, the horrible words splattered across the screen, blood-red against the black background, looking more ominous than ever.

Dare #5: *Kill an animal, and tell me which method you chose and why. Don't forget to upload videos/photos.*

If this was the first dare of Level Three, what could she possibly expect next? She shuddered, her brain flashing visions of dead kittens, puppy dogs, bunnies, and birds. The image of the poor frog her teacher had tried to make her dissect in science class last year, but which she'd flat out refused to do. There was no way she could do this. She even hated killing mosquitoes, flies, or spiders. While she might be able to work up the nerve to kill a snake, that was no help since there weren't any snakes in Ireland.

Was this actually the portal to one of those terrorist sites where they lured kids into following whatever cause they espoused? Was that what she'd gotten involved in? And how compliant had she shown herself to be? She'd already broken the law for them, but to kill an animal? No. No way.

She didn't want to play The Game anymore. She needed to talk to Amy and figure out how to get out of this mess. With shaky fingers, she texted her friend.

Can you talk?

Within seconds, her phone rang. Hayley reached for it faster than the lightning that split the sky outside.

"Hey, what's up?" Amy's voice sounded odd, preoccupied, as though she wasn't feeling well.

"Amy, can you talk?" Hayley's own voice was hoarse from crying and vomiting. Imagine the mess she would be if she actually attempted to fulfill that horrific dare.

"Yeah. What's wrong?"

"How do I get out of The Game? How do I delete my account and everything I posted there?" Her words tumbled over one another.

"What? Listen, I don't know why you're so freaked out, but

you can't delete your account," Amy answered cautiously. "It doesn't work that way. This is the Dark Web. You can't delete information from there. Why do you want to leave The Game?"

"Because it's sick! Do you know —" Hayley's voice was little more than a sob. "Do you know what the first dare from the third level is?"

"I do." Amy's dry, short reply left a wall of silence between them.

Hayley swallowed, goose bumps covering her skin. "Do you mean ... Amy, did you do that? Have you —"

"Get the fuck off your high and mighty throne, Hayley. I did what I fucking had to do. Was it easy? No. Am I sorry I did it? Hell no. I'm one step closer to the goddamn money. One step closer to getting out of this shithole and moving to California. I'll win that prize and become an actress like I've always dreamed of."

"But ... How could you?" Hayley's voice was a mere whisper. This cruel, angry person wasn't the Amy she knew.

"Don't tell me you're squeamish over this. You, who broke into a house to see a real crime scene? I thought you had more balls than that."

"I didn't kill the woman. I just filmed the crime scene. It's not the same as killing a defenseless animal," she argued, sensing Amy was as disappointed with her as she was with her friend.

"What did you think? That earning fifty grand would be easy? For fuck's sake, you eat chickens, pigs, even lambs every time you sit down to a meal. Do you think they grow in a supermarket? *The lamb chops in aisle four are ready for harvesting. Butcher to aisle four,*" Amy mocked harshly. "Grow a pair, will you?" She paused, collecting herself. When she spoke again, her voice was so calm it was blood-chilling. "Listen, Hal, you've got to understand something."

"What?" Hayley asked, her voice small. How could Amy talk

about killing an animal as if it were nothing? She wasn't stupid enough to accept that buying meat in the market was the same as killing something. Sure, her ancestors had hunted wild animals for food, but damn it. This was the twenty-first century, and she wasn't going to start hunting for the pleasure of the kill.

"Most of the people who invent this kind of game are fucked up," Amy said, bringing her back. "But they've got the money."

"I don't care about the money anymore," Hayley said loudly, angry her friend couldn't understand how she felt. "I'm not going to kill an animal for a game! How could you do it?"

"Shh," Amy said sharply. "Do you want your mom to hear you?"

"She's not home from work yet."

"Okay. About The Game, you have to understand that it's not just about the money. People like this are sick, and that means dangerous. You don't know what they'll do if you quit The Game. They know all about you, Hayley — where you live, what you look like, who your family is — they know where to find you. Do you understand what I'm telling you?"

Hayley swallowed, her throat clogging with tears. "God, Amy, what have we gotten ourselves into? How do we get out?"

"We finish it. It's the only way."

"I'm not doing it! I can't. I'll go to the police."

"And tell them what? There are thousands of dare games like this on the internet. Ever heard of the Blue Whale? What good did the police do to all of those who finished that game by killing themselves?"

"Suicide? Are you crazy? Is that what this is?" Tears ran down Hayley's cheeks.

"Calm down, for fuck's sake. No, this isn't a suicide pact. Sheesh! You didn't overreact like this when you lived here." Amy's tone was filled with fury. "No one can stop The Game; you have to accept it once and for all. Once you're in, you're in.

They own you. You have to complete all the dares. If you don't ..." Her words trailed off, and the silence was worse than anything she could say. It left the rest to the imagination.

"What animal did you kill?" Hayley whispered, feeling this whole conversation was surreal — wishing it were.

"The neighbor's yappy dog," Amy replied defiantly. "It wasn't easy, but it's done. The fucking neighborhood should give me a prize for shutting the damn thing up. Look. This doesn't have to be hard. Find a stray cat, feed it poison, and take a picture of the corpse. Just get on with it. Keep your eye on the money, Hal. That's all that matters. I've got to go. We'll chat later."

She ended the call. Hayley put the phone on the nightstand and threw herself on her bed, great sobs wracking her body. She'd lost Amy's respect and friendship, but there was no way she could kill an animal. She felt trapped, desperate. How could she get out of this sadistic Game without getting hurt herself?

12

"I think you might be right about our killer being a professional assassin, one the judge could have hired to murder Dr. McKenna," John said, maneuvering the car through the traffic.

He focused on his conversation with Aidan, controlling his breathing carefully. He couldn't ignore the raging storm since he barely had any visibility beyond the windshield. The wipers swept frantically at the rain, and his fingers clenched tighter on the wheel with each roar of thunder, each bolt of lightning. He'd hoped getting through a storm would become easier in time — it hadn't.

To be fair, he had to admit this had been another difficult day. He and Aidan had visited Brian McKenna to inform him he was free to make funeral arrangements. John could've called to tell Mr. McKenna he could now claim his wife's body, but that was too impersonal, and he identified too closely with the man to do it that way.

Although the McKenna house had been cleaned and there were no signs left of the murder, Brian had opted to stay with his neighbors. John could understand that. It had taken days before he'd been able to go into their home after Shanna's death — and she hadn't died in it.

He forced his mind back on the case. "The killer probably picks up whatever he needs in the country where he has a job, which would explain why he used four different guns. If it wasn't for the Ace of Spades, we wouldn't have seen the connection. Jenna might never have found him."

"I agree." Aidan twisted in his seat to face him. "It's much easier than traveling with a weapon these days when everyone and his mother is on the watch for terrorists. But how are we going to prove the judge hired him if we can't find the blighter? Where are we going, by the way?"

"To see that graphologist I mentioned. I discussed the idea with the chief inspector. He called earlier. The man's expecting us."

"Good idea. The more we can learn about the bastard, the better. We've got precious little as it is."

RALPH LANDRY WAS the most renowned graphologist in Ireland. It took John and Aidan half an hour to find his office — or was it a workshop? — in the historical city center, tucked in an old building that had been a drugstore more than a century ago. Since they couldn't drive a car through the cobblestone alley meant for pedestrians, they had to walk through the rain, which didn't improve John's mood.

Once they reached the handwriting expert's office, John gave him the basics and waited while the man analyzed what little evidence the Garda had.

"So, what's your first impression, Mr. Landry?" John asked after a while.

Landry didn't raise his head, still looking closely through a large magnifying glass at the playing cards arranged in front of him.

Since they didn't have the physical evidence from the other cases, all John could show him was the actual card left by Maureen's killer and the high-resolution photos of the others sent with the electronic files. It was far from the best, but the graphologist said he could do a preliminary analysis since this was an emergency.

Finally, when John's patience had all but lapsed, Landry lifted his face to look at him, eyes sober behind his large, horn-rimmed glasses.

"There is very little to work with here," he began in his raspy drawl. "I usually need a larger sample of writing, at least a few paragraphs, and I'll still need to see the originals, not just the photos. Based on this, I can't give you an official opinion; however, as far as I can tell, each of these cards was signed by different individuals."

"What?" Aidan, who'd been pacing the room, whirled around.

John wasn't a man to lose his professional demeanor easily. He wouldn't have made it to the rank of detective inspector otherwise. But when the graphologist's words penetrated the layers of fatigue and foreboding that fogged his brain, his heart skipped a beat.

"Bloody hell!" His gaze connected with Aidan's across the room. "We'd better pray this is one killer smart enough to ask four innocent people to write on these cards for him without explaining why they were doing it."

"Or we have four different killers," Aidan finished.

The silence in the room was deafening. John's mind couldn't process this new information. He didn't know where to begin assessing the potential complications of this case, which seemed to grow more tentacles by the day. He shoved his fingers through his wet hair, savagely rubbing his scalp.

"Are you sure?" he asked the graphologist.

Ralph Landry shrugged his thin shoulders. "No," he admitted. "I wouldn't be 100 percent certain even if I saw the original cards. As I told you, there simply isn't enough writing to analyze. I do know there are at least two writers, and this one was written by a left-handed person," he said, indicating the file from Italy. "While this has been scribbled by a right-handed one. There's no question about it," he emphasized, placing one finger on the card left on Maureen McKenna's body. "Each symbol is written in a different style. This one is drawn with uneven edges, unlike this other one, which is traced carefully and with less pressure." He demonstrated as he spoke, showing John the patterns he saw on each piece of evidence. "Here, we have someone who tried to do a neat job but elongated the second horizontal line more than the others. The fourth one looks as if the author started tracing the G with the vertical line, not in the usual way."

Aidan walked over to stand behind Landry, looking over the man's shoulder to get a better view of the documents spread over his desk.

"Can you tell us anything about the people who drew these symbols? Or about the symbol itself?" Aidan asked.

Landry reached for his magnifying glass and bent over the photos once more. He studied each one for a few more minutes, moving back and forth between them. Finally, he shook his head.

"As I said, it's very little to work with. Other than what I've already told you, I really can't offer an educated guess regarding age, character traits, or anything pertinent."

John pressed his fist against his mouth, willing the other man to read more from the scribbled symbols. Not that it would make much difference if they hadn't been written by the killer or killers. He tried to inject patience into his voice to mask his desperation.

"Mr. Landry, at this point, anything you tell us might help, even if it doesn't seem pertinent."

"I'm sorry, I truly am. If you get the original cards, bring them to me, and I'll have another look. That's the best I can do."

John nodded and thanked him, then gathered the evidence bags.

Once outside, the dark skies seemed eerier than ever. Just what he needed — a bloody storm and a case he didn't have a clue how to solve.

"What now?" Aidan asked, getting into the car.

"We go back to the beginning. If this is one contract killer or a team of them, they had to be hired somewhere, somehow. Let's hope Jenna can use her magic and figure out how."

JOHN HAD BEEN GOING over the four crime reports since early afternoon, and nothing made any more sense than it had earlier. He hadn't eaten, his throat was scratchy because of dehydration, and a vicious headache radiated within his entire skull.

It took him several moments to realize someone was pounding on the office door.

"John, I need to speak to you, now," a bleary-eyed Jenna said, cracking the door only open enough to shove her head inside the office. "You too, Aidan. My office."

She didn't wait for them to follow her. The urgency in her voice was so compelling they didn't have a choice. John rushed after her, Aidan at his heels.

"I found your killer," Jenna said without any preamble. "And it isn't the murder for hire you had me looking for. It's far worse than that. I don't know his or her identity yet, but I do know why he or she killed Maureen McKenna."

Things were happening so fast John's mind spun. He sat on the edge of a chair next to Aidan, who was anxiously rubbing his palms up and down his thighs.

John fixed his gaze on Jenna. "I'm listening."

"Okay. So, I was searching for killers for hire on the Dark Web. Ye wouldn't find them at an employment site. While I was at it, it occurred to me that when I searched for that symbol, I only searched the regular channels, the surface web," she said, gesturing as she spoke. "That's how I tracked down the other murders. I spent all afternoon digging for your assassin — which is not nearly as easy as digging through your average internet layers — and I discovered THE GAME."

Her eyebrows arched high above the rimless glasses she wore. As he listened to her, John's apprehension increased. Several times, he had to remind himself to breathe.

"This is a game for teenagers between fifteen and eighteen years of age," Jenna continued. "Apparently, it's a dare game, which starts with innocent dares such as *Take a Selfie* but ends with *Kill John Doe*."

"Holy shit," Aidan cursed, repeating the words several times.

"Oh, aye." John couldn't agree more. "Holy shit, indeed." He stood and walked over to the small window, suddenly feeling claustrophobic in this tiny room. The storm clouds were heavy, with thunder rumbling in the distance and lightning flashing intermittently. "Teenagers? For God's sake, Jenna, are you saying teenagers are killing innocent people as part of a game?"

He turned abruptly to face her. "Tell me you know who runs this bloody game."

She took off her glasses and rubbed her eyes, her posture reflecting defeat. "Wish I could. I'm not even close to finding the bastard or bastards in charge. They're smart. I can't track them down by myself. I'll get the whole team working on this, but … it might take days, weeks, even months."

"And while we sit on our arses waiting, someone else could die at any time," Aidan concluded.

"Unfortunately, yes." Jenna bit her lower lip. Worry lines creased her young, beautiful face. "I'm sorry, but that's the way of it. Digging on the Dark Web takes time — lots of time — and this looks bad."

John paced the narrow room, feeling more like a caged animal than ever. He needed to put this into perspective. Panic wasn't an option. They finally had a lead, a real lead. He just needed to pursue it in the best, fastest, most effective way possible. He turned to Jenna once more.

"Do you know how he targets his victims? And how, for the love of God, does he convince these ... children to kill people? Where are their parents? Why hasn't anyone gone to the police with this?"

"I can't answer either of those questions yet," Jenna said apologetically, raking her fingers through her red curls in a gesture of frustration. "I suspect he or they offer the teenagers a money prize. Bored kids, dissatisfied with their lives, will do just about anything for kicks these days. As for why no one's gone to the police, there are all sorts of methods of manipulation — social engineering, threats against them and their families ... Don't forget, there are a lot of disenchanted teens out there. Some may be doing this to feel accepted, to gain praise from their peers, to be one of the cool kids, if only in the virtual world."

"Jesus, Mary, and Joseph! How do they get so fucked up?" John was about to explode. "Four people are dead because some teenagers have a popularity contest going?"

Jenna nodded sadly. "It seems unbelievable, I know, but this is the society we live in. I worked a case once where a lunatic persuaded seventeen kids to kill themselves. It was in a forest outside of Waterford. I still have nightmares when I recall the scene we discovered that night. We caught the bastard, but ...

we were too late to save any of the children. The youngest was eleven years old."

All at once, her gaze reflected all the horrors she'd seen in her short years, and John felt sorry for the loss of her youthful innocence. This job could suck the life right out of you. As a city cop, it was impossible to preserve a rosy, optimistic perception of the world.

John noted the way Aidan's gaze softened when he looked at Jenna. In another time, another place, perhaps his partner might've reached out and taken her into his arms, making her forget if only for a moment all the horrors she'd seen, showing her some of the beautiful things that made life worth living. But this wasn't the time for romance.

"We have to get to work so we can prevent stuff like that from happening again," John said briskly. "What's the next step, Jenna? How do we locate this son of a bitch?"

"Well, first, we don't know if the Game Master is one person. There could be several people involved, whether creators of The Game or just admins, but for now, we'll call our suspect *he*. I'll brief the team in the morning, and we'll start working on this. We'll use reverse engineering, but we have to be very careful. We don't want him to know we're on to him. If he catches us, he could disappear, close down the site, fall off the radar, and we could lose him for good."

"Why wait until morning?"

"John, it's past eight," she said patiently. "Your case isn't the only one the Cyber Division is working on. Everyone has gone home. Besides, I'm so knackered I can't see the screen clearly. I'm no good to you now."

John glanced at his watch, chagrinned. He hadn't realized how tired he was, too, until now. Or maybe he'd subconsciously wanted to delay his going home to that damn empty apartment. A flash of lightning made him step casually away from the window before the following thunder roar reminded him the storm was still going strong outside.

"I'm sorry, Jenna. You're right. I lost track of time. Go home and rest. We'll pick this up in the morning."

"You've done a great job, kid," Aidan said, getting to his feet.

Jenna's pale cheeks bloomed pink. "Thanks. My job isn't nearly done. I'll do my best to find this creep."

"And when you do, we'll see the bastard and those who followed his sick orders get everything they deserve," John vowed.

AMBER WAS EXHAUSTED, achy, and wet. Sitting at a desk eight hours a day, then walking several blocks from the bus station — tonight in the pouring rain — was a far cry from the lifestyle she was accustomed to. Not that she hadn't done plenty of walking in New York, but she used to be in better shape thanks to her gym membership.

Maybe she could find a nearby gym soon. Hayley might like to go with her. Besides being good for her health and development, it would be a great opportunity for them to bond as mother and daughter, maybe make some friends as well. And it would give her another opportunity to keep an eye on Hayley.

When had playing warden become part of her job as a mother? She supposed it was normal for teenagers to sneak out sometimes and lie to their parents about it — she'd done it often enough herself — but the circumstances were different now.

She hadn't read anything new about Maureen McKenna's murder, although she scanned the news every day, hoping to learn they'd caught the killer. Maybe she was hoping the hunky detective would come knocking at her door again to give her the good news personally.

She shook her head. God, she was too old and jaded to have such fantasies. Every night when she went to bed, she lay awake, remembering the number one therapy for insomnia, the thing all magazines recommended: think of something pleasant, a happy memory, or something nice in your life.

It was hard to think of anything nice in her life right now. Everything had revolved around her family and her marriage, but now all of those memories were tainted by Dean's affair. So what did she have left other than a little fantasy about a sexy man she probably would never see again?

For the second time in a week, she'd been so lost in thought she almost walked past her house. Scoffing, she stopped herself just in time.

It would've been cheaper to rent a flat, but Hayley had always lived in a house, and she wanted her daughter to have a backyard where she could sit in the fresh air and listen to music, the way she had back in New York.

She was rummaging through her purse, looking for her key, when she spotted a tabby cat perched on the stone railing that edged their old-fashioned veranda. Judging by its size and battle-scarred face, this guy must be king of the neighborhood.

"Hi there," she said, hoping she wouldn't scare him. "Come to inspect the newcomers?"

The cat — far from being afraid — watched her with cold green eyes, in that superior way innate to felines. As she reached out to let him sniff her hand, he tilted his pink nose toward it in a gesture fit for royalty, and his white whiskers twitched. Deciding she was acceptable — for a human — he let her stroke his head, then tipped it back, allowing her to scratch under his chin.

Amber couldn't stifle her giggle. She loved animals, especially cats. They'd adopted one when Hayley was five, but her daughter had been so heartbroken when he'd died six years later that she and Dean had decided against getting another pet for a while. The years had passed, and they'd been too busy with other things to think about pets.

Now, as she caressed the cat's soft fur and listened to his tentative purring, Amber decided she and Hayley had been deprived long enough. Sometimes, animals were better company than people. They didn't demand nearly as much work as most relationships did.

"Hey, big boy, if you don't have a home, you're welcome to bunk here with us. Let's see if you would like some sour cream." She winked, remembering that had been their cat's favorite treat.

She didn't pick him up, well aware he could have fleas or other parasites. If the stray decided to stay, she would have to take him to a vet, but for now, she'd take things slowly. She walked to the front door and unlocked it, continuing to talk gently to the cat. He must have sensed her good intentions because he followed her, intrigued.

"Wait here." She could swear the intelligent green eyes understood.

The moment she took off her shoes and stepped onto the cool parquet floor, she sighed contentedly. She looked around, but Hayley wasn't downstairs. Putting away her umbrella, she dropped her purse onto the sofa, padded to the base of the stairs, and called out.

"Hayley, I'm home."

"I'm taking a nap," Hayley's muffled voice came from her bedroom.

A nap? At this hour? Puzzled, she checked her wristwatch, but she already knew it was six-twenty. Despite the rain, she and Hayley were supposed to go and buy groceries. They'd talked about it only a couple of hours ago. Maybe she wasn't keen on going out in the rain.

"You might want to come downstairs. There's something I

want to show you," she called out from the kitchen, dolloping thick sour cream on a saucer.

Stepping outside, she heard the muffled rumble of thunder. Hadn't the damn storm ended? Carried by the wind, a red candy bar wrapper fluttered past the gate.

Her furry companion waited patiently on the doormat. He dropped all pretense of indifference and mewed shamelessly when he smelled the sour cream. Laughing, Amber put the saucer in front of him, watching him dive in. He lapped away enthusiastically, his whiskers becoming creamy-white in seconds.

Amber sensed rather than heard Hayley behind her and turned to see her daughter standing in the doorway. Although Hayley tried to hide her reddened eyes by looking down at the cat, Amber realized her daughter had been crying. Was it something she'd done? God, was she so miserable and alone here that she was sinking into depression?

"Who's this?" Hayley asked before Amber had time to speak. "Where did you find him?"

"On the veranda. He looked as if he was standing guard outside the house. By the size of him, I'll bet he would be as good as a guard dog."

"He looks like he could eat a guard dog," Hayley said, a reluctant smile teasing at her mouth. She knelt to stroke the cat, whose sudden purring took on an engine-like quality.

"I thought that if he wants to stick around, we could adopt him," Amber said, watching her daughter for a reaction.

Hayley's dark face lit up. "Really? That would be awesome!"

"I know. You wouldn't be alone all day anymore." Amber gazed into her daughter's eyes, wishing she could read her mind. "What's wrong, honey?"

"Nothing."

Hayley lowered her eyes, continuing to stroke the cat, who

was licking the last traces of cream. Her face was pale, and Amber noticed her hand trembled on the cat's fur.

Fear tightened Amber's belly. "Hayley, I'm not asking you to tell me what's wrong; I'm *demanding* to know," she said, getting to her feet. She could only hope she sounded authoritarian instead of panicky. "Why have you been crying?"

"I haven't," Hayley snapped, jerking to her feet as well.

Her abrupt gesture startled the cat, who jumped away. Looking into his big, scared eyes, Hayley crumpled. Her eyes welled up, and she let herself slide down on the veranda floor. She reached for the cat.

"I would never hurt you," she murmured over and over until he accepted being cuddled in her arms.

Amber's anxiety increased as she watched the scene. Dropping to her knees beside her daughter, she smoothed Hayley's hair away from her face.

"Talk to me, honey. What's wrong?"

"I can't tell you, I just can't ... I can't tell you."

Hayley's repeated words were knife wounds in Amber's heart. Her daughter was having a meltdown, and she had no idea why. She felt helpless and terrified at the same time.

"Sweetie, you can tell me anything. I'm your mom; you're my baby. Whatever's wrong, we'll fix it together."

"You can't fix this, believe me. No one can."

The hopelessness in Hayley's voice was absolute, increasing Amber's fear. This wasn't an ordinary teenage crisis, like a huge pimple or a boy's rejection. This was something far more serious.

"Hayley, everything has a solution," she said, keeping her tone measured. "We'll find it together, I promise you, but you have to tell me what the problem is. I'm here for you, always have been, always will be. Now, take a deep breath and tell me what it is." Her voice held more confidence than she felt.

Hayley's teeth were buried savagely in her lower lip. She

made an effort to dislodge them and breathe — once, twice, three times. When she'd calmed a little, she began speaking, her eyes resting on the cat in her arms.

"I have this friend in New York. Her name's Amy. You don't know her. We used to hang out together, but I didn't tell you because I knew you wouldn't like her. Anyway, she started playing this dare game, and she told me I should play it, too. There's a $50,000 prize if you finish the game."

Amber had a sick feeling in her stomach. As someone with a degree in Information Technology, she was up to date with most things and knew what kind of games kids today played. A dare game could mean anything from cutting oneself to committing suicide. It was incredible how many teenagers fell prey to sociopaths who invented these twisted games and manipulated kids using social engineering. Her baby had gotten involved in such a thing. And she'd been worried about Hayley sneaking outside ... It seemed that staying inside was far more dangerous.

13

Amber's stomach muscles were so tight she could barely breathe. It took all of her self-control to listen in silence as Hayley confided in her.

"It sounded like harmless fun, so I created an account and started playing. At first, the dares were simple stuff, like take a selfie, do something you've never done, take something from a store without paying for it, get a tattoo ..."

Hayley glanced up at her, seeming surprised she wasn't breathing fire by now. In fact, Amber was, but now wasn't the time to vent her rage. Obviously, control, obedience, and manipulation were the goals here. She had to shut up and listen, or she would never hear the whole story.

"Anyway, this was only for the first levels," Hayley resumed, taking longer and longer pauses. It seemed that every word she uttered caused her immense pain. "The first dare in the third level was ... to ..." She gulped several times. "To kill an animal."

Amber gasped. "My God, Hayley, you didn't —"

"No! I could never do that, Mom, never," Hayley cried.

Her daughter's firm reply allowed Amber's heart to start beating again.

"I wanted to quit The Game, delete my account, but Amy said I couldn't, stating that the people who manage the game know everything about us now, and they would hurt our families and us. She said the only way to get out was to finish the game."

Amber huffed out a sigh of relief, dragging a heavy hand through her hair. At least her daughter hadn't done something she couldn't live with — although her stomach was still tight at the thought of the other dares she'd completed. Shoplifting was a crime, for heaven's sake, and — God help her — getting a tattoo at her age. But there was hope for her misguided child. Hayley had stopped herself from doing something truly monstrous.

Amber knew all the pressures and tactics people used to scare impressionable teenagers. Most of the server administrators of these games, the Game Masters, were sick bastards but not nearly as powerful as they tried to appear.

"Honey," she began, speaking as calmly as she possibly could under the circumstances. "What you did was very wrong, but the fact that you *know* it was wrong is good. No one will harm you, I assure you. Show me the link to this game, and I'll make sure —"

"You don't understand," Hayley said in a whisper. "That's not the worst of it, Mom."

Her brown eyes lifted to Amber for the first time. They were so filled with desperation that Amber's heart started pounding again. Even the cat was still as though it sensed something terrible.

Hayley swallowed audibly. "That's not the last dare. Amy called me earlier, totally freaked out … She got access to the final level forum, and … she saw the last dare. You have to kill someone to win The Game."

Amber watched in horror as Hayley turned over her phone and showed her the picture Amy had sent.

Dear God! She pressed a fist against her mouth, feeling she couldn't draw enough air into her lungs. What was her baby mixed up in?

"These people have to be stopped, Hayley. You understand that, don't you?"

Hayley nodded.

"We need help to do that." Hands trembling, Amber reached for her purse and pulled out her cellphone, then rummaged through her things until she found Detective O'Sullivan's business card.

"Who are you calling?" Hayley asked, tears sliding down her cheeks once more.

"Detective O'Sullivan. He needs to know about this."

She keyed in the number and waited as the phone rang, praying he was still at work.

"Hello." He sounded exhausted, almost defeated.

"Detective O'Sullivan?" Amber's voice was hesitant.

"Yes. May I help you?"

"I don't know if you remember me. My name is Amber Reed; I live across the street from Maureen McKenna —"

"Of course I remember you, Ms. Reed."

She paused for a moment, taken by surprise. She didn't think he would remember her. Squaring her shoulders, she continued. "I need to talk to you urgently about Mrs. McKenna's murder. I have vital information you need to know right away. Should I come to the police station or —"

"Ms. Reed, are you at home?"

"Yes."

"Stay there. My partner and I will be with you as soon as we can." He ended the call.

Amber stared at her phone. Something in the detective's urgency told her things would get a lot worse from this point on.

Fifteen minutes later, the screech of tires announced their

guests. Hayley was curled up on the sofa, holding her knees and looking miserable. Having paced the room in silence, Amber rushed to open the door before the detectives knocked.

"Ms. Reed, this is Detective Aidan Connor, my partner," John introduced the other man. "We're both very anxious to hear what you have to tell us about the murder."

"Please, come in."

Minutes later, Amber sat next to Hayley on the sofa, her hands clasped tightly in her lap, listening as her daughter confessed what she'd done as part of the game. Grim-faced, the men sat on kitchen chairs she'd placed in front of the sofa. One of them would ask a question now and again, but for the past ten minutes, the only sound in the room had been Hayley's tentative voice.

Every word was a punch to Amber's gut. How could she not have realized all of this was going on? How horrible a parent was she that her daughter had turned to crime and violence like this?

When Hayley reached the part where she'd broken into Maureen McKenna's house, Amber bit her lip, willing herself to remain quiet. Any reaction she displayed might inhibit Hayley, and any information her daughter could provide the police was valuable. That much they both understood. Everything seemed surreal. How had they ended up involved in this mess?

"Yesterday, after I uploaded the photo with my new tattoo ..." Hayley paused, glancing apologetically at her mother. She moistened her lips and blinked rapidly, then focused back on detective John O'Sullivan. "That was the last dare in the second level. Then I got a message welcoming me to level three, and ... the first dare was to kill an animal, tell which method I used, and why."

"And you had to film this?" John asked, his expression carefully neutral.

"Yeah, that's how the dares work. You have to prove everything you do by uploading the pictures or videos."

"What did you do then, Hayley?" Detective Connor asked.

Hayley slumped deeper between the sofa cushions, shoving her legs under herself.

"I slammed the laptop shut and called Amy. I would never do such a thing, ever!" she emphasized, her voice thin, almost to the breaking point.

"I'm glad to hear that," John said, shifting his body to lean slightly forward in his chair. He looked intently at Hayley. "That's not only illegal, but such cruelty is a grave sign of mental illness. Has Amy done this?"

When several seconds had passed, and there was no answer, Amber turned her head to look at Hayley. Her eyes had filled with tears, and she was nodding soundlessly, staring down at her hands. She squeezed her phone so tightly that her knuckles were as white as marble.

"How do you know? Did she tell you?" Detective Connor asked.

Hayley nodded again. "She said it wasn't a big deal. I told her I wanted out of this game, that I wanted to delete my account and everything I'd uploaded on that website. But she said I couldn't, because the person or people who created this game know me, know everything about my family and me, and if I tried to quit or told anyone about The Game, they would hurt me."

She sniffed back tears, wiping her eyes with the back of her hands. "I was simply going to stop calling her. Anyway, she was angry with me for being a wimp. I just wasn't going to go back to The Game; I didn't plan to access it ever again — not that it would stop them from hunting me down if they wanted to." Her chin trembled. "A couple of hours later, Amy called me. She was so freaked out I didn't understand what she meant in the beginning — until she sent me this."

She turned her phone around so the detectives could see the screen. Amber closed her eyes briefly. That image was going to haunt her forever. It was a miracle she hadn't fainted the first time Hayley had shown her a screenshot of Maureen McKenna, her eyes as wide as the bloody hole in her forehead. A playing card was lying on her chest in a pool of blood. The thought that her daughter might be involved in *any* way in this nightmare was enough to drive Amber into the deepest, darkest oceans of despair.

To her amazement, the detectives didn't seem shocked. Either they were so exceptional at their jobs they'd trained their features to the point they could remain almost robotic, or ...

"Did you know about this?" The thought was voiced before Amber realized she'd spoken aloud. But when John's steel-gray eyes turned to her, she faced him squarely.

"You don't seem surprised," she reasoned. "Did you know about this ... this Game?"

John glanced at his partner as though consulting him about how much he should tell her.

Finally, he replied, "We've learned about The Game today, but the fact that you and Hayley contacted us and actually have access to this website is an incredible stroke of luck. I think it will help us catch this person or persons considerably quicker. How much do you know about this Game, Ms. Reed?"

Amber lifted her hands, palms up, glancing at Hayley.

"Only what my daughter told me. I had no idea this *Game* existed until today. To be honest, it's still such a shock I can't —"

Her shoulders slumped in utter defeat. She was tired to the bone, worn out to her very core. Her exhaustion was more than physical. To her dismay, she was ashamed to admit it, but right now, in this particular moment, she was tired of being a mother, ashamed of the fact that she'd failed at what she'd considered her most important job.

She'd always tried to protect her child from the viciousness of the world, but today it was as if all of her hard work had been in vain. How could one woman expect to shield her child from the horrors of a society gone mad?

Eventually, she lifted her head and stared at John, then at Aidan. "I have a degree in computer science, specifically information technology," she said wearily. "I'm a website developer, and my work revolves around computers, so I know quite a lot about what happens on the internet. But this is too much to accept, even for me. People manipulating teenagers into committing murder? How is this possible? And, most importantly, why are they doing it? For kicks?"

Her voice rose involuntarily, and she forced herself to temper it. Stressing Hayley further wouldn't accomplish anything. Besides, the two detectives weren't to blame for any of this. Judging by their faces and wrinkled clothes, they were more exhausted than she was, and the responsibilities of their jobs far surpassed hers.

"We don't know the reason behind this website yet," John answered. "But like I said, now we have a very important asset. The question is: will you collaborate with the Garda to assist us in solving this case?"

Amber gaped at him. "Of course we will. We're the ones who contacted you. What do we have to do?"

John glanced at his watch, but she had the impression he didn't really register the time. "I would like to take Hayley's laptop so our cybercrime experts can analyze it; however, we have to treat this case with kid gloves. If indeed the Game admin or admins are monitoring the players, they might track the device and see the laptop is located at Garda headquarters. We can't risk moving it yet. Tomorrow morning we'll talk to Detective Jenna Darcy, our cybercrime expert, and she'll come here to take a look at Hayley's laptop. She'll tell us what to do next. It's very important that you don't touch it until then," he told Hayley, stretching out the words.

Hayley nodded several times. "I won't. But who's going to protect us until morning? What if they already know I've talked with the police? By morning, my mom and I could — What happened to Mrs. McKenna can happen to us."

Aidan leaned forward, supporting his hands on his knees.

"Hayley, I don't think you're in any immediate danger. If you keep away from the internet and don't tell anyone what you told us, the Game admins can't know you contacted us."

"Yes, they will! They know everything! Maybe Amy has told someone already. I don't know ... I can't trust her anymore. She was so far gone that she might've done something crazy. You have to stay with us or send someone to protect us!"

She was half-shouting, half-crying, so John reached out to touch her shoulder.

"Okay, relax, lass. We'll see what we can do." He shifted his eyes to Aidan. "It's too late now, but first thing tomorrow, I'll arrange to have an unmarked patrol car stationed in front of the house."

"What about tonight?" Hayley wailed, her round eyes pleading. "Who's going to stay with us tonight?"

"I will," John said soothingly.

He hitched his thumb in the general direction of the street where their car was parked. "I'll bunk in the car. Aidan, can you get a cab home?"

There was an unspoken exchange between the two men, one Amber couldn't understand, but only seconds later, Aidan nodded.

This probably wasn't the usual police procedure, indulging the fears of a teenage girl, but Amber was immensely grateful to John O'Sullivan for doing this. They obviously had a hell of a case on their hands. If the person who'd killed Dr. McKenna was in the area, and he probably was, she and Hayley really could be in danger.

"What about Amy?" Aidan asked. "We need to contact her parents right away."

"Right you are," John agreed. "Hayley, can you give us Amy's full name and address?"

Hayley looked at him from under wet eyelashes. She appeared calmer now that the detective had guaranteed them protection.

"Her name is Amy Fielding. I don't know her exact address, other than the name of the street. I'll write it down for you," she said, getting to her feet to search for a notepad and pencil.

"Would you contact Mr. and Mrs. Fielding asap?" John asked Aidan.

Hayley returned with a piece of paper.

"Amy lives with her mom," she said, scribbling down Amy's information. "I don't know where her dad is, but her mom is ..."

She looked up at the two detectives, an awkward expression dragging at her features. "Amy's mom is cool and everything, but she's not, like ... Very responsible."

"I thought I was responsible, and look how that turned out," Amber muttered bitterly.

She hadn't meant for anyone to hear, but when Hayley darted her a hurt glance, she stared her daughter down.

John was the one to interrupt the tense moment. "What do you mean by that, Hayley?"

Hayley fidgeted with the paper in her hand, then handed it to the detective. "She ... Umm ... does a lot of drugs and lets Amy do whatever she wants."

Amber closed her eyes and turned her head away. How the hell had she found herself in this situation? It wasn't bad enough her daughter had a friend she knew nothing about; this girl had gotten them involved in a twisted game of multiple murders. As a result, Hayley had been sneaking out of the house, had broken into a stranger's home, shoplifted clothing, and had gotten a tattoo. Had she done drugs as well?

How smug of her to criticize the crappy moms whose kids made the evening news for doing God knew what crazy things. Now she was as bad — if not worse — than all of them put together. She never would have imagined things could get so out of control.

She broke out of her thoughts, refocusing her attention on the detectives, who were discussing something about Amy, child protection services, and keeping the case out of the press at all costs. After they conferred quietly for a few more minutes, Aidan took the piece of paper with Amy's address and stood.

"Thank you for your cooperation, Ms. Reed." He shook her hand as she got to her feet. "Hayley, you did very well to tell your mother about this. I hope you learned a lesson today. Detective O'Sullivan will tell you what to do next. Have a good evening."

Amber's eyes followed him to the door. When he closed it, there was a moment of silence in the room.

"It's vital that neither of you talks to anyone about this," John said. "If the press gets wind of it and leaks that the police are investigating the matter, several things could happen. For one, the killer will be warned and have time to vanish, and he — or they — may seek revenge. I don't think you're in any danger now," he added, looking at Hayley. "But you have to promise you won't tell anyone about this game or that you've spoken to the police."

Hayley nodded.

"I need your laptop and your phone, Hayley," John said.

"My phone? Why?"

"Because in a moment of panic, you may be tempted to call Amy or someone else, and we can't risk that."

Still feeling surreal, as if this couldn't be happening, Amber stood beside the couch, her arms wrapped around herself. She jumped when John spoke to her.

"Ms. Reed, would you please bring Hayley's laptop?" He turned to the girl, his hand extended, palm up. "Hayley, switch off your phone and give it to me."

Amber waited until Hayley handed John the phone.

"Hayley, come upstairs with me. It's time for bed anyway." Turning to John, she smiled faintly. "Detective O'Sullivan, I'll be right back."

She followed Hayley up the stairs, aware of every creak in the old wooden steps. Had they creaked the night Hayley had left the house? Why hadn't she heard them? She could've put an end to this before it had even started. If only ...

The silence between herself and Hayley was heavier than ever. All the progress she'd thought she'd made was a smokescreen, a curtain of lies. Would she ever reach Hayley? Probably not — at least not deep inside where it mattered. As if they hadn't had enough trouble before, now their lives could be in danger. Would she ever be able to trust her daughter again?

Hayley pushed open the door to her room and sat on the bed. She reached out, took the laptop from her nightstand, and gave it to her mother, handling it as if it were a bomb.

Amber was about to leave when she noticed a tear spilling down from Hayley's bent face. Her heart broke yet again. With so many pieces floating around her chest, she marveled it could still beat.

"I'm sorry, Mom," Hayley whispered, her face hidden by the thick, brown curtain of hair. "I never thought ... It was supposed to be something fun to help me spend a lonely summer; that's all."

Another tear fell on her small, defenseless hands that were clutched restlessly in her lap.

Amber's own eyes stung. She sat on the bed and reached

out to stroke her daughter's hair, then tucked a rebel strand behind her ear.

"I know you're sorry, Hayley. I'm sorry, too. If I'd been a better mother, maybe none of this would've happened."

"No!" Hayley angled her head to gaze at her. "You are a good mom. You never left me, not like Dad did. No matter how much crap I've given you, you're still here. I hope you always will be." Her voice broke on the last word.

Amber reached out to enfold her in her arms. God, she had grown so much, and yet she was still the baby who had developed inside her — her little girl, the one person Amber loved more than anything.

"I will always be here, honey. Even when you'll be a woman and have children of your own, you will be my baby forever. Nothing will ever change that. You're a part of me — the best part."

She sniffed back tears, gently rocking her daughter, who'd curled up in her lap as if she was boneless.

"I'll never let anything bad happen to you, Hayley, but you have to help me take care of you. You're almost an adult now; you have to learn right from wrong."

"I know. I know what I did was wrong. If only I could turn back time and undo it —"

"You can't. That's the first thing you need to understand about being a grownup. You can't change things, so you have to think really hard before you do something, before you make any decisions. You'll make mistakes because you're human, but you need to learn to deal with them. Some you can fix, some you just live with."

She sighed, continuing to caress her daughter's hair, enjoying the scent of her skin. Remembering the tattoo Hayley had shown her earlier made her cringe. But at least she was thankful she hadn't chosen some grotesque symbol or had half of her body scarred. The tattoo was an artsy little thing. Maybe in a while, she would actually come to like it, although that was too optimistic a thought right now.

Hayley sat up slowly, and Amber brushed gentle fingers over her face.

"Don't cry, honey. We did the right thing, and we'll continue to do what the police tell us to. We'll help them catch this maniac."

Hayley nodded, shifting herself to curl up under the covers.

"I love you, Mom."

Despite the circumstances, a wave of joy enveloped Amber. She couldn't remember the last time — if ever — she'd heard those heartfelt words from her daughter. Before she started crying again, she bent to kiss Hayley's forehead.

"I love you too, sweetie. Now get some sleep. Will you be okay?"

Hayley's beautiful brown eyes were blurred by a layer of red, but she nodded bravely. "I will."

"Okay then. Goodnight."

Amber switched off the light and left the door ajar in case Hayley had a nightmare or called to her during the night. Tucking the laptop under her arm, she went downstairs once more.

14

As she descended the stairs, Amber realized the storm had moved away, leaving behind only the patter of tiny drops rhythmically striking the roof. Stepping into the living room, she found John in front of the window. He'd opened it, and she was grateful for the clean, crisp air that filled the room with the smell of ozone.

"Here's Hayley's laptop," she said, placing it on the coffee table.

He turned around to face her. "Thank you."

She noticed how tired he looked. His skin was pale under the beard stubble, and his eyes were bloodshot as if he hadn't had a good night's sleep in days.

"Are you hungry?" she asked impulsively. "I could fix you a sandwich or something."

"No, thank you. I —" His mouth curved in a slight smile, a flash of soft lips and white teeth that transformed his face. "Actually, I would love a sandwich, thank you. It would be really kind of you, Ms. Reed."

All at once, Amber was so aware of his masculinity she grew flustered. Grateful for the excuse, she went to the kitchen and started to make two ham and cheese sandwiches. She added tomato and lettuce, then topped it off with mayonnaise.

Back in the living room, she paused in the doorway to observe her guest — her protector — who was standing at the window, his back to her. She'd had more important business to attend to since he'd arrived, but now she allowed herself a minute to admire his tall frame, broad shoulders, and muscular legs.

The dark blue shirt and jeans fit him like tailor-made clothes. The matching clean-cut waterproof vest enhanced the length of his back. It had been raining when he and Aidan had arrived. Amber noticed the sleeves of John's shirt were still damp. There was something about the way they clung to his rounded biceps and strong forearms that made her stomach feel weightless — and not because she was hungry.

She cleared her throat, wishing she could clear her mind just as easily.

"I hope you like ham and cheese." She set the two plates on the coffee table.

He turned away from the window, retracing his steps to the chair he'd sat on earlier. "I was prepared to gnaw on me own boots tonight. These look delicious, ma'am, thank you."

"It's nothing. I should thank you for staying here, for my daughter's sake. You must be exhausted."

"It's my job," he stated simply, then took a bite of his sandwich. After he chewed and swallowed, he added, "Besides, I've spent as many nights in that car as I have at home, so it's not a novelty."

Amber paused, sandwich in mid-air. Before she could talk herself out of it, she voiced her sudden thought.

"Please, there's no need for you to sit in the car when we have a perfectly comfortable couch. You can sleep here."

His surprised gaze shifted to meet hers, making the knot in her stomach tighten. She hoped he didn't think she was coming on to him. God, she should have shut up. Why was she preaching to her daughter to think a thousand times before making a decision when she didn't do it herself?

"It's very kind of you, ma'am, but I'm not here to sleep," John said. "I need to be awake in order to protect and serve."

She was relieved to see a glint of amusement in his expression, and she smiled back.

"You did say we're probably not in any immediate danger. I happen to agree. Besides, I doubt anyone can get past you, even if you're asleep."

She'd meant it as a compliment, and the curve of his lips proved he'd taken it as such. They finished their sandwiches in silence, then she collected the plates and went to get a couple of soft drinks.

"I'm glad you contacted us immediately after Hayley told you about The Game," John said seriously, uncapping his drink. "This piece will help us solve the puzzle. I'm afraid we'll have to inconvenience you further. I'm not sure yet, but based on what we know, our computer specialist will have to work from here for a few days."

"Here, meaning my house?" Amber asked, puzzled. "But why, since Hayley has a laptop that can be transported anywhere?"

"If the killer monitors the players' locations — and I believe he does — he'll notice if the location changes. It's easy to find out it's at the Garda headquarters, and if he puts two and two together, he'll know Hayley talked to the police. The last thing we want is for the killer to know we're tracking him."

Amber took a sip of her Sprite. "Do you know if it's a man or a woman? Are we dealing with only one person?"

John shook his head.

"Why do you call him the killer?" Amber continued. "Those teenagers are the ones who committed the murders."

"They did, and they'll be punished for it, but the person

who created The Game and set those dares, the person who manipulated the teenagers into committing murder, is the intellectual author of the crimes. We need to find him — or them — in order to stop this."

Amber's hands were cold as ice as she squeezed the can of Sprite between her palms. "Do you know why he or they are doing this?"

He expelled a long breath. "No. When we find the motive, it'll be the biggest break in this case. It's very important we have Hayley as a witness. She's actually had contact with this sick bastard, even if it's only virtual contact."

A shudder crossed through Amber. The thought of her little girl having "contact" with a serial killer was unbearable. She thought she didn't have any tears left, but she felt one sliding down her cheek. She averted her face quickly, but the gesture didn't escape John. It was reassuring to know his reflexes and sense of observation were sharp even when he was dead-tired. Still, she couldn't help being embarrassed when he stood, walked around the coffee table, and sat beside her on the sofa.

"Look, Ms. Reed, I know this situation is terrifying, but I assure ye we'll do everything within our power to catch this person as quickly as possible. We have competent people, and we have assistance from Interpol as well. Thanks to you and Hayley, it's only a matter of time before we find him. In the meantime, we'll keep you and the lass safe, I promise."

His words, spoken in that deep voice with its melodious accent, calmed Amber. She turned her head slightly to look into his eyes. There was warmth in them and an almost hypnotic quality she hadn't noticed until now. She hadn't had the chance to look at his face closely enough to see how alluring his mouth was amidst the salt-and-pepper five o'clock stubble. She'd thought his hair was gray, but at a closer inspection, she saw most of it was brown. The sprinkle of silver enhanced his classical features — high cheekbones and a roman nose — lending him a distinguished air. She was shocked to realize she longed to brush her fingers over that shallow dent in his chin.

She became aware of the fact that he was studying her, too, when he reached out a gentle hand to wipe a tear from her cheek. His touch was not only comforting but sexy as hell. In fact, being so close to him made her dizzy. It had been such a long time since she'd enjoyed the touch of a man, a strong male presence, the weight of a man on top of her ...

Sensing the blood rush to her face, she looked away quickly, raking her shaky fingers through her hair. Thank God she'd put on makeup this morning before she left for work, though it had probably worn off long ago. Without it, she always felt she looked washed out.

"I'll get you a pillow and blanket. Please, no more arguments," she added, getting to her feet. "You can't sleep in the car. If anything were to happen, I think we would be safer with you inside the house rather than out there."

Without waiting for a reply, she dashed upstairs. She didn't have a spare pillow, so she grabbed hers from the bed and dug up one of the new blankets from the closet. As she descended the stairs, she saw John was taking off his shoes, placing them next to the sofa.

Looking up, he smiled at her. "Thank you. This is unusual, but I'm grateful for your hospitality."

"It's an unusual situation." Amber arranged the pillow on the sofa, then set down the blanket at the other end. "I guess we all have to adapt until ... until our lives get back to normal." She darted him a glance. "Should you call your wife and let her know you'll be staying here?"

As his gaze fixed on her, inquisitive and unblinking, she straightened slowly. After several seconds of uncomfortable silence, she gestured vaguely to his wedding ring hand. "I thought ... I mean, it's obvious that you're married, so I thought your wife might be worried ..."

He looked down at his hand, brushing his thumb over the gold band. Then he arranged his features in an impassive expression and met her eyes again.

"My wife died five years ago."

Although he'd stated it matter-of-factly, Amber had seen the pain in his eyes. She could have kicked herself a thousand times for being so tactless, so stupid.

"Oh ... I'm so sorry. I didn't know ... What happened to her?" she blurted out, feeling like a nosy idiot for the second time in as many minutes. But somehow, she had to know. Not because of morbid curiosity, but because she genuinely wanted to know.

John took off his vest, then draped it over the back of a chair. His shoulders hunched in an almost defensive posture.

"It was one of those situations most people only see on the news because it happens to one person in millions. My wife was that person." As he spoke, he seemed to relive that tragic moment as if it were yesterday. "She was a journalist, always on the lookout for the next exciting story. Five years ago, a new drug started to circulate on the black market. It was said to be energizing, when in fact, it caused anxiety, paranoia, rage ... Even a few milligrams could turn the user into a dangerous madman. This guy, Seamus Walsh, thought it might be fun to experiment. According to statements, he was a habitual drug user but a peaceful fella. He didn't react well to the new drug. That evening, the neighbors heard him shouting, his wife screaming, their two kids crying, so they called the Garda. I remember there was a terrible storm that day. Shanna was heading home, and on her way, she drove by Walsh's house. She saw two police cars, so she stopped to see what was going on." He raised his eyebrows in a bitter, cynical gesture. "I used to joke with her about that saying, curiosity killed the cat. I never thought it would happen to us. Long story short, Walsh had a gun and a pocketful of ammo. He shot his wife, kids, and anyone nearby. Several Gardaí were wounded, one was killed ... and Shanna was mortally shot. By the time I got there, she had died, and Walsh had killed himself."

Tears filled Amber's eyes as she listened to him. What were the odds for something like this to happen? One chance in millions indeed! It seemed that God, or fate, or whatever force governed these things, wanted Shanna to be that chance. For the world, she'd been an unfortunate casualty. For John, *she* had been the world.

Amber felt strange, grieving for a woman she'd never known.

"I'm sorry." She sat back on the sofa, her damp eyes still on him. "I'm so sorry. I had no idea ... It was tactless of me to ask. I didn't mean to bring back this horrible memory."

He sat too, far enough to keep some distance between them. "It's okay, you couldn't have known. You were only being thoughtful. Things like this happen."

"It's not fair. Things like this should never happen to good people."

He smiled sadly. "That's what I used to think. I've asked myself countless times, why Shanna? Why me? Why did it have to happen to us when there are so many bad people out there who deserve it more, and yet they live long, happy, and carefree lives?"

Amber didn't have an answer for him. She'd asked herself similar questions when the life she'd known had ended. However, this was a real tragedy. Compared to John's story, her life was a fairy tale. She moistened her lips, torn between doing the polite thing and leaving or doing what she thought was the human thing and staying. She had no idea if John wanted to talk about this, but in case he did — or needed to — she felt compelled to stay. Not only for him but because she wanted to know more about this man.

"How did you meet?" she asked softly.

The ghost of a smile brushed his face. "We met at a crime scene. 'Twas about nine years ago. I'd just been promoted to sergeant, and she was a persistent reporter who refused to leave the scene until I answered a few questions. I did, only because she was so damn beautiful," he added, gazing distantly toward that bittersweet memory. "She ended her questions by asking me if I wanted to have dinner with her."

Amber smiled. Shanna must have been quite the woman.

"We went out that night, and after that, we were officially a couple," John went on. "We dated for almost two years before I convinced her to marry me. She didn't believe in papers; she believed commitment was in one's heart, not written on a contract. But in the end, I wore her down. We had a huge wedding, one of those three-hundred-guests affairs. Turns out Shanna was like any other woman when it came to her wedding," he added with a trace of humor that vanished in his next sentence. "For three years, I was the happiest man alive, and then ... The world ended. At least for Shanna and me."

"I can't imagine losing the person you love so tragically." Amber swiped at her eyes.

Embarrassed, she stood abruptly. She had no right to snoop around in this man's life when her own was so messed up. She had to go before she made a fool of herself.

"Thanks again for staying here tonight, Detective. Goodnight."

As she made to head for the door, he stopped her by placing a hand on her arm.

"Ms. Reed. There's one more thing we need to clarify."

"What's that?"

"Until we speak with the cybercrime specialists and decide

what to do next, I want you and Hayley to be protected. That means you should stay at home, both of you."

She gaped at him for a second, then spread her arms widely. "But I have a job. I've been working there for less than a week. I can't take vacation time now, especially since I have no idea how long it will be until you find this creep. I'm not in any danger."

She saw his jaw clench and took it as a sign of stubbornness.

"I'm not willing to take any chances," John said. "Until we know more about this individual or group, we can't risk anything. You and Hayley are key witnesses, as is Amy Fielding. You can take a few days of medical leave for now. It's important the media doesn't find out about this, so you can't tell your boss the truth yet."

"What if I lose my job?"

"You won't, I promise. After we close the case, I will speak to your supervisor and explain the situation. Until then, you're under police protection and have to stay home."

Amber opened her mouth to speak. She didn't know any delicate way to ask the next question, so she decided to be blunt. "What happens if you don't solve the case?"

John's steely eyes glinted. "Ah, that *we will*. Ye have my word. And we'll solve it as quickly as we can. Any minute, another person might die. Trust me, when you have that kind of responsibility on your shoulders, it's a hell of a motivation to find a killer and make sure he's punished."

His fierce expression boosted her own confidence in him. She nodded, as much in consent as a sign of approval. She even managed a small smile.

"Okay, I'll call in sick tomorrow." She gazed around the room, lightly propping her hands on her hips. "Do you need anything?"

"No, thank you. I'm good."

"Well, goodnight. If you need me, I'll be in my bedroom. It's upstairs, to the left of the staircase."

She was walking backward as she spoke, wishing she would shut up and stop embarrassing herself. When her bare foot stepped on a foreign object, she lost her balance and would've fallen had John's lightning-fast reflexes not stopped her. He wrapped a strong arm around her waist to steady her.

"I'm sorry, those were my shoes you stumbled on," he apologized.

"I should've looked where I was going."

"I should've placed them somewhere else."

Their voices dropped to whispers, adding a sense of intimacy to their position. Amber's heart raced. She could hear her breath grow faster as her body remained pressed against his. Since he'd removed his vest, she clutched a fistful of his shirt. The taut muscles beneath her hand made her want to explore more. She wondered if his eyes had darkened because he felt the same curiosity, the same need.

But this wasn't the time or place to explore anything. It was a crisis situation, and her priority was the safety of her daughter, not the desperate cry of her hormones. Lowering her eyes, she drew away slowly. She sensed the same reluctance from him when he let her go and stepped back.

If regret had a voice, it would have uttered a frustrated cry instead of the quiet "Goodnight" she threw over her shoulder before rushing upstairs.

In her room, Amber filled the tub and added her favorite lavender oil to it. Immersing herself in the water, she tried not to think about the man sleeping on their couch, a man who touched her in ways she couldn't understand and yet had missed so much.

She had no doubt he would protect her and Hayley until his dying breath. She believed him when he said he would close the case sooner now with Hayley's help, but she still felt antsy, restless.

Getting out of the tub, she dried off and put on her lightweight pajamas. Sitting in the center of her bed, she turned on her laptop and did a web search for Shanna O'Sullivan.

The first image to pop up on the screen showed a beautiful blond woman with piercing blue eyes and a gorgeous smile. Scrolling down the page, she found the headline she'd expected.

ONE MORE CASUALTY OF SUNDAY'S BLOODBATH IN DUBLIN: TRAGIC DEATH OF NEWS BROADCAST JOURNALIST SHANNA O'SULLIVAN.

Amber clicked on the article dated five years ago, and read it twice, barely breathing. It was more or less what John had told her.

Shanna O'Sullivan, wife of detective John O'Sullivan, had been twenty-seven at the time of her death. Without any warning, a drug addict had taken his wife and children hostages, and despite the police's best efforts, no one could reason with him. He'd killed his family, a police officer, and journalist Shanna O'Sullivan. The Garda thought the gunman was shooting randomly, and Mrs. O'Sullivan's death was a tragic accident.

As she read, Amber's eyes overflowed with tears. No wonder John had looked haunted as he'd spoken. This tragedy had marked him for life. She knew terrible things happened every day, every minute, but learning it had happened to someone she knew changed things. He'd never even had the chance to bring Seamus Walsh to justice. That must eat at him every day. A quick, self-inflicted death wasn't punishment enough for that man.

She'd thought Dean's cheating was a tragedy, but she'd been wrong. *This* was a true tragedy.

A second photo filled the screen, one of Shanna with John

by her side. From the caption beneath it, Amber knew it had been taken at an award ceremony. Had Shanna won an award in journalism? It wouldn't matter because, for her, the most precious prize in the world had been the man smiling proudly at her side. God, how awful it must be for John to look at this photo, to reach out for his wife in the night and realize she wasn't there and never would be again.

Slowly, she swiped away tears, then reached out blindly to grab a tissue from her nightstand and blow her nose. Sighing, she closed her laptop and switched off the bedside lamp.

Curling up under the sheets, she reached out for the spare pillow on the other side of the bed — the side that no one used. Instead of placing it under her head, she cradled it in her arms. Her thoughts, filled with sorrow and regret, lingered on John.

She'd thought she'd known the pain of losing the love of her life, but in her case, fate had been much more merciful. The fact that Dean had cheated on her had killed any love she had for him, even more so now that he planned to marry his partner in adultery. John, on the other hand, had to live every single day with the agonizing loss of his soul mate.

Squeezing the pillow tighter to her chest, overwhelmed by sorrow and loneliness, she closed her eyes. If somewhere in the dark recesses of her mind, she'd somehow harbored a crazy, tiny hope that she and John might get together, it was gone now. There was no way she could compete with the beautiful Shanna and the love she'd seen sparkling between them in that photo. Shanna's death had crippled John's soul. He was a troubled man who could never love again the way he loved his wife. And Amber would never settle for second best.

15

It was still dark when John pried his eyes open. He lifted a stiff arm to squint at the phosphorescent numbers on his watch, noting it was 5:20. He desperately wanted coffee and a shower, in that order, but he couldn't leave yet. He'd promised Hayley. God help him. Those puppy-dog eyes had melted his heart. When she'd pleaded with him to stay and protect them, he couldn't refuse.

And her mother ... She was a fine thing, for sure. It took a special kind of woman to stay on his mind, especially when he had the most difficult case of his career to solve. Thank Christ he was good at multitasking.

Shanna had been the only other woman able to steal her way into his mind, into his thoughts, and make him crazy with wanting her. He stared into the dark. All he had awaiting him now was an empty apartment.

Even though he hadn't slept much because the couch was too small for him and he ached all over, last night had been the best night he'd spent in a long, long time. The pillow Amber had given him carried her scent, a sensual, surprisingly bold perfume. He'd had more than one erotic dream as he'd slept with his face half-buried in it, the silky fabric soft against his cheek.

But his attraction to Amber hadn't been the sole reason for his restful night. Knowing she and Hayley were upstairs — soundly sleeping thanks to his presence — was strangely comforting. It was good not to be alone for a change, to feel needed.

He heard a faint noise upstairs, then saw a sliver of light creep across the staircase. A moment later, Amber descended the stairs, her graceful silhouette outlined by the dim light.

John felt his body stir behind his fly. He liked everything about this woman — her messy hair, her gorgeous eyes, those sexy toes she probably wasn't aware of. Even the way she moved her hips was alluring as she'd walked cautiously around the house, afraid to wake him. And he was deeply touched by the compassion he saw in her eyes when he'd told her about Shanna.

But despite his interest in her, he couldn't do anything about it. Not yet, not until they found the criminal mastermind behind The Game. He couldn't afford any distractions. Someone else could die at any time unless he ended it and locked the killer away.

Amber disappeared into the kitchen. Suppressing a groan, he sat up. He rubbed the back of his neck for a couple of minutes, stimulating the circulation into the stiff muscles. He still wore his holster, and it had dug into his hip bone. He could feel the ridges across his skin.

Standing, he rotated his shoulders several times before brushing his fingers over his face and hair. He hoped he looked better than the Beast, and he was just as apprehensive about facing the Beauty.

He smelled the coffee before he reached the kitchen and closed his eyes briefly, inhaling the strong aroma. God bless the woman! It was as if she'd read his mind. He pushed the door open, then raised his hands in a harmless gesture when Amber jumped and whirled, clutching a hand to her chest.

"It's me," he whispered. "Sorry if I startled you."

"I thought you were asleep."

She pressed her back against the refrigerator, taking a few gulps of air. John did his best to ignore the taut nipples behind her beige cotton T-shirt and the long slender thighs outlined by matching track pants. With her fresh face and disheveled hair, she looked as if she was Hayley's big sister. Hayley's *hot* big sister.

Looking away, he told himself his mouth was watering for the coffee, not the woman.

"I just woke up," he said.

"Did you sleep well?"

He nodded.

"Would you like some coffee?"

"That would be grand, thank you."

Smiling, she invited him to sit at the table.

As she turned and reached up into a cabinet for cups, John's eyes lowered to her round, perfect ass. Jesus, Mary, and Joseph. This woman would drive him crazy if he spent any more time with her.

"Sugar?"

At his blank look, she elaborated, "Do you want sugar in your coffee?"

"Oh, no, just black. Thank you," he added as she placed a full mug of rich, dark coffee in front of him before sitting across the table from him.

She toyed with the handle of the mug for a while, using the tips of her fingers to trace its rounded shape. Outside, the light was beginning to grow, shades of orange and pink promising another sunny day.

"So, what's the plan for today?" Amber asked. Worry clouded her eyes. She didn't look as if she'd gotten much sleep.

John sipped the delicious, scalding coffee before he answered. "As soon as I finish my coffee, I'll order a car stationed in front of your house 24/7. I'll go home to shower and change before I go to the office. After I brief my superiors and my team, we'll be back here to let you know what's next. In the meantime, call your workplace and say you're sick. Don't tell them anything else, please. It's vital we keep this out of the media."

She nodded, staring into her coffee cup, seemingly far, far away.

"Is there anything wrong?" he asked, realizing how stupid his question was, given the circumstances.

Amber didn't seem to think so. She took a while before she answered. "It's just ... I don't know how to react. Last night I kept hoping I'd wake up, and this would all be nothing more than a really bad nightmare. But I'm awake now." Her lips twisted bitterly. "And it's dawning on me that it's real. I keep wondering where I've gone wrong, how I failed so completely as a mother."

"You didn't. Hayley is a normal, typical teenager, curious about things. She didn't know what she was getting into, but what matters is that she knew when to stop. She knows right from wrong. That's the biggest proof you're doing a good job as a parent."

She gazed into his eyes, and John could see she wanted to believe him.

Looking away, she shrugged softly. "It's been a very difficult time for her. Her father and I divorced recently, then I've uprooted her and moved us across the ocean. I think what affected her the most, though, was the news that her father is remarrying."

John pondered the information for a few moments, curious to know more. He'd shared his loss with her. Would she be willing to do the same? Perhaps it would help her to talk.

"How do you feel about it?" he asked.

She moved her head dismissively. "I don't care. The moment I discovered Dean was having an affair, it was over for me. I could never forgive this kind of thing."

"Nor should you. I realize it's none of my business, but how did you find out?"

She chuckled humorlessly. "Well, I did a little police work of my own. At the time, I considered my marriage as rock-solid as ever. One day during my lunch hour, I decided to visit an expensive lingerie shop — not a place where I usually shopped. In the past, Dean had bought me gifts from there a few times, and I thought I would pick up something sexy to surprise him."

John swallowed with difficulty. Imagining her in a sexy negligee made his salivary glands go into overdrive.

Unaware of his thoughts, she went on. "Instead, I was the one surprised. I was browsing around when I saw him with his secretary. I thought he might be there to buy me a gift. Can you imagine such stupidity? Even that would've been odd, but once he put his arm around that tall, skinny redhead and whispered something to her, I understood. At times, I can still hear their laughter."

Without thinking, just reacting, he reached across the table and covered her hand with his. Her fingers were icy cold.

"I was numb inside, but I managed to get out of there without them seeing me," she continued, her gaze staring into the past. "I didn't go back to work. Instead, I drove home, hoping to find proof that I'd simply misread the situation, you know? The last thing I wanted was to become a cliché. No such luck. It only took a few minutes of fishing in his jacket pockets to find more evidence than I needed — a hotel business card, a receipt for a diamond necklace I knew nothing about, a handkerchief stained with red lipstick. Needless to say, I never wear red. The most incriminating proof was the box of condoms since we didn't use them. Suddenly, it was all too clear — all those late nights working at the office, the sudden trips out of town ... I couldn't believe how naïve I'd been." Her eyes were dry and cold, her jaw rigid. "From then on, I've done my best to erase him from my mind. Actually, perhaps erase isn't the proper word. Thanks to him, I have my daughter, the greatest accomplishment of my life. So I can't say I wasted the seventeen years we were together. We were young. Maybe it simply wasn't meant to be. In the end, I have no regrets."

"He sounds like a fool to me."

He hadn't meant to say that aloud. Or had he, subconsciously? Trained as he was to control each of his reactions, deep down inside, he must've wanted to voice that remark, if only to see her gaze slide up to meet his, as it did now. A man could drown in those golden, whiskey-toned eyes.

But he was a cop, and drinking on the job was forbidden. Scraping back his chair, he stood and took his phone out of his pocket. He speed-dialed the station and waited for someone to answer.

"This is Detective O'Sullivan. I want an unmarked car for surveillance at Stanford Street, number —" He raised his eyebrows and glanced at Amber.

"Thirty-four," she supplied.

"Number 34," he said into the phone. "One Garda is enough per shift; arrange for three shifts a day. I'll brief the first officer when he gets here. Make it fast, thanks."

As he shoved the phone back into his pocket, he finished his coffee in one gulp.

"Okay, I'm off when the guard arrives. I'll be in touch as soon as I can. In the meantime, I have one more important task for you." He pressed his palms against the table and stared at Amber. "Please make sure neither you nor Hayley touches her laptop. Don't switch it on. The same goes for her phone. Can I trust you with this, Ms. Reed?" He used her last name to remind himself that he was on duty and she was a witness he needed to protect.

She stood and nodded. "Absolutely."

"Thank you, and thanks for the coffee."

John went back into the living room, sat on the couch, and put on his shoes. Then he pulled on his vest, rearranging his gun under it. He tried not to be unnerved by Amber, who stood in the doorway watching him get ready to go. The scene was strangely domestic — a cop getting ready for work while his wife watched, patiently waiting to shut the door after him, the way Shanna used to do every morning.

Raking his hands through his hair, he turned to Amber. "I'll be waiting for the Garda in my car. I need to make some phone calls. Don't open the door for anyone unless you know them."

"Okay. Thank you, Detective."

He smiled. She'd slipped into professional mode, too. Bobbing his head to acknowledge her softly spoken words, he left the house. Amber locked the door behind him.

The fragrant morning air was slightly chilly for this time of year, a pleasant change from yesterday's oppressive heat before the storm. It cleared his head as much as the coffee had. Getting into his car, he took out his phone. It was only six. He regretted having to wake up Aidan and Jenna, but it had to be done. After receiving copious groans and moans from each of them in turn, they agreed to meet in his office at 7:30.

The Garda arrived a few minutes later, and John gave him instructions on how to handle this witness protection operation. He knew the young officer, believed him to be competent, which made it slightly easier for John to give him this responsibility. Satisfied Amber and Hayley were safe, he drove to his flat, grateful the traffic was so slight.

Once home, he undressed, threw his clothes into the hamper, shaved, and brushed his teeth before stepping into the shower. He winced at the faint aroma of sweat tickling his nostrils as he lifted his arm and reached for the soap. While he washed, his mind worked to find the best strategy to approach the case.

Clean and refreshed, he dried himself, rubbing his hair with a towel until it was almost dry, using his fingers to tame it once he'd finished.

Opening his closet door, he noticed he only had two clean shirts left. He'd have to do the washing, but domestic chores were the last thing on his mind right now. He picked the light-gray shirt, donned a pair of black jeans, and breathed in relief when he managed to dig up matching clean socks.

Passing through the kitchen, he spotted an overripe banana on the table. He should have something in his belly to keep up his energy. Shanna would urge him not only to eat the fruit but to make himself a sandwich and add yogurt to his breakfast. The sandwich Amber had made for him last night had been delicious. He wondered what she was having for breakfast.

He shook his head, annoyed with himself for allowing memories and other distractions to confuse him. Time was running out. Someone could die at any minute. Grabbing the banana and his car keys, he locked the door behind him.

He peeled and ate the fruit as he jogged down the stairs. By the time he reached his car and headed to headquarters, it was already 7:15.

He was grateful to find both Aidan and Jenna waiting for him. Jenna, legs crossed, sat at his desk. Aidan paced the room, an unlit cigarette between his teeth.

"Morning," John said. "Sorry I woke you so early, Jenna, but as I'm sure Aidan told you, we had a major breakthrough in the case last night."

"If what he told me is right, that's an understatement." The creases on Jenna's forehead deepened, her face a worried mask. "I'm going to need serious help with this. Where's the girl's laptop?"

"I left it at home with her mother, giving strict instructions neither of them should touch it. I didn't know if it was safe to move it, in case the Game Master is monitoring its location."

"Good thinking," Jenna said.

"The Game Master?" Aidan asked, eyebrows raised.

John gave a dismissive shrug. "In lieu of sick motherfucker, it's all I could think of. Anyway, Jenna, what do you think? Will you be able to trace him?"

"I have no idea. I need to see the website as a player, the codes ..." She chewed absently at her lower lip. From the way her eyes were darting left and right, she was thinking fast and furiously. Suddenly, she jumped to her feet. "Let's go. I need to get some equipment, then we need to get over to this kid's house. Is the mother cooperating?" she asked John.

"Totally, but I still need to write my report, brief the chief —"

"You can do that after I've had a look," Jenna said. "You'll have more info. Besides, we have no time to lose."

She hurried out of the office, so wired that her energy seeped into John, infusing him with the need to act, to follow the lead they had, to start the hunt. It was the same determination that drove him to pursue suspects and cases with mindless perseverance. He followed her out, and Aidan closed the door behind them.

Within ten minutes, John and Aidan loaded the trunk of their vehicle with boxes filled with the electronic equipment Jenna insisted she needed.

As soon as he got behind the wheel, John started the engine, pressing the accelerator before his passengers had time to close their doors.

"Jenna, do you have enough data on this Game Master to share it with a profiler?" John asked.

"Not yet, but once I have a look at what's what, I hope I will."

"Can't you make an educated guess?" Aidan asked from the passenger seat, his tone almost reproachful.

John looked into the rearview mirror in time to see Jenna roll her eyes before aiming a murderous glance at the back of Aidan's head.

"Can't ye get it through that thick skull of yours that I can't venture any guesses until I actually access that website? I need to see the URL format, the coding, the digital dust — if he's left any."

"Jesus, calm down. Don't throw all that geek stuff at me. I was just asking," Aidan mumbled, staring out the window.

"It's not geek stuff; it's technical terminology, something you obviously know nothing about," she replied through her teeth.

"Cut it out," John barked at them. "I don't need any more casualties on my hands."

When they reached Amber's house, he parked behind the squad car, then checked briefly with the Garda, who informed him no one had come or gone.

"Good lad. Stay at your post," John instructed.

After unloading the boxes from the trunk, the three of them walked to the house, John in the lead. He knocked at the door, Aidan and Jenna flanking him. A few seconds later, the peephole darkened.

"Ms. Reed, it's Detective O'Sullivan."

Amber unlocked the door and opened it tentatively, then wider when she realized he wasn't alone.

"This is Detective Jenna Darcy from our Cybercrime Division," John said. "You know Detective Connor. May we come in?"

"Of course. It's nice to meet you, Detective," Amber acknowledged Jenna in a hurry before stepping out of the way to let them inside.

John walked straight into the living room. Amber had tidied the couch but had left the pillow and blanket folded in the corner. Was she hoping he would be spending the night again?

"Is that your daughter's laptop?" Jenna asked briskly, pointing at the device on the coffee table.

"Yes." Amber's hands fidgeted nervously with her phone. She'd changed into a pair of faded jeans and a blue shirt. "Is there anything you need?"

"Just your cooperation, ma'am, which is much appreciated." Jenna flashed her a quick smile. "Where is your daughter? I'll need to speak to her."

"She's upstairs. I'll get her right away."

John watched Amber hurry up the stairs. Next to him, Jenna was getting to work, removing a laptop from one of the boxes they'd brought with them. Kneeling next to the sofa, she placed the laptop on the coffee table next to Hayley's, then switched it on. While it was booting, she dug into the box and took out a couple of other devices and a USB cable.

Not knowing what else to do, John sat beside Aidan on the sofa, one of them on each side of Jenna, watching her in silence, not knowing what was going to happen next.

16

John looked up to see Hayley slowly coming down the stairs. Amber walked behind her. The young girl appeared uncomfortable with the police team setting up camp in her living room.

"Hayley, this is Detective Jenna Darcy," John said, trying to put her at ease. "She works with the Cybercrime division and needs to speak with you about The Game. Why don't I bring in a couple of chairs so that you and your mum can sit while we talk?"

Standing, he went into the kitchen. He was on his way out, carrying a chair in each hand, when Amber entered. Only his quick reflexes prevented him from crashing into her.

"Sorry." She put out a hand instinctively to help him with one of the chairs.

He held it out of her reach.

"No worries, I have it."

He was about to step forward, but Amber stood her ground.

"Is there a problem, Ms. Reed?"

Her lips parted as if she were trying to choose her words but couldn't find the ones she wanted.

"Um ... Well ... Detective Darcy seems a little abrupt. Does she blame Hayley because she played this monstrous game?"

"No, of course not. On the contrary, she's as grateful as I am that you and Hayley contacted us as soon as you did. Believe me, Ms. Reed, you can't realize how critical to the case your help is."

Her lips curved faintly, and her eyes traveled up to meet his. "I think, given the circumstances, you should call me Amber. It saves time."

His heart skipped a beat. Perhaps it was inappropriate, but ... What the hell? He'd slept on her couch, and they were facing an extremely grave situation together. What difference did a title really make now?

He returned her smile. "Aye, that makes sense, Amber. Then you must call me John."

He'd nearly forgotten the chairs he held in each hand. As he moved, one of the metal legs scraped the floor, breaking the silence.

"Come on, lead the way," he said, nodding toward the living room.

Jenna was already questioning Hayley in a friendly, non-threatening manner. John was relieved to see the girl was more relaxed. She smiled at him when he placed a chair next to her, and he returned her smile.

He placed Amber's chair beside the sofa, close to the spot where he sat, so it wouldn't be in the way — or so he told himself. Doing his best to ignore Amber's shapely legs outlined by skinny jeans, he focused on the job at hand, watching as Jenna masterfully interviewed Hayley.

"So you've never had direct contact with the Game Master like you do when you use a chat or a messaging service?"

Hayley shook her head. "No. I only received standard messages on the screen whenever I got a dare or finished one. Oh, and the form I had to fill out when I created my account."

She proceeded to describe the data she'd been required to provide.

"Hmm." Jenna chewed thoughtfully on her unpainted fingernail. "Okay, come here, sit next to me." She patted the rug, moving closer to the coffee table. "Show me how you logged into The Game website."

Hayley knelt down beside her, reaching for the mouse.

"Please make sure you write down your username and password for me," Jenna told her, not taking her eyes off the screen.

As the webpage opened, she frowned. "This is it?"

"Yup," Hayley replied. "Not too fancy, is it?"

Jenna propped an elbow on the table, staring at the screen. A frown of frustration creased her forehead.

"What's wrong?" John leaned forward to look at the laptop's screen. What was he supposed to be looking for?

"This is the skimpiest website I've ever seen," Jenna said, gesturing vaguely. "Isn't there a forum? Where are the dares? How do you see other players?"

"There's a forum where the Game Master posts the coolest dares," Hayley answered. "Each player can only see posts from those on the same level or the levels below, but only after they complete a dare. Since I haven't completed the most recent one, the forum button is locked. Do you see? Last time I saw a boy steal a car. Amy is Level Three now — I guess it's the final level, because she was able to see ..." She swallowed, her face paling. "She sent me screenshots of the forum and a photo of ... the murdered woman."

Her voice was shaky. As he glanced at the teenager, John knew she would be marked for life by those images. She would see them in her nightmares for months, probably years, to come.

"Do you know Amy's username and password?" Jenna asked.

Hayley shook her head silently.

Jenna shifted her body around to look up at John. "I could move much faster if I could access the website as a Level Three player."

"Technically, I reached Level Three," Hayley said. "But I have to complete the next dare before I can see the next step — and I can't." She turned to John, her eyes pleading with him to understand.

"Lord, no. It's not just that we don't expect you to do that, lass; we severely punish people who do. We need to contact Amy Fielding," John said. He looked over at Aidan sitting at the other end of the couch. "Did you manage to reach her mother last night?"

Aidan's lips were a grim line. "I did. Amy ran away from home sometime yesterday. Her mother has no idea where she is."

Hayley gasped, darting an anxious gaze toward Amber.

Jenna looked at John and mouthed a single word, "Fuck."

He could empathize. They needed Amy and that password. He suspected Amy was just another misguided teenager and hoped nothing bad had happened to the girl.

Aidan continued. "Her mother wasn't too coherent, but I gathered she hadn't seen Amy since yesterday morning. She didn't tell me if she filed a missing person report, so I contacted the New York Police Department and asked them to look into it. They promised they'd get in touch with us as soon as they find anything."

Jenna blew out a long breath, pulling her red curls back into a ponytail and securing them with the elastic band she wore around her wrist. "Alright then, let's see what we can do."

Cracking her knuckles, she got to work on Hayley's laptop, which she'd connected to her own with a cable.

The rest of them sat in silence, watching her hands fly over the keyboard and the green writing that flashed across the black screen. Jenna's occasional mutters and groans, along with the click of the keyboard, were the only sounds in the room. Minutes dragged by while they all sat there waiting, wishing Jenna would suddenly scream, "Hooray! I found the bastard!"

Sweat trickled down John's back. Waiting had never been his strong suit. Especially when any minute could mean another dead body.

AMBER WATCHED HAYLEY, alarmed by the waxy pallor of her face. Call her selfish, but at that moment, she could only thank God her daughter was here with her, that she hadn't crossed the line her friend had. She said a quick prayer for Amy Fielding, a girl she didn't know and who'd unknowingly gotten herself and Hayley into this mess. She was a victim, like so many other teenagers. It wasn't the girl's fault her mother was a druggie or that society hadn't been able to offer her a chance at a better life.

Half an hour passed, and as much as she wanted to know what was happening, Amber knew better than to break Jenna's concentration. She understood enough about coding to keep quiet while a pro was at work. She could see Jenna trying to drill down to the source of the website, but the layers were more complex on the Dark Web than on the surface internet, where any good hacker could take apart a website piece by piece in a relatively short time.

Besides, she couldn't complain about having to sit next to John, listen to his steady breathing, and inhale the musky, oriental scent of his shower gel. She adjusted her head slightly to study his profile, hoping he wouldn't notice. Freshly shaven, he looked younger, not as rugged or tired. Although his features were strong, his alluring lips promised sensuality. His gray eyes were trained on Jenna. The impatient way he squinted from time to time amused Amber. Clearly, he liked to be in control, and it was obvious he had no idea what Jenna was doing, which pushed him to the limits of frustration.

"She's trying to find the source of The Game's website," she whispered, inclining her head slightly.

As he turned his head toward her, a faint shiver slid through her body. His face was so close to hers she felt his breath when he spoke.

"I forgot you know about these things. How long does it take to find the source?"

She smothered a laugh. "It can take a few minutes, a few hours, a few days, or longer. It all depends on how skilled the hacker is, as well as the hacked."

The sofa cushions rustled as Aidan shifted yet again. Amber had noticed him fidgeting the last ten minutes, reminding her of a kid who needed to go to the bathroom.

John followed her gaze, and his lips twitched in amusement. "He's trying to quit smoking," he whispered. "Sitting and waiting is not his favorite thing to do right now."

"Oh, that sucks. Been there, done that, own the T-shirt."

Noticing his raised eyebrows, she explained. "I used to smoke two packs a day when I was in college. Then, when I got pregnant, I had to quit cold turkey. Added to the crazy mood swings brought on by pregnancy, it was a nightmare."

"And even more commendable. Aidan is trying to give up gradually, but I can't say I see any significant results."

"I can hear ya, you know." Aidan got to his feet. "Are you making any progress, kid?" he asked Jenna, staring a hole in the top of her head.

She didn't spare him a single glance. "I'm trying, but having the lot of you breathing down my neck doesn't help. Why don't you all find something else to do?"

There was a collective sigh of relief, and everyone jumped to their feet. Aidan dug a pack of cigarettes out of his pocket and power-walked to the front door, saying he would be outside on the porch.

Amber arched her stiff back, making a mental list of what she had to do that day. She desperately needed to go shopping for groceries. Having such a small refrigerator and freezer would take some getting used to. People tended to buy more fresh food here, and that was a good thing. There was also laundry to do, but flaunting her dirty underwear in front of John and two other strangers wasn't appealing. It would have to wait. How long before her life would return to normal? If it ever did.

"I found your parental control program," Jenna said. "I've disabled it for now."

At her words, Amber glanced down. She had no reason to feel uncomfortable, so when Hayley gave her a reproachful, outraged look, she directed an intimidating stare right back at her daughter.

"A lot of good it did me," she told Jenna, not taking her eyes off her daughter. "I haven't had a chance to check it since we got here. I would never have believed that oversight could lead to this."

Hayley lowered her gaze, stood, and headed toward the stairs. She stopped and turned around.

"Can I call Amy?" she asked.

Amber glanced at John.

His forehead creased for a moment before he nodded.

"That might be a good idea. It might help us locate her so that we can get her some protection, too. Go ahead and call her, Hayley, but make sure you act naturally. No mention of The Game, of the police, of anything," he instructed, raising his index finger to accentuate his words. "Just casual chat, ask her how she is, tell her you're okay, normal conversation. If she asks about The Game, tell her your laptop is broken. Can you do that?"

Hayley nodded, bending to retrieve her phone from the coffee table. She speed-dialed Amy's number and put the phone to her ear, biting her lips as she waited. Half a minute later, she shook her head, putting the phone back down. "Her phone's off."

"Bollocks," John muttered under his breath. "I hope the NYPD finds her soon."

"Go on up to your room, honey," Amber urged her daughter. "Detective Darcy will call you if she needs any more information. Now, let's all leave her alone so she can work quietly."

After Hayley left the room, Amber looked up at John. Since he was at least three inches taller than her, she had to tilt her head back to look him in the eyes.

"Do you think something's happened to Amy?" she whispered.

"I hope not. I think she's just scared out of her mind, but that doesn't make it any less dangerous for a sixteen-year-old girl to venture out alone on the streets of New York City."

Amber couldn't suppress a smile. "You say that as if New York is Hell. Have you ever been there?"

"No. But from what I hear, it's close enough."

"I'm from New York. Do I look dangerous to you?"

She was teasing him, but the slow once-over he gave her sent heat throughout her body and made her smile fade. His gaze was disconcerting not because it was lascivious or naughty but because it was dead serious.

"It depends."

They could have stayed that way for a small eternity, their gazes locked, had Jenna not cleared her throat loudly.

"Can I have some silence, please? Thank you."

Her irritated tone ushered them out of the room and into the kitchen to seek refuge. Through the window, they saw Aidan chatting with the Garda who was on duty, puffing away at the cigarette dangling between his lips.

"I have to go and buy food," Amber said, staring into the dismally empty fridge. She turned to John. "Could I go out for a bit? I'd like to take Hayley with me. Get her out of here for a little while. We won't be more than a couple of hours."

He gnawed at the inside of his cheek. He didn't seem to like the idea.

"I don't think the two of you should go out alone. We don't know what to expect right now." He hesitated, slapped his hands against his thighs, and stood. "But you need to eat. Come on, I'll take you."

Amber's lips parted in surprise. She hadn't expected this, but she wasn't disappointed. Secretly, she'd hoped for an opportunity to get to know him better, maybe continue the budding friendship she'd sensed over coffee this morning. She had no idea if he felt the same way or whether this was only a coincidence, but she didn't care. She smiled gratefully.

"I'll go get dressed and tell Hayley. Thank you."

She climbed the stairs quickly, stuck her head in Hayley's bedroom to give her the news, then dashed to her own room. She decided not to change her clothes. She didn't want John to think she was trying to impress him. She applied mascara and the pale-cocoa lipstick she preferred. She was brushing her hair when Hayley walked into her room without knocking.

"Is the detective really coming with us?"

"Yes. Is that a problem?"

"I need to buy pads and ... stuff," Hayley muttered, her cheeks blooming red.

Amber snuffled a laugh. "Don't worry. He won't pay attention to what we buy. I'll distract him when we get to the tampon aisle, okay?"

Hayley's mouth twitched in amusement. "Okay. Let's go. I'm starving. Are you making shrimp tonight?"

"We'll see."

When they reached the main floor, John was talking to

Jenna. Amber saw the woman's eyebrows arch while she listened to John. A foxy expression brightened her young, beautiful face, and Amber was shocked by the pang of jealousy spearing her. Was the stunning redhead involved with John on an intimate level? He was a widower, but he was also a man with normal appetites. Since he'd told her about his wife's death, it hadn't occurred to her he might be in another relationship right now.

Hayley nudged her, and she realized she'd stopped at the base of the stairs. Walking slowly into the living room, she fought to hide her conflicting emotions. She had no claim on this man. If there was going to be anything between them — even just friendship — she had to let things evolve naturally. Dating wasn't something she really understood. Dean had been the only man she'd had sex with. She'd rushed into that relationship, and it hadn't ended well. If she ever got into another one, she would take her time.

Following Jenna's gaze, John turned around and saw them.

"Ready?" he asked.

When they nodded, he looked at Jenna.

"We'll be back as soon as we can. Call me if there's any breakthrough." He turned to Amber. "Where's your car?"

"I don't have one yet. I've been using the bus and taxis."

"We'll take mine then," he said. "If there's an emergency, there's the Garda with a car outside."

On the veranda, John exchanged a few words with Aidan, then they headed to his vehicle, a non-descript sedan in desperate need of washing. John opened the passenger door for Amber, then ushered Hayley into the backseat.

"Where to?" he asked.

Fastening her seatbelt, Amber named a nearby supermarket.

"I've never been in a police car before," she confessed.

John smiled. "That means you've been a good girl."

"Yeah. Boring, huh?"

His eyes sparkled with humor. "Not in the least."

It only took a short while to reach the supermarket. Shopping with John proved to be an unexpectedly pleasant experience. During the last years of their marriage, Amber had given up trying to make shopping with Dean fun. He used to trail alongside her, broody and bored, shrugging disinterestedly whenever she asked his opinion about something. Not to mention he never helped with the cart or the packing.

John seemed to enjoy the experience. He insisted on pushing the cart, offered his opinion when asked, and moved discretely away when they had to pick up personal items.

"I'll buy more frozen shrimp," Amber told Hayley as they reached the seafood freezers. "It's faster and easier to cook."

Amber turned to John. "Do you like shrimp?"

He nodded. "I've had it on occasion. I usually stick to the basics for myself — frozen pizza, potatoes and bacon, the usual easy-to-make Irish food."

She smiled back at him. "I'm impressed. I don't know too many men who can cook for themselves."

"You don't know many men, period," Hayley put in, grinning when Amber's cheeks burned. "Why don't you stay for dinner tonight?" she asked John. "Mom makes the best Alfredo shrimp-and-spinach pasta."

Amber looked from Hayley to John and back. She was grateful to her daughter for issuing the invitation. It was as though Hayley had read her mind. Wanting to make the offer more tempting, she smiled warmly at John.

"That would be great. We would love to have you, that is unless you have a prior engagement," she added, slightly flustered.

John seemed surprised by the invitation. He divided a gaze between her and Hayley. Although he didn't display any blatant emotion, Amber could've sworn she saw joy, yearning, possibly even gratitude in the depths of his eyes. Her heart contracted with a curious mix of feelings. This man had to be lonely, and if she could offer him company, was that so wrong?

"That would be grand, thanks," he said a moment later. "But you'll have to let me help."

"We'll work something out," Amber promised.

They picked up the rest of the groceries, then loaded everything into the trunk.

Feeling good about things for the first time since she'd learned about The Game, Amber smiled as she got into the car for the ride home. Call her an idiot, but she took a second to hope this ghastly story might lead to something positive after all.

17

"I hope Jenna's found something," John said, driving efficiently through what Dublin considered rush hour traffic. "How does this drilling down thing work again?"

Amber explained as much as she could about online tracing, using simple terms and analogies. Jenna's knowledge of these things was immensely superior to hers, but she did her best to paint a basic picture.

"From what I can tell, she's using snippets of code to search for the Game Master on the Dark Web. Each top-level programmer has his own style of coding, which is unique. Like a fingerprint," she said, inspired. "With this information, a good hacker can find out if a certain style of coding is used in other places on the web. Besides, there's no such thing as the perfect crime."

He nodded. "Sooner or later, everyone makes a mistake."

"Exactly. There was a website on the Dark Web a few years ago, specifically created to facilitate drug deals by connecting users with sellers. After a while, as it began to grow popular and profitable, it started to allow more shady deals, like gun traffic, and ... other stuff," she added vaguely, remembering her daughter was listening. She didn't want to discuss human trafficking, child pornography, and contract kills in front of Hayley. "Anyway, do you know how the FBI discovered the identity of the guy running it?"

It was a rhetorical question. She took a deep breath and continued, "First, they used infiltrating agents who posed as users to get close to him. It took them almost a year, but during that time, the website's creator got cocky and began to make mistakes — he used his personal email address, used his own photo on a fake ID, boasted publicly about running his international multimillion-dollar drug marketplace, used his real name when he asked for coding advice ... Huge mistakes, pieces of a puzzle the FBI put together. He's currently serving two consecutive life sentences with no chance for parole."

John slowly shook his head. "It's unbelievable what some people will do for money."

"It's not just the money. For some, it's a community service or a form of protesting against the establishment they don't believe in. For others, it's just a way to get cheap thrills."

"I wonder what it is for our guy," John murmured. "We certainly don't have years to track him down."

"Haven't you alerted Interpol or asked for help from the FBI?"

"We did inform them; that's protocol. If Jenna doesn't find anything soon, they might take the case away from us. There's no room for egos or politics in a situation like this."

They completed the trip home in silence. When they reached the house, Aidan was still chatting with the Garda on duty in the unmarked car.

He came over to help them with the bags. "All done?"

"Yep." John nodded. "Anything from Jenna?"

"Nothing. She's still in there," Aidan replied, jutting his chin toward the house. "I think —"

He didn't finish the thought. Jenna hurried out the front

door. The moment she spotted them, she rushed toward them, her features set in a dark frown that didn't seem to bode well.

"John, Aidan, I need to speak to you now," she said.

Amber hesitated only a second before taking the bags from John and motioning for Hayley to help her. Something had happened, but what? She was dying to know what Jenna had found, but this was probably classified information. She would ask John about it later — if she had the chance.

Leaving the detectives to talk outside, she and Hayley headed toward the house.

"Look who's back," Amber said, smiling.

The motley cat sat perched on the railing. He meowed when they walked past him, then stopped as though sensing something was wrong.

"Start putting these away," Amber told Hayley, setting the bags on the counter. "I'll take some food out to that poor cat."

Digging through the items they'd bought, she unpacked the half dozen smoked sausages, broke off a generous piece from one, and went outside.

The cat smelled the meat immediately, and this time nothing in the world could stop him from demanding to be fed.

"I'm sorry I didn't buy any kitty food for you, but I wasn't sure you'd come back."

The cat jumped down, and she bent to give him the sausage. He purred and chewed with equal enthusiasm. Amber stroked his head absently, all the while watching the trio engaged in conversation outside her gate. Jenna was talking, gesticulating, and the two men listened, their faces frozen in disbelief.

"God, what's happened now?" Amber murmured, barely aware that she was talking to herself. She'd been doing a lot of that lately. She pressed her hand to her stomach, where a tornado of stress and anxiety had taken permanent residence.

The cat finished the sausage. He licked his lips copiously,

then sat and lifted one paw to groom his whiskers. Amber reached out to stroke his chin but stopped when she saw Jenna and the men returning to the house. Startled by the sudden crowd, the cat scrambled away, his claws making a scratching sound on the stone steps.

Amber stood quickly, studying the inscrutable faces.

Jenna paused in front of her. "Ms. Reed, I'll have to take Hayley's laptop and phone. We'll return them to you as soon as possible." She turned to John and Aidan. "Help me gather my equipment and write Ms. Reed a receipt for the items, will you?" she added over her shoulder to her partners.

Aidan followed her into the house, but John hesitated even before Amber touched his arm to stop him.

"What is it?" she asked, staring intently into his eyes. "Has Detective Darcy discovered the identity of the Game Master?"

He shook his head. "No. She's found something else."

"What?"

"I can't tell you that. I'm sorry." His gaze was apologetic. He rummaged through his pockets. "I'll write you a receipt for Hayley's laptop and phone."

"Don't worry about that now. But why do you need her phone?"

"So she won't contact Amy or anyone else and give us away. Besides, it can be traced, too."

He moved to go inside, but she stopped him again. It wasn't easy not to be angry with the whole situation.

"When will you tell me what's going on? When can I return to work?"

John gave a slight shake of his head. "I don't know. As soon as I can, I promise."

Jenna and Aidan emerged from the house carrying the boxes. While they were busy loading the equipment into the car, John covered Amber's hand with his.

"I have to go," he said. "I don't know if I can come to dinner tonight, but ... I'll call you and let you know, okay?"

Amber's hand was swallowed by his warm, larger palm. Excitement, worry, and fear all radiated from him into her, making her heart beat faster.

"Okay."

He squeezed her hand once, and she rushed inside, closing the door. She leaned her forehead against it, breathing hard.

Jenna must've found something of epic proportion. What the hell could it be? Would John tell her about it over dinner? Disappointment filled her at the thought he might not come after all.

Shoulders slumped, she was about to turn toward the kitchen when she realized Aidan and John were still on the porch steps. The other detective must have returned to tell John to hurry up.

Pressing her ear to the door, shamelessly eavesdropping, Amber listened.

"John, I understand you like this woman, but do you think it's smart to get involved with her now when you need to keep a clear, objective head? We can't afford any distractions."

"Do I look fucking distracted? I have the right to a private life, but that has never interfered with my work. Now let's move. Every minute is vital."

She listened to their footsteps, then heard the car doors slam and tires screeching. Exhaling the breath she'd been holding, she unglued herself from the door. As she walked slowly to the kitchen, her mind worked faster than a hamster in a wheel. A thousand thoughts assaulted her, a thousand suppositions about what Jenna might have found and how this thing could get any worse. But amidst all that darkness was one glowing glimpse of joy. John liked her. It was probably crazy, possibly foolish, but there it was. She couldn't ignore this attraction, not now that she knew he felt it, too.

"So essentially what you're saying is that this individual, in addition to having created a game through which he motivates teenagers to kill, has another website where people *pay* him to kill other people?"

John's voice sounded incredulous to his own ears as he tried to grasp what Jenna had been explaining to Aidan and him for the past ten minutes. Paying attention to the traffic was instinctive as he drove mechanically toward the police station. All his focus was on Jenna.

"Yes. That's how he chooses his victims," Jenna said, gesticulating widely as was her habit. "That's the whole purpose of The Game. He invented it so he could make vast amounts of money without getting his hands dirty."

"Does this mean someone out there hired the Game Master to kill Maureen McKenna?" Aidan asked. "And someone else paid him to kill Frank Baxter? And so on?"

"Bang on!" Jenna confirmed. "For example, I hate that floozie with the big tits who works in Missing Persons," she said, ignoring Aidan's snort. "I want her dead, so I find this website and pay to have her killed. The people who pay for the contract have no clue it isn't their hired assassin doing the job but a clueless teenager manipulated through a game. Leaving the playing card over the bodies is how the players prove to the Game Master that the job is done."

"Holy shit! Can this get any sicker? Do you know what this means?" John asked, narrowly missing an oncoming bus. "It means all of these people who paid for the kills are murderers as well. Those are the intellectual authors of the crimes. There are four that we know of, but we can't be sure how many others there are. We don't stand a chance of finding them all and discovering why they hired someone to kill the victims."

"Our best shot is to uncover the Game Master's identity,"

Aidan said. "Can you do that?" he asked Jenna, looking over his shoulder.

"I don't know."

Glancing into the rearview mirror, John saw her shrug helplessly.

"How much time do we have before the FBI and Interpol elbow their way into this case?" she asked.

"Practically none," John answered. "It's their right to handle this, as much as it is ours. The murders have occurred all over the globe. I'm sure it's what the chief will order when we brief him."

"But we found this bugger!" Jenna protested. "If it weren't for us, no one would know about this serial killer."

"I know, lass," John said patiently. Part of his job as lead investigator was to play devil's advocate. "But this is international. The guy could be anything — Irish, American, Chinese, Russian, African, or whatever — and he's operated in different countries. There are laws and protocols we have to respect. After all, the only thing that matters is catching this bastard and stopping him from arranging to have more people killed."

"That's my purpose too, John. But *I want* to find him," Jenna said, stabbing a finger at her own chest. "I'm so close I can feel it. It's personal now. Give me until tonight — tomorrow, at the latest. If I don't have anything definitive by then, ye can bring in whoever you want to."

Her green stare — as determined as it was pleading — met John's in the rearview mirror. He gritted his teeth, torn between duty and instinct. The two didn't always go hand in hand, but so far, his instincts hadn't failed him. After all, she was only asking for a few hours. Not that something tragic couldn't happen during those few hours, but he doubted foreign authorities would move faster. They were doing all that was humanly possible to find and apprehend this killer.

"Okay," he said. "Give it your best shot. In the meantime, I'll talk to Chelsea Campbell and see if she can sketch a psychological profile for us. Aidan, we also have to bring Henry Connelly in for a formal interview. I'd bet my life he's the one who paid to have Maureen McKenna murdered."

"Feckin' gobshite, you're right! Since he was alibied, I set him aside." Aidan snapped his fingers. "I'll send a couple of uniforms after him asap. What about McLean?" he asked, referring to their Chief Inspector.

John expelled a heavy breath. "I'll brief him tonight. I'll start the report now and add the data as we gather it."

They arrived at headquarters in a cloud of dust, the passengers getting out before John could turn off the engine. Jenna opened the trunk and grabbed the two laptops.

"Leave everything else, for now. I don't need it. I'll be in my office," she said, rushing into the building.

John noticed the back of her white shirt was damp with sweat. Another hot summer day, monumental not because of the temperature but because of the explosive case unraveling piece by piece. He hoped to God they had something substantial by nightfall.

He and Aidan sat squinting for a moment in the blinding sunlight — a pair of cowboys engaged in a deadly duel against a faceless enemy, waiting for the showdown at high noon as if they were in an old western movie. But he wasn't imagining the torrid heat and dry air. Reality was scarier than any vision.

John burst into action.

"Make sure Connelly is here asap. I'll go and find Chelsea," he told Aidan, on his way to his office to get the case file.

Chelsea Campbell had a degree in criminal psychology and volunteered for the Garda when she wasn't seeing patients at her private psychology practice. John had teased her about making money by listening to dissatisfied wives bitch about their husbands, but he was aware her reputation was excellent, and she took her job very seriously.

She didn't have an office at headquarters, only a cubicle in a space she shared with a couple dozen officers. John prayed she would be here, sitting next to the window, under the huge Ficus plant she'd brought in her first day at the Garda. He'd worked with her a few times but never on a case of such magnitude. Nevertheless, he had confidence in her abilities.

His muscles relaxed a fraction when he saw her petite, busty silhouette framed against the window. Sighing, he walked over, focusing on her mass of shiny blond hair as if it were the light at the end of a tunnel.

"Unless you're busy saving the world, I need your help, Chelsea."

He dragged a chair from an unoccupied cubby and sat next to her. She was thumbing through a thin file, which she put aside immediately and focused her unusual blue-violet eyes on him.

"What is it? Sounds urgent."

"Aye, ye have no idea."

He handed her the file, opening it to reveal the scattered pages of his scribbled notes, which he hadn't had the time to type and print out.

He filled his lungs with air and started talking. "Criminal mastermind builds a contract killing website but is unwilling to get his hands dirty, so he develops a dare game through which he manipulates teenagers into killing his victims as the final task to win The Game. When the job is done, he collects the fees from the hiring parties, and each teenager who completed this final dare receives a money prize."

Chelsea's lips parted in shock, but she didn't utter a sound for a full thirty seconds. When she was able to speak, her usually calm and modulated voice was shaky.

"Are you serious? No, wait. I'm sorry." She lifted a hand to rub her forehead. "I'm wasting time with stupid questions. Of course, you're serious. It's just that ... This sounds really far-fetched."

She expelled a breath, then opened the file, her eyes moving over the text and crime scene photos.

John relayed the rest of the information they had.

"I need your professional opinion about this person, The Game Master," he concluded. "We have no idea if it's a man or a woman. Anything you can tell me is important."

"Got it. Let me read this carefully, please."

He waited quietly, making a supreme effort not to move, not to tap his foot, not to distract her in any way. He wished he could create a bubble of silence so the other officers sharing the space wouldn't disturb them. Each noise seemed exaggerated in his mind. Keyboards clicked, printers hummed, phones rang, people talked, but none of this appeared to bother Chelsea. Her eyes were fixed on the pages, moving methodically as though they were a device that scanned and absorbed all that data.

Once she finished, she flipped back to the beginning of the file and lifted her face away from the sheets. Her gaze was distant, as though she was trying to remember something.

"I would say it's a man. Not that women aren't calculated or smart enough to devise such a plan, but the feel of the murders, the simple, no-nonsense method suggests it's a man, including his choice of the playing card." She spoke in careful sentences, sometimes seconds apart, but her tone was precise and sure. "He's highly intelligent, which makes him cocky. I can't say for sure, but I would place his age between twenty and forty. He's skilled in computer sciences and social engineering. Keeps up to date with technology. He chose to market The Game to teenagers because he knows they're easily manipulated, through both money and flattery, and capable of committing murder. Most importantly, teenagers are the least likely to talk to their parents or the police about the game and are vulnerable to threats."

She lowered her gaze to the file in her lap and turned a couple of pages. "If you look closely, all dares are meant to select the smartest, most ambitious, and eventually most cold-blooded players, which indicates he also knows quite a lot about psychology. And this symbol here ..." She pressed her index finger on one of the playing cards, where the symbol was drawn. "I assume this is like a ... logo of The Game. It's basically a letter G, but with that horizontal line crossing it, it resembles a currency symbol."

"Currency?"

"Yes. Dollar sign, Euro sign, Pound sterling ... The main money symbols used worldwide have one or two lines crossing them, vertically or horizontally. But this is just a long shot. I might be wrong; however, money is very important to him. And in my opinion, there's a chance his name starts with G. The fact that he chose an Ace of Spades as his signature, so to speak, indicates he considers himself powerful. He fancies himself a leader, a winner, an *Ace*. He's certainly a megalomaniac — confident, vain, and believes himself to be above the law. He lacks any trace of empathy and remorse. Probably considers himself a very successful, clever businessman."

"He rather is," John remarked dryly. "Jenna Darcy is working to find out more, but I'll bet he's made a lot of money using this scheme. We have to stop him."

"I agree. He'll escalate; he'll want more money in less time. But I think at this point it's not just about financial gain, it's also about the thrill. He's done it at least four times, in at least four countries, and gotten away with it. He might imagine he's invincible, which makes him weak. That's your advantage," she said, lifting her face to his.

"I sure hope so. A lot depends on Jenna now." He flexed his

right hand, wincing when his knuckles cracked painfully. "Anything else you can tell me? Any clue on his nationality?"

She pursed her lips, frowning as she looked back down at the file. "I couldn't tell you his nationality. The fact that he operates worldwide might indicate he's multilingual, but I can't be sure. It's almost certain he speaks English well since it's a universally accepted language, especially on the internet. Other than that, I can't tell you anything else," she concluded apologetically, handing him the file.

John took it, feeling as if it weighed a ton. Chelsea had provided him with good information, but nothing earth-shattering. He knew better than to believe a miracle would happen to help him crack the case.

"Thanks, Chelsea, you've been a huge help."

He stood, giving her a grateful half-smile.

"Let me know if there's anything else I can do. And please keep me posted. This case is one of a kind."

"Tell me about it."

He was just making his way toward the exit when Aidan entered, his dark eyes scanning the room.

"I've got Connelly in an interview room," he announced when he reached John.

John felt a spark of hope. In addition to Jenna's hard work, they might have another button to push if Connelly was guilty. He knew the guy was an old fox, an ex-judge who knew all the tricks of the trade and wouldn't be easy to crack. But they had to start somewhere.

"Good job. What's his state of mind?"

"Hostile, but underneath I sense he's uneasy," Aidan replied. "Don't know if it's guilt or the instinctive reaction people have when dealing with the guards."

John made a derisive sound. He had a flashback to his childhood, when he used to feel the same, not even knowing why. "We'll find out. Did he mention a lawyer?"

"Not yet. He knows that would make him look guilty as shite. Now he's playing it as though we're harassing him because he was the only one who had a recent public altercation with Maureen McKenna."

"Let's see if he sticks to that story."

18

As he and Aidan entered the interview room, John studied the elderly man. Connelly sat at the table, his back straight, his posture rigid. He seemed thinner than the last time they'd spoken, paler, his bushy eyebrows drawn into an intimidating scowl. His countenance was as imposing as it had been previously, but John could see the chinks in his armor. Although he appeared perfectly composed, keeping his hands clasped in front of him, the pressure of his grip had discolored his nails. The man was out of his element, and he knew it.

"Mr. Connelly, thank you for coming in for formal questioning in the case of Maureen McKenna's murder. You are not obliged to say anything unless you wish to do so, but whatever you say will be taken down in writing and may be given in evidence." John recited the man his rights, placing the case file on the table and sitting in the chair facing Connelly. Aidan remained standing.

"Did I have a choice, detective?" Connelly replied, his voice an echo of affected dignity. "I thought you understood I had nothing to do with this after you called my daughter to check my alibi."

"It seems that's no longer relevant. Tell me, Mr. Connelly, are you familiar with the Dark Web?"

John watched him like a hunter stalks his prey. He saw the flash of fear in the man's hooded eyes and knew his swift approach was as efficient as a cobra's.

I've got you, you son of a bitch!

Connelly recovered to a degree, but he clenched his hands tighter, no doubt to stop them from shaking.

"I have no idea what you mean."

John gestured casually as if he were talking about the weather. "Sure you do. The Dark Web is the internet's underground, the place where anything is possible, no matter how shady. Drugs, modern slavery ... Contract killing."

He allowed the words to hover between them, his unblinking gaze drilling relentlessly into Connelly's. He could almost hear the old man's heart pumping faster and faster, now that he realized he was trapped.

"That's how Maureen McKenna was murdered," John continued. "Someone hired a killer on the Dark Web to assassinate her. Did you set up the deal, or did someone help you?"

Connelly managed to appear shocked. Was it because he was innocent, learning about this just now, or was it because the bastard was guilty as sin and couldn't believe they'd caught him?

"Are you insinuating that I —"

"Did you find this website alone, or did someone recommend it to you?" John wasn't going to fall for his act, nor was he going to give him time to breathe. He leaned forward, forearms planted firmly on the table, hurling the questions at him faster, harsher. "Was it your daughter? Did she help you cook up this plan?"

"I don't know what you're talking about," the judge fought to sound offended. "Do you have any proof of this?"

"Is that why you used her as an alibi? Because she's actually your accomplice in the murder of Maureen McKenna?"

"She knows nothing about this, and neither do I!" Connelly lowered his voice, dragging his composure around himself like a cloak once more. "You can check my financial records if you want. You'll see I haven't paid anyone to —"

"There are dozens of ways to conduct a transaction like that. I'm sure you've learned that in all the years you were a judge."

Sweat beaded on Connelly's forehead. His face, once pale, was now a furious red.

"John, come on, he's old," Aidan said, sliding smoothly into the role of good cop.

"I don't give a fuck how old he is. Maureen McKenna will never have the chance to reach his age because this man chose to play God and end her life."

"I didn't kill her!" Connelly's breathing was shallow and wheezy. He pulled at the collar of his starched white shirt as if he couldn't get enough air.

"As good as. If we charge you with murder, no judge in this country will acquit you. Do you know what her death did to her husband and sons?" John shouted, opening the file and shoving the photos of Maureen's body toward Connelly.

The old man took one look before averting his gaze. He grimaced, his boney chest rising and falling rapidly.

"She ... She was responsible for my wife's death."

"No, she wasn't. Your wife's own negligence killed her, not Maureen McKenna. And I think you realize that now. But it's too late. She's already dead — because of you." John stared at the elderly man's tortured expression.

Connelly lowered his head, spreading his hands wide on the hard, cold surface of the table. A minute later, he shook his head.

"I didn't kill her, nor did I pay anyone to do it," he said, weakly but decisively.

John's eyes burned holes in the top of Connelly's bent head. He stood abruptly, walked around the table, and stopped next to the judge.

"Fine. If that's the way you want to play it." He turned to his partner. "Aidan, find Mr. Connelly's daughter and bring her in for questioning. She must be the one who found the website and handled the transaction."

Connelly's head snapped up, his eyes haunted. "No! My daughter has nothing to do with this, I swear."

John slammed his palms on the table and leaned forward, his face inches away from Connelly's. "Then start talking. Every minute that website is functioning, someone else could get killed. And I will hold *you* responsible. Tell me what you know, and I might offer you a deal. Cost me more time, and I swear you'll be very sorry."

Connelly held his gaze for a few seconds longer, then his shoulders slumped in defeat. All at once, his breath seemed to leave him, along with the iron will he'd displayed earlier. He was smart and experienced enough to know there was no way out of this.

"I found the website myself," he confessed quietly.

"How?" John asked.

"As you pointed out the other day, I had to deal with a lot of different people in my career — some of them shady but useful. I asked around, and I got the link to the website."

"We need names, Mr. Connelly."

"I don't have any names. On the Dark Web, everyone is anonymous. I left a message on the website with Maureen McKenna's name and address, which I'd gotten from the phone book. I was given a price and —"

"How much?" John interrupted.

Connelly gave a small shrug. "It wasn't money; it was

bitcoins. I ... A few years ago, my daughter advised me to invest some money in bitcoin. I made the transfer right away. You can get the details from my computer. After a few days, I received the —" He stopped, rubbing a hand over his face as though to wipe away a terrible memory. "I received the photos of Dr. McKenna ... dead. It was proof the job had been done."

John stared down at Connelly, a shattering rage building inside him. He knew all too well the damage one human being could inflict on another, but this cold-blooded transaction in human lives was too much for him to stomach.

Aidan, knowing him as well as he did, must've sensed it and placed a hand discretely on his shoulder, stepping forward to take the lead.

"Do you know this man's name, Mr. Connelly? The man who runs the website? Or are there more?"

Connelly shook his head. "I have no idea what his name is or if there are several individuals operating this website." He huffed out a breath. "After my wife's death, I went crazy. I realize that now. You may think it's an excuse to get a lighter sentence, but it really was a case of temporary insanity."

He lowered his head again, plowing his trembling fingers through the gray hair at his temples.

"I don't imagine either of you can understand what it's like to lose the love of your life like that, but I needed someone to blame, someone to pay for the loss in order to maintain my sanity." A bitter grimace slashed his face. "What a fool I was ... The murder didn't bring Harriet back, didn't ease the pain of her loss, and I've been haunted by demons from the moment I saw those photos."

John clenched his teeth so hard his jaw hurt. His anger was palpable, an entity enveloping him, as dark and absolute as a sarcophagus. He understood all too well Connelly's rage, pain, and insanity. Part of his anger was directed toward himself because, for just one second, he'd allowed his own trauma to surface and cloud his judgment, making him feel sorry for the son of a bitch. But it was just a second. The memory of Brian McKenna's echoing cries was enough to bring back his objectivity.

He moved closer to the former judge, speaking down to his bent head. "You can spin it like that if you want to. You can plead temporary insanity, but that's only a pretext. You're a pathetic excuse for a human being. *You are a murderer.*"

Aidan opened the door and signaled to the two Gardaí who were waiting outside.

"Stand up," John barked. "Henry Connelly, you are charged with the murder of Maureen McKenna and multiple counts of conspiracy to murder." While John continued the accusation, the young officers moved in to handcuff the man. He didn't resist, staring down at the floor as the guards led him away.

"Well done, John, as always."

John turned to Aidan, acknowledging his praise with the shadow of a smile.

"We're far from done yet. We need to get a warrant and confiscate Connelly's computer asap. If the bitcoin transaction can be traced, we might not need more than that to discover the Game Master's identity."

"I'll get the warrant. Why don't you check up on Jenna and see if she's made any progress?"

Aidan had barely finished the sentence when Jenna burst through the open door, hair disheveled, cheeks flushed, a glorious and triumphant expression on her face.

"I found him! His name is Gareth James Reilly. He currently lives in Chicago, but he's an Irish citizen, so we have the right to ask Detective Coldwell or the FBI or whoever has jurisdiction over cybercrimes to apprehend him, then extradite him to Ireland to be questioned and tried here. We've got him, guys. We fucking got him!"

AMBER NEVER REALIZED how slowly minutes and hours could crawl. From the moment she'd become a teenager, she'd rarely had free time. She'd been busy with her studies in high school and college, busy with work, whether it was a steady job or freelancing, and later busy as a wife and mother. She couldn't honestly say she'd ever been bored — she hadn't had time for that. On those rare occasions when she could've done nothing, she opted to work, as much for the pleasure of it as for the money.

Today had to be the longest day of her life, precisely because she had nothing to do. She couldn't focus on anything, couldn't direct her thoughts anywhere else other than to John and what he and his team were doing. She'd never been a patient person, and now she was more aware of that character flaw than ever before. She sat on the sofa, tapping her fingernails against her front teeth, staring at her phone and willing it to ring.

It didn't, of course. So much for the power of the mind — her mind, anyway. Standing, she paced to the window, looking outside into the night. What was John doing? Had they found the killer? He'd called around seven to apologize and say he wouldn't be able to come to dinner. He either ignored her questions or hadn't heard them, but she pleaded with him to call at any hour once he could tell her why he'd left so abruptly. She had no idea if he'd heard her begging words before he ended the call.

Now it was past eleven, and sleep was as far away from her as the moon. Hayley had been just as affected as she had by the day's events. She'd confessed that she was particularly worried about Amy. Amber had tried to reassure her, but the words sounded hollow and meaningless even to her.

Anxiety was a living presence in the house. Sitting on the

sofa, pretending to watch TV, Amber had opted to make them both some valerian tea, hoping its calming properties might relax them.

Relieved when she saw Hayley's eyelids droop, she'd gone upstairs with her and tucked her in, comforting her as best she could. At least one of them would get some sleep tonight.

She showered, brushed her teeth, applied body lotion and face cream, then shimmied into a short, black nightgown. It was too hot for pajamas. The silk felt good against her skin, soothing it just as the valerian tea had soothed her nerves. She didn't think she would sleep, at least not deeply, but thanks to the tea, she no longer felt as though her skin was too tight and itchy.

Leaving the light on in the hallway, she checked on Hayley again. She tiptoed to the bed, closing her eyes in a thankful prayer when she saw her baby was sleeping soundly, her breathing steady, her budding chest rising and falling gently. She caressed her hair, fingers moving lighter than a butterfly's wings, then turned around and closed the door carefully behind her.

She was about to get into bed when she remembered she'd left the TV on downstairs and her phone on the sofa.

Cursing under her breath, she padded down the stairs, feeling her way in the semi-darkness. The only light came from the TV screen, but she knew her way through the house by now. Turning off the set, she inhaled deeply. Despite everything that had happened, she felt at home here. What would Hayley think if she were to buy this house? She had enough money from the divorce settlement to do it. But maybe now wasn't the time to think that far ahead. They had to wait and see what was going to happen.

Bending to retrieve her phone from between the sofa cushions, she jumped when it rang in her hand. She quickly tapped the screen to answer.

"Hello."

"Hi, it's John."

She held her breath for a few seconds, her heart beating madly. If he'd called at this hour, it meant he had important news. Was it good or bad?

"I'm sorry, did I wake you?" His voice was hesitant. "You said to call whenever I had information —"

"No, I was waiting for you to call. What happened? Can you tell me?"

"Aye, I can. Actually ... I'm parked in front of your house."

"What?"

Dazed, she dropped the phone onto the sofa and hurried to the front door. Her hands shook as she unlocked it. She stepped out onto the porch, then went down the three steps, unmindful of her bare feet and skimpy attire.

Streetlights diluted the darkness, but it took her eyes a few moments to adjust. When they did, she saw John emerge from his car. He didn't slam the door, yet the sound echoed loudly on the quiet street. The full moon peering through the tree branches bathed everything in a silvery glow. As he walked toward her, John was only a silhouette in a haze of misty light.

"Hi."

"Hi." Her eyes scanned the street, doing a double-take. "The Gardaí's car is gone! Does that mean ... You're spending the night here again?"

He shook his head. "There's no need."

"You caught him?" she whispered, her voice trembling hopefully.

"Sort of. Um ... Can I come inside? I'll tell you all about it if you're not too sleepy."

"Of course. Believe me, I'm wide awake."

Unable to distinguish his features in the dim light, she saw only the glint of his eyes and his white smile. She found herself grinning back, flooded by happiness and an immense feeling of relief.

Hurrying into the house, she barely gave him time to shut the door before flinging her arms around him. At that moment, John was more of a superhero in her eyes than Superman himself.

"Oh, my God, you're a genius! I'm so relieved this nightmare is over."

Her gesture was an unconscious one, a natural reaction to the joy she felt, knowing the ordeal was over. She could breathe again without the unbearable pressure of fear and worry.

When John's tightened his arms around her, Amber's head cleared. She was suddenly aware of every inch of his body pressed against hers, of his warm palms fanning her back. His skin was separated from hers only by a thin layer of silk. The floor was cool under the soles of her feet, yet her body was warm, almost feverish. Each inch of her exposed skin was aware of every texture pressed against it — the denim of his jeans, the soft cotton of his shirt, the holster of his gun touching her hip.

His stubbled cheek rubbed against her face as he turned his head to look at her. She couldn't see his eyes, but she felt them burn into her soul a moment before he bent his mouth to hers. And then ... Oh, God! Her most erotic fantasies hadn't come close to picturing the way he kissed.

There was no hesitation as he pressed his lips to hers — only desire, need, raw sexuality. His tongue delved into her mouth, and she drew it in, stroking it hungrily with her own, arching her body toward him, as his hands moved over her back, her shoulders, her hips.

As he cupped her ass, his fingertips touched her bare buttocks under the short nightgown. He pulled her more tightly against him, and she felt his straining erection behind the fly of his jeans. She wanted him so badly it hurt. A moan vibrated in her chest.

He must have thought it a protest because he tore his mouth away from hers. "I'm sorry, Amber."

His breathing was fast and ragged. He started to release her, but she tightened her hands around his waist, gripping handfuls of his shirt. The darkness had an eerie, intoxicating quality to it. Combined with his pure maleness, which she'd craved from the moment they'd met, it made her reckless. She would implode if he let her go now. She didn't remember wanting anything or anyone so badly.

"Don't stop unless you want to," she whispered, staring into his eyes.

It only took a heartbeat before he reclaimed her mouth, this time without restraint. Then he lowered his lips to her neck, scraping the sensitive skin with his teeth.

"Where's Hayley?" he asked.

"She's asleep upstairs."

"What if she wakes up?"

"She won't."

Amber breathed the words into his ear, her skin erupting into goose bumps under his skillful hands. For the first time in years, she wasn't just a mom, but a woman, engulfed by needs she'd thought long forgotten. This wonderful, overwhelming man had reawakened her, making everything more vivid than before. She would never get enough of him.

Still kissing her passionately, he pressed her against the door, tracing kisses down her chest and over the delicate curves of her breasts. Her nipples ached to be kissed, and she barely managed to stifle a whimper when his mouth closed around one through the lacy cups of her nightie.

"Wait," she whispered, breathing shallowly. "Upstairs. My room. Take off your shoes so we don't make noise."

Silently, he toed off his footwear.

Amber guided him up the stairs, moving on tiptoes, her fingers laced with his. Opening the bedroom door, she motioned him inside and closed it silently. She turned the key softly, separating them from the rest of the world. They might only have this one night, but tonight was for them.

19

The bedside lamp bathed the room in warm, dim light. John removed his gun and holster and placed them on her dresser, all without taking his scorching gaze off her.

Amber was self-conscious as she turned to face him once more. It had been a long time since she'd done this — stood half-naked in front of a man. And that man had always been Dean, no one else. A man who'd left her for another woman. For a split second, her mind flashed back at the busty, pouty, bold Lena.

Would John like her? Would he prefer she had bigger breasts, curvier hips, fuller lips? She'd read somewhere that men liked long hair in a woman, but she hadn't been thinking of seduction when she'd chopped hers into a short, unruly bob. What if he didn't like it?

Judging by the intensity with which he watched her, he loved everything he saw and was dying to touch what he couldn't see. He covered the distance between them in a single stride and drew her in his arms, lowering his mouth to hers.

It had been more than a decade since she'd had what she'd thought of as good sex, but now she realized Dean had been a mild breeze compared to the tornado John stirred inside her. His hands moved confidently over her body; his mouth so skilled it sparked sensations wherever he kissed her. One moment they were standing, the next they were on the bed, and she reveled in the pressure of his body on hers. His lips traveled down over her breasts, his tongue teasing but urgent, kissing away any trace of doubt she might've had.

Reaching down, she fumbled with his belt and the zipper of his jeans. She didn't recognize this ardent woman, who lacked inhibition as she pushed aside his underwear and folded her hand around him. He gasped, then slid his hand between her thighs. His erection became even firmer when he found her wet for him.

She helped him discard her panties, then started to work frantically on the buttons of his shirt. Revealing his skin, she lifted her mouth to his muscled chest, kissing him without pattern or technique, her senses drunk with lust. She flicked her tongue over one taut nipple, drawing it into her mouth. It was too much for him. Lowering her head to the pillow, he took her mouth hard then, in one swift movement, raised her hips and pushed himself inside her.

She sank her teeth into his lower lip so she wouldn't cry out as wave after wave of mind-blowing pleasure assaulted her. Her body shuddered, tensed, squeezed, and in less than a dozen strokes, she was reaching the most volcanic climax she'd ever experienced. And so did he. On the final high, hard push, he kissed her, so tenderly she felt he was giving himself to her as she had to him, on a level that was much more than sexual.

"I'm sorry about your wife. She was so beautiful, so young ..."

Amber hadn't meant to voice the statement, but as they lay together naked a while later, she felt she was unable and unwilling to hide anything from him. Not after they'd made love again, tenderly, deepening the connection the tumultuous sex had started.

He shifted to look at her, and she raised her head from his chest. The nightstand lamp cast an edgy shadow over his face, sharpening his features. His eyes were full of questions.

"I'm sorry," she repeated, afraid she'd screwed up big time. Too late did she realize she couldn't have known how beautiful Shanna was unless she'd snooped around in his life.

She withdrew slightly and lifted herself on one elbow, so she could watch his face. "After you told me about it, I did some research regarding her death. I didn't mean to pry into your life. I just ... I liked you. I wanted to know more," she confessed, tracing her finger over the pattern of circles on the pillowcase.

Her face burned with embarrassment and guilt. Had she gone too far? After all, she barely knew him. Maybe he'd kept the details to himself for a reason. She wouldn't blame him if he stormed out of her house right now. And out of her life.

The thought was so daunting she glanced back at his face, her eyes searching his insistently. To her joy, a reluctant smile curved his beautiful mouth.

"I can't say I blame you," he said. "I researched you, too, although at first, I was only following up on a potential witness. But after we met, I wanted an excuse to see you again. At the time, it seemed as if circumstances were against us."

She returned his smile, relieved with his reaction to her confession. Then she became serious again.

"Your wife was stunning. You looked so happy together in the photos I saw. I ... I don't understand why such terrible things happen."

He was quiet, his eyes distant, lost in memories no one should experience. The sheets rustled as he rolled onto his side to face her. Reaching out, he stroked her damp cheekbone with his thumb.

"Hey, what's wrong?"

She shook her head, unable to describe her feelings. Slipping back into his embrace, she sheltered her face in the hollow of his neck. His steady pulse was reassuring, warming every cold, dark place inside her. She would have given anything to be able to soothe him just as easily.

"When my marriage ended, I couldn't imagine anything more devastating than being betrayed by my life partner. You see ... He was the only man I'd ever been with. But now I realize how weak and silly I was. John, I would do anything to take this pain away from you."

"You have."

She wasn't sure she'd heard him correctly.

"You've taken the pain away," he repeated, lifting her chin to look at her. "I don't know how or why this hasn't happened with anyone since Shanna died, but ... it's different with you. It's not just that false feeling of sexual release when the bad things inside you are dulled for a short while." He moistened his lips as though searching for words. "When I lost Shanna, I felt as though my soul had died with her. Even when I began dating again, I felt empty inside. I just went through the motions, you know? But you ... I'm alive again when I'm with you." He sounded puzzled at his own revelation. "That night when I slept here, and I knew you and Hayley were close, counting on me, trusting me, I felt I was part of your family. The same happened when we went shopping together. It was as if I belonged with the two of you. I can't imagine how big a wanker your ex-husband must be for letting you and the lass go."

Moved to the core, Amber sniffed back more tears. She

lifted a hand to caress his cheek, letting the tips of her fingers meander over his handsome features. "Maybe we've been all given a second chance."

He lowered his mouth to hers, and she sank into the tender kiss. But a moment later, she drew away, struck by a sudden realization.

"Wait. Not that I'm not enjoying this, but you promised to tell me about the case. You said you caught the guy. What happened?" she asked frantically, pushing herself up, the sheet clutched to her chest.

"Right." John let out a long breath, obviously trying to reorient his priorities. "Yes, we've identified him. His name is Gareth James Reilly. He's thirty-three, originally from Galway, Ireland, but currently living in Chicago. Turns out The Game was a cover-up for a contract-killing business."

Her mouth gaped as he told her how Reilly had created The Game and used teenagers to do his dirty work while he collected the fees and accepted more contracts.

"Holy crap!" She was unable to get her head around this horrendous plan. "No wonder he wasn't caught until now. Who would have thought of something this complicated?"

"Gareth Reilly did."

"Yeah ... How did you find him?"

"Jenna kept digging at it, determined to find the man, and she did. She discovered an old blog he kept about being an entrepreneur." He scoffed. "Appropriate, eh? Anyway, she matched some of the expressions he used in his writing, but what gave him away was the way he constantly misspelled a word — he spelled *cleaver* instead of *clever*. Not a common mistake, so Jenna latched onto it immediately. She said from there it was a piece of cake to match his coding style and confirm he'd created both websites, then determine his identity and location."

"Wow." She rubbed her forehead, where information tumbled and tangled into the beginnings of a headache. "But you said he's in Chicago. I'm confused. How will you arrest him?"

"Once we knew his name, we talked with Detective Maggie Coldwell in Boston. She and a team from the FBI raided Reilly's apartment, apprehended him, and confiscated all his electronic devices. Since the man's an Irish citizen and we cracked the case, we have the right to try and convict him. At least, we have priority over jurisdiction. We're working on extraditing him and getting him brought here, along with all of his equipment. As soon as she has that, Jenna will trace the people who paid him to kill the victims, as well as the teenagers who committed the actual killings. They'll all face trial and conviction."

"Amazing." Amber raked a hand through her disheveled hair. "This is incredible."

"Tell me about it. I may be able to explain it now, but it took Jenna the better part of an hour to explain it to Aidan, the chief, and me. We don't speak geek," he added, grinning. "But to summarize, The Game was a very select operation. Reilly devised an algorithm to recognize the players who had the potential to serve his purpose. The first set of dares was given automatically through the server, but he monitored the players himself as they moved closer to the top-level until they were given the most important dare: killing the target he set. He kept a profile for each of the players, monitored their social media, and knew everything there was to know about their lives. The moment they signed into The Game, he created a file, and all the information from their online presence and social media was linked automatically. The algorithm analyzed everything about them: their data, their photos, the music they liked, movies they watched, posts they wrote. Based on this, he made the initial selection, and the player was accepted or rejected."

Amber was quiet, still trying to digest all this information. It seemed straightforward when described so meticulously. She understood why Hayley had been accepted into The Game. She liked dark rock, was a fan of horror movies, read thriller novels, and wore mostly black. Since the divorce, she'd been rebellious, too.

Amber shuddered at the thought of her baby girl's life under the virtual microscope of a sociopath who had the ability to pull together an operation of this magnitude.

Feeling her tremble, John reached out and pulled her closer.

"Hey, it's okay now. It's over." He massaged her scalp with gentle, calming motions. "Jenna and the rest of the Cybercrime team have managed to block all access to Reilly's websites, both The Game and his blog."

"Thank God for that."

She rested her head against his shoulder, stroking his chest absently. Despite the few gray hairs mixed with the dark ones sprinkled over his torso, he had the body of a thirty-year-old man — not one of those waxed and oiled male strippers, but the body of a real-life man — toned, firm, and dusted with the perfect amount of hair. He didn't have bulging pectorals or a bulky six-pack, but each subtle line of his muscles was well-defined. Her gaze traveled down over him, pausing on each taut nipple that made her mouth water, continuing over his flat abdomen and sexy navel, where the white sheet contrasted with the silky patch of hair.

Desire stirred inside her once more. Even if they had only this one night together, it was a memory she would cherish forever. Although the clock on the wall showed it was three, she was wide awake. She squirmed closer to him, tangling her legs with his. The hair on his thighs and calves felt masculine and erotic against the sole of her foot as she slid her leg up in a lazy caress.

"You're a real hero, John, you know that? No one else was able to figure out this case."

"Thanks, but I can't take all of the credit. It was a team effort, and Jenna is the true champion. I don't think she's slept four hours since this started. Come to think of it, neither of us has."

She looked up, noticing the deep shadows under his eyes. "I'm sorry I kept you up," she said, then buried her face in his chest and began to giggle when she heard the pun in her words.

He chuckled. "Never apologize for such a thing. I've had a whale of a time. A great time," he explained, seeing her puzzled expression.

"Oh ... Me too. A big, huge, amazing whale of a time," she said, grinning. Some of his Irish expressions were hilarious and so damned irresistible.

Suddenly, her maternal instincts kicked in, pushing aside the nymphomaniac drunk on sex she hadn't known lived inside her. Poor man, she'd sucked up all of his energy — and then some.

"Have you eaten anything?"

He shook his head.

"I saved some pasta and shrimp for you."

His face brightened, softened somehow, showing a lot more emotion than her cooking deserved. "How did you know I would be here? Even I didn't know."

She slipped out of his embrace, reaching for her nightgown. "I didn't. I just hoped you'd come over. I'll be right back," she whispered, shimmying into her nightie on her way to the door.

She was self-conscious of his gaze on her, anxiously trying to cover her thirty-eight-year-old body. She did her best to keep it slim and firm, but ... She'd never met a woman with no stretch marks and cellulite. Would he think she was sexy if he saw her exposed in bright light?

One look over her shoulder stroked her ego as thoroughly as his hands had caressed her body. His eyes darkened, his pupils dilating as he watched her. His Adam's apple moved as he swallowed slowly, and the sheet stirred below his waist.

Hiding a grin of satisfaction, she unlocked the bedroom door carefully, wincing at each tiny noise. She wished she could slither down the stairs as silently as a snake, but she did her best to tiptoe delicately.

In the kitchen, she hastily took out the casserole of food, stuck it into the microwave oven, programmed it, and watched the display, counting down the seconds with it. She pressed the stop button before the timer could beep, grabbed the casserole, a fork, and a few napkins from the counter, then turned to the door.

She almost dropped everything when she saw her sleepy daughter in the doorway, rubbing her eyes like a little girl, hair disheveled.

"Hayley!"

"Mom? What are you doing?"

Oh, God! Oh, crap!

What was she supposed to do now? How was she supposed to handle this? Guilt choked Amber as she looked into her daughter's big, innocent eyes. They were illuminated only by the light emanating from the microwave oven, the door of which she'd forgotten to close.

She had brought a man into their home and had sex with him while her daughter slept in the room next door. What had she been thinking? How could she explain? Could she lie her way out of this? No, that would be the coward's way out, and no matter what else she might be, she wasn't a coward. Nor did she want her daughter to grow up to be one. She had to take responsibility for her actions, no matter the consequences.

She cleared her throat. "Sweetie, what are you doing up?"

"I woke up thirsty and wanted some milk," Hayley said around a yawn. "What are *you* doing up?"

Amber's knees were rubbery. She wasn't ready, but the moment of truth raced toward her.

Squaring her shoulders, she reached out and switched on the light, feeling ashamed and exposed under its glare. Pulling out a chair, she sat at the kitchen table, shoving the dish of food away. She had to handle this the way she'd been taught, the way she believed everyone should — with honesty.

"Please sit down, honey."

Hayley moved forward, her expression growing increasingly anxious as she sat across from her mother.

"What's wrong? Has something happened? Have the police found Amy?"

There was a trace of hope in her frightened voice, but Amber shook her head. "I don't know."

Hayley slumped into the chair, her elbows sliding along the table, as she shoved her hair out of her eyes. "Then why are you awake?"

Amber moistened her lips. How to start? As seconds went by, Hayley lifted her head and stared at her. She had to say something.

"John doesn't know anything about Amy yet, but they caught the man ... the Game Master."

Hayley's eyes widened, her face brightening with an incredulous smile. "They have? Oh, my God! That's great. Detective John's so smart, and Detective Darcy is, like, a genius. How did they do it? Who is he?"

"He's an Irishman who lives in Chicago. He created The Game to —"

Amber stopped, shaking her head. There was only so much shocking information a sixteen-year-old girl could absorb at once.

"I'll give you the details later. The important thing is that they've arrested him in the United States, closed The Game website, and they'll bring him here to be tried."

Hayley's lips parted, still curved into a smile. "That's such great news! I didn't expect them to find him so soon. I've read about these things on the net, and sometimes it takes the police years to catch people like that." She paused to take a breath. "So, how did you find out? Did Detective John call you?"

Oh, boy! God, if you hear me, please give me strength and the right words.

"Uh ... Yes, he did call." Amber's stomach clenched. "And then he came to tell me ... Face to face."

Hayley's eyebrows drew together in a puzzled frown. "At night?"

Amber had never been able to hide anything from her daughter. As Hayley had grown up, she'd developed an uncanny ability to read her mother's mind, a talent Amber heartily wished she didn't have. It wouldn't be hard now. Guilt was stamped all over her face.

Hayley shifted her gaze to the casserole of leftovers, then back to Amber's face. For the first time, it seemed she noticed her attire and messy hair. Amber knew her body must be covered in whisker burns, maybe even a bruise or two. John hadn't been gentle the first time — she hadn't wanted him to be. But although she was sure her daughter wasn't sexually active yet, she wasn't so naïve as to miss the signs.

Hayley swallowed, her eyes growing cold. "Where is he now?"

Amber's silence was louder and more eloquent than anything she could say. Her gaze was locked on Hayley's. She held her breath while she analyzed each of her daughter's facial expressions — suspicion, denial, comprehension.

"He's here, isn't he?" Hayley asked, her voice dropping to a furious whisper. "You've slept with him?"

The words were an ugly accusation. Amber couldn't bear

the way Hayley gaped at her, as if she were the dirtiest of whores. Her daughter was old enough to understand, to judge her, but Amber felt the need to justify herself.

As Hayley's chair scraped against the kitchen tiles and she jerked up to her feet, Amber reached out and caught her hand, pinning it against the table.

"Hayley, listen to me. Please." Maybe it was all her desperation concentrated on this last word that made Hayley sit back down. Her eyes were averted, her inner turmoil hidden, but Amber tightened her grip, willing her daughter to look at her.

"Hayley, your father was the only man in my life. I would've stayed and been faithful to him forever, even though he didn't always make me happy. I *never* looked at another man. He was the one who betrayed me."

"So now you're going to turn into a slut to pay him back?"

Tears welled in Amber's eyes. To hear those vicious, nasty words from her own daughter tore her apart.

"I'm not a slut, Hayley. I'm just a normal woman who has the right to rebuild her life." Tears ran down her cheeks, but she continued, her voice as broken as her heart. "I did everything I could to make your father happy and to make you happy. He's moved on. I've tried to make up for his absence as much as I could, but I'm not just your mom, honey. I'm a woman and, before tonight, I've been lonely and miserable, more than you can possibly imagine. You're a young woman now. You've dated a little. You know what it feels like when a boy you care for feels the same way about you." She paused to sniffle back tears, her gaze still burning into Hayley's. "Don't you think I have the right to be happy and loved, too?"

Hayley's eyes were glassy, but Amber couldn't tell what emotions struggled inside her daughter's heart. At least her gaze was no longer darting contempt, so maybe Amber's plea for understanding was hitting home.

"Does Detective John make you happy?" Hayley asked.

Amber relaxed her grip on her daughter's hand, allowing herself a small, tearful smile. "Yes. Really happy."

"Was this the first time you two ... ?"

Heat rushed to Amber's cheeks as she nodded again, staring at the table.

Hayley withdrew her hand slowly but without any sign of anger. When she glanced up, Amber saw her frown.

"But isn't he married? He wears a wedding ring."

"His wife died five years ago." She explained about Shanna. By the time she finished, sorrow had replaced Hayley's accusing expression.

"Poor man."

"Yeah. He loved his wife very much," Amber said, staring down at the table. "He suffered so much. Now it feels like we have a chance to move on together. He likes you a lot, by the way. And that has nothing to do with the way he feels about me."

Hayley lifted her head. "Really? Did he say that?"

"Yes. He said he felt he was part of our family when he was with us."

Hayley was silent for a while. Then her chin pointed at the casserole. "Is that for him?"

Amber bobbed her head.

"Is he in your bedroom? Naked?" Hayley asked in a ridiculously low whisper.

Amber had to press a hand over her lips to stop herself from laughing. Hayley's mouth began to twitch in amusement.

"No, I'm dressed. Hello, Hayley."

John's deep voice startled the living daylights out of them. He slowly stepped into the kitchen, walked around the table, head bent as if he had no idea how to deal with this situation either. Reaching the window, he looked out into the night. A few seconds later, he let the lacy curtain drop and turned to face them both.

"I'm sorry you found me here in the middle of the night like this," he told Hayley, sliding his hands into his pockets. "I just want you to know I would never do anything to disrespect either of you. I —" The words seemed to stick in his throat as he struggled to put his emotions into sentences. "I care very much for your mother and for you, lass, but ... There's no excuse for me being here like this. I'm sorry. I'll leave now."

20

"No!" Amber insisted, standing abruptly.

She was surprised to hear Hayley echo her plea.

"You don't have to go," Hayley added. "I understand about you and my mom. And ... I'm okay with it, I guess." She glanced up at John from under her long lashes.

As she stared at her daughter's beautiful brown eyes connected with the hesitant, grateful, gray gaze of the man she cared about so much, Amber's heart contracted. Love flooded her for these two wonderful people she was blessed to have in her life. No matter what happened between John and her, he'd unknowingly helped her connect with her daughter on another level.

"Thank you, Hayley," John said quietly. "It's very mature of you to say that. I appreciate it. If your feelings about this should change at any point, please tell me, aye?"

Hayley offered him a shy smile. "Okay." She pushed the casserole of food in front of a chair and motioned him to sit down. "Eat. My mom's a great cook, and she saved this especially for you."

He smiled too, enveloping both mother and daughter in such a tender gaze it almost made Amber cry again. This was a deeply emotional moment for all of them.

John sat and opened the casserole, his eyebrows arching appreciatively. Amber propped her chin on her hand and just watched him, stifling a laugh when she saw Hayley do the same. Glancing up, John seemed as uncomfortable as an inexperienced actor on stage.

All at once, the tension was broken, and they all laughed.

"This feels like a standoff," he remarked after the giggles subsided. "If I didn't know ya two were related, this would have convinced me. Alright then, let's see."

He took a bite of shrimp pasta, chewing slowly as if he were analyzing each texture and flavor.

"Not bad," he said, grinning at them. When he saw them pout, he chuckled. "Ah, I was just acting the maggot. It's excellent."

As he ate, Amber poured Hayley a glass of milk and told her the entire story behind The Game and Gareth Reilly. She'd debated about giving her an abridged version but decided against it. If she wanted to protect her, she had to make sure Hayley knew the unlimited, unimaginable dangers that lurked on the internet.

By the time she'd finished the story, punctuated by John's addendums from time to time, Hayley was looking both awed and terrified.

"I can't believe someone would think of such a twisted plan," she said, shivering.

"Ye have no idea how sick people can be. That's why you need to be careful, Hayley," John said gravely, pushing the empty dish aside and mouthing a *thank you* to Amber. "Never access the Dark Web again. Only enter sites you're familiar with when you're on the internet. If you must use social media — although I, personally, don't get people's need for it —

make sure only your friends have access to your information. Never befriend people you don't know. If someone wants to get in touch with you, check their profile, see when they've created it, what they post ... Jenna will give you more pointers on how to recognize scammers, spammers, and other criminals."

Hayley toyed with her empty glass, scraping her fingernails over the subtle decorative ridges. "I still can't understand why no one else went to the police."

"Apparently, Reilly contacted the high-level players personally and threatened them by saying they could easily become victims instead of players. He made them believe they had no choice but to go along, finish The Game, and get paid."

"So he actually paid them?" Amber interjected.

"Yes, in bitcoin. I imagine he thought of himself as a fair businessman, which is a good thing since it'll make it simpler to trace the payments, find the kids who did the deeds, and make sure they pay for what they've done."

A sudden shiver shook Amber. Maybe it was the late hour and her fatigue that made the situation seem so sinister. This case was like a Hydra — the more heads you cut off, the more grew from the stumps. How would the police ever tie up all the loose ends?

"When this hits the media, how many of the sickos out there will be inspired by Reilly?"

John stood, a grim expression clouding his features. "I don't know. That's what I'm most afraid of. There will be people who will idolize the son of a —". He stopped, glancing at Hayley, then cleared his throat. "In any case, he'll rot in jail."

"Are you sure?" Hayley asked fearfully, unfolding her legs from under her and getting to her feet.

"Yes. We have him cold. The evidence against him is indisputable."

"But what if —"

They all froze when a phone started ringing somewhere in the house.

Amber was the first one to react. "That's mine. Who the hell could be calling at this hour?"

She dashed into the living room, lifted the ringing phone, then gaped at the display, blinking twice to make sure she'd read it correctly. Why the hell would Dean be calling at this time of night?

"Hello?" she said.

"Can you explain why the fuck our daughter's name is in the news, related to a multiple murder scandal?" Dean demanded furiously.

Amber's knees gave out, and she collapsed onto the sofa. "What are you talking about? What news?"

"I just saw a breaking news announcement on TV. They said that an international serial killer who operated via an internet game for teenagers has been arrested and that sixteen-year-old Hayley Jones was instrumental in his capture. Amber, what the hell is this about? Were they really talking about our daughter?"

His shouts reverberated in her ear. How could this be in the news already? Hadn't John said it had to remain quiet? Had some other Garda member spoken to the press? Or had it been some publicity-hungry member of the FBI?

She took a deep, fortifying breath. "Dean, I was going to tell you about this once it was all sorted out. It's the middle of the night here. I had no idea it was already on the news. I only found out about Gareth Reilly's capture a few hours ago. I don't know what the reporters said or how much they know, but I'm going to summarize this for you. Gareth Reilly created a game for teenagers to —"

"Have them kill people. Yes, I know all that. The whole story was on TV. What I want to know is how my daughter got involved in such a mess."

"Well, she started to play this game, without knowing what it was about —"

"And you let her?"

"I was at work," she shouted back, her control snapping. "I have to work so I can raise our daughter, the one you abandoned for your secretary, remember?"

He was silent for a moment, so she lowered her voice. It wouldn't do any good for her to lose her temper, too.

"Dean, I had no idea what was going on, but when Hayley realized what The Game was about, she told me, and we went to the police."

"So that's it? Are you sure she didn't kill anybody?"

"Jesus! Of course, she didn't. How can you believe that?"

"I have no idea what I believe, Amber. I never thought Hayley would do anything like that, but I realize I don't even know my own child."

Amber raked a hand over her face. She could hear the genuine pain in his voice, and she understood. She'd felt the same not so long ago. Despite his betrayal, Dean had been a good father.

"It's not true, Dean. She's a teenager, and our split-up was hard on her, but underneath it all, she is our sweet baby girl. It's just ... you could make more of an effort to improve your relationship with her, to show her you care."

"Of course I care. I'm really sorry about what happened, Amber. I know I made a mess of things, but I love Hayley. That won't ever change. Can I talk to her?"

Amber chewed on her bottom lip. Raising her head, she saw Hayley and John were standing together in the doorway. John had one hand on Hayley's shoulder. Amber felt a surge of joy, noticing Hayley's body was angled toward John's in the subliminal acceptance of his care and protection.

"Hold on." She held a finger over the phone's microphone.

"It's your dad. He wants to talk to you," she whispered to Hayley. "He found out about The Game from the news."

Both Hayley and John stared at her in shock, then glanced at one another. Hayley looked at the phone, a weary, almost frightened expression on her face. But John squeezed her shoulder reassuringly.

"It's okay, lass. Talk to your dad. We'll be right in the kitchen if you need us."

Reluctantly, Hayley took a few steps forward and reached for the phone. Amber handed it to her, then stood up and went to John.

She let him lead her into the kitchen, giving Hayley some privacy. As soon as they cleared the doorway, he took her shoulders and turned her to face him.

"Are you sure he said the story was on the news?"

She nodded. "You didn't know?"

"Of course not. I would never have given Hayley's name out to the press, for God's sake!"

"Do you think she's in danger?" Amber asked, assaulted by a new wave of anxiety.

John shook his head, then rested his forehead against hers. "I don't know. This might complicate things and make it harder for us to apprehend those teenagers. If I ever find out who leaked this to the press, I'll break the arsehole in half," he swore through gritted teeth.

Taking a step away from her, he consulted his watch. "I have to go. I have to sort this out. Hopefully, tomorrow we'll have Reilly in custody, along with his computer and other electronics. Once Jenna has them, she'll discover the identity of the teens and the people who hired Reilly. Then we can cooperate with the various police departments to have them all arrested. Until then, we have at least twenty-four hours during which those teenagers are going to be on the loose. If they watch the news, they've already been warned."

"They might run and hide," she finished his thought.

"Exactly. I'll send the patrol car back, just to be safe. I think the worst is over, and I know we'll catch those boyos, but until then, we have to keep a close watch on Hayley. I'll be back tomorrow as soon as I can."

He cupped her face between his rough palms and kissed her softly. His lips were warm, his touch calming and comforting. Amber had never felt as safe with anyone as she did when she and John were together.

"Okay. Shouldn't you get some sleep?" She creased her brow in concern.

"I'll catch an hour or two when I can. Don't worry."

"I can't help it."

His eyes moved tenderly over her features, then he kissed her again. Even after he let her go, she felt the effect of his kiss throughout her entire body, burning hotter than liquid lava.

"I'll have a police car outside in ten minutes, and I'll call you as soon as I have any news. I don't want you and Hayley to worry." He brushed his thumb over her chin. "You both get some rest. All will be well, I promise."

She nodded, watching him walk out. The moment he was gone, pessimism reared its ugly head, invading her again. Would this nightmare ever end? She'd read once that crying helped people get through crisis situations by releasing stress. She desperately wanted to collapse to the floor and have a good cry, but she couldn't afford that luxury. Taking a fortifying breath, she walked into the living room, back to her terrified daughter and furious ex-husband.

ON THE WAY out to his car, John fished his phone from his pocket. Silence reigned, the moonlight silvering the neat houses and trimmed hedges. He imagined the people inside snuggled together in their beds, feeling safe and warm on this cool night. He glanced across the street at the McKennas' house. All those destroyed lives because of one man. Because he'd had the money to pay someone to take Maureen's life. Just because he'd wanted to. No one should have that kind of power.

After climbing into his car, he was surprised to see his hands were shaking. He hadn't realized how angry he was about that media leak. What made him madder than anything was that, in all probability, he might never find out who the dirty tooth was, and that was unacceptable.

He called headquarters and ordered a patrol car, giving the dispatcher Amber's address. As he waited for the car to arrive, he called Detective Maggie Coldwell.

"Detective O'Sullivan." Her voice sounded breathless. "It's been a long night here. I was about to leave for home."

"Have you seen the news?"

"I did. At first, I thought it might be someone from your unit."

"I can assure you it wasn't. Besides, the story was broadcasted in America, for Christ's sake! Do you have any idea who's responsible for this?"

"None, but I can swear to you it wasn't me, nor anyone from my team. Hell," she swore softly. "You know how these things work. It could've been anyone — some enterprising freelancer in the right place at the right time, or maybe even Reilly's lawyers trying to set the stage for an insanity plea."

"Lawyers?"

"Yep, he has two."

"That motherfucker." He swallowed his anger. "How's the extradition process coming along?"

"I have good news about that." Detective Coldwell's voice lost its tired edge and grew cheerful. "Tomorrow — actually today, by your time — you should have him in your custody, sometime in the afternoon."

"That's great news." John felt the knot in his stomach loosen just a little. He looked forward to grilling the fecking bastard. "What about his equipment? I need it urgently to track down those teenagers. I'm afraid broadcasting this story may have catastrophic results. They might vanish as soon as they see the news. It's only a matter of time before the story appears in more countries."

"I've already thought of that, so our Cyber unit started on his servers. I have the names of two of the teenagers: Angela Craft, seventeen years old, from Boston, and Antoine Simon, eighteen, from Paris. In fact, I've just dispatched a couple of detectives to detain Craft and contacted Lieutenant Hugo Gaspard with Antoine Simon's information, demanding that he be arrested asap."

"How come you didn't inform me immediately?" John asked angrily.

"It's only been minutes since I emailed everybody, including you. I guess you haven't checked your emails, but I was about to call you anyway. I'm doing the best I can to cooperate, Detective. We're all tired and overworked, but we have to stick together."

John sighed, knowing she was right. If this was to go down well, he needed all the help he could get.

"Thanks. You did a grand job. So, we still have a loose killer in Italy and one here in Ireland."

"Yep. But my team is still working on tracing the bitcoin Reilly used to pay the teenagers. I'm hoping they'll have the other two names by the time Reilly and his lawyers are escorted to the airport." She waited a beat. "They're claiming he's insane."

John scoffed. "Go way outta that! That defense should be fun to crack."

"I don't know. Genius and insanity often go hand in hand. Rodney Alcala, California's infamous *Dating Game Killer*, had an IQ of 170. Stephen Hawking and Albert Einstein only clocked in at 160. It doesn't seem like a solid defense to me, but the lawyers are two of the best in Massachusetts. You'll have to come at him pretty strongly."

"You bet I will. This dryshite won't get away with doing time in a cushy institution, watching TV, and listening to Zen music."

"I trust you. You sound like a real badass."

He could hear the grin in her voice and found himself chuckling. In the distance, he saw the lights from the police car moving into the curve and heading toward him.

"Thanks again, Detective Coldwell. Keep me posted, and I'll do the same."

"Will do. Good luck with interviewing that bastard."

"Thanks."

He slipped the phone back into his pocket and climbed out of the car, just as the police cruiser rolled to a stop. John walked over, pleased to see two of the officers who'd previously been on this duty.

"Good morning, Sir," one of them said, rolling down the window. "A bit early to be awake, isn't it? What's up? I thought the perpetrator was behind bars."

"Not quite." John told them briefly about the media leak. "I don't know how likely it is that the teenager who killed Maureen McKenna will try to get retribution on Hayley and/or her mother, but it's better to be safe than sorry. I'm hoping to wrap this up soon."

"No worries, Sir," the Garda behind the wheel answered. "We'll be here as long as it's necessary."

"Thanks, lads. I'll go catch a couple hours of sleep, then pour more grease on those wheels."

As he drove away, John realized how tired he was and how

off his reflexes were. He wasn't twenty anymore; that was for damn sure. He'd put in eighteen-hour days back in his prime after only an hour or two of sleep. Now, he needed at least seven hours a night to be fully functional — and when was the last time he'd gotten that?

He was getting old; that was the truth. Although he hadn't felt old when he'd been in bed with Amber, desire pumping in his veins. Only thinking of caressing her body, of burying himself deep inside her, had him hot all over. He'd been afraid he was attracted only to her domestic, maternal side, but tonight had extinguished all of his doubts.

She was sexier than he could have ever imagined. Why that idiot husband of hers had felt the need to have another woman was a real puzzler. But then, a woman was only as good in bed as the man who inspired her — or didn't. Dean Jones sounded like a boring, pompous prick with a tiny dick and a tinier ego, in desperate need of a pea-brained woman who would devote herself to reassuring and worshipping him. Amber could never be that small. She had too much personality for a man like Jones. Probably too much sexuality as well.

"His loss, my gain," he muttered, grinning cockily.

Reaching his building, he parked in his usual spot along the sidewalk, climbed out, and locked the car. The two flights of stairs that led to his flat seemed to have grown higher, longer. He wiped his feet on the dusty doormat, unlocked the door, then switched on the lights in the hall. He hung his jacket, ditched his shoes, and took off his gun holster as he crossed the living area and walked into the bedroom. He moved his tired eyes around the small apartment, taking in the basic furniture and simple setting. White walls, black tiles, a black sofa, and white counters in the open kitchen he rarely used. Funny. It was as if he hadn't been here in a long while.

He brushed a finger over the round glass coffee table in the living area, leaving a clean trace amid the thick layer of dust.

The place needed cleaning, but one thing he was grateful for was the primarily cloudy Irish sky. The light was milky gray most of the time, hiding the dust. Shanna had hated dusting and cleaning their house, but she'd done it religiously. She'd needed cleanliness and being surrounded by shiny surfaces and fresh scents. Probably because she'd grown up in a dirty dump, which neither her philanderer father nor her alcoholic mother had ever cared to clean.

When they'd gotten married and moved into a brand-new house, John would watch her for minutes at a time as she strolled from room to room, admiring their new furniture, the white walls, the pristine sheets she stroked with a lover's caress. She'd had air freshener cans in every room, and all around the house, she placed bowls filled with dry leaves, which she called potpourri.

He smiled fondly at those memories. He undressed in the bathroom and threw his clothes in the hamper. Back in the bedroom, he lay on the bed, wearing only his boxers. He was too knackered to shower. He rolled onto his stomach, drawing a corner of the blanket to cover himself partially. Dawn was breaking, but he was too beat to get up and close the shutters. His last coherent thought was of Amber, beautiful-as-a-dream Amber.

"Forgive me, *mo ghrá*," he whispered to the framed photo of Shanna, which had kept watch over him for the past five years, silently smiling at him from his nightstand. "Is it wrong of me to fall in love again?"

A tear formed at the inner corner of his eye, but he was already asleep before it could fall.

21

It seemed mere minutes had passed when the ringing phone jolted John awake. He was in the same position he'd been in when he'd fallen into bed. Sunlight stabbed his eyes as he cracked them open and reached for the phone on his nightstand.

"Hey, are you still alive?" Aidan's raspy voice sounded in his ear. "You do know it's almost ten?"

"Ten?" John rolled onto his back, wincing at the stiff pain in his shoulders. "Bollocks! No, I ... I only got home a few hours ago."

"Ye sleeveen! Solving the most complicated case in the Garda's recorded history and spending the night with the hot MILF. You're flying it, mate."

"Aye, your mum drained the life out of me last night," John said dryly, making Aidan burst into laughter. "So, did Jenna bring you up to date with everything?"

"Yep, so did Detective Coldwell. She sent out a memo this morning — well, last night, actually. Reilly's plane will land at 15:40 this afternoon. We're bringing him straight in to interview. I hope you're ready, old boy."

John's eyes narrowed and not from the light. "He and his fancy lawyers will be in tatters when I'm done with them. Give me an hour to get there. In the meantime, I want ye and Jenna to gather up every scrap of information about Reilly — what his parents did, where he grew up, his grades in school, if he has a police record, previous arrests, aliases, psychiatric record, and financial situation. I want to know everything about this son of a bitch, right down to the size of his cock."

Aidan chuckled. "If anyone can do it, it's Jenna. I have to admit having help from Boston PD made a huge difference."

"Strength in numbers. I'll see you in an hour."

He put the phone down, then pushed himself into a sitting position. He needed strong coffee and a hot shower to wash away this false sense of being hungover.

Should he call Amber? In the light of day, last night's events seemed remote somehow. Not to him — his feelings toward her were just as intense, but he had surprised her with his sudden visit at a vulnerable moment.

Maybe she'd acted spontaneously and regretted it today. Christ, he hoped she didn't. Still, he needed to give her time to sort out her emotions. Besides, they both had a lot to deal with. Better to give her space while he focused all of his energy on breaking Gareth Reilly.

As he showered, shaved, and went about his morning ritual, he outlined the interview strategy in his mind. He still didn't have all the facts, which was not only frustrating but dangerous as well. Timing was crucial.

He wasn't hungry, thanks to Amber's delicious cooking, but he munched on a slightly old waffle he'd found in the back of the fridge, then washed it down with strong coffee. He made a quick call to check that things were fine at Amber's house. It bugged him that Maureen's killer was at large. That kid — whether it was a boy or a girl — was a loose cannon. It was unlikely he or she would come after Hayley, but he'd learned no one was 100 percent predictable.

He texted Jenna to make sure she started working on Reilly's computer as soon as it arrived in order to learn the identities of the two remaining teenagers.

After he donned a pair of clean jeans and a slightly wrinkled shirt, he took off in a hurry, locking the door behind him.

Driving to work, he used the hands-free function on his phone to make a few calls. First, he checked with the Boston PD to see if Angela Craft was in custody, which they confirmed. Same thing with Antoine Simon in France. Lieutenant Gaspard, who sounded unusually subdued, informed him Simon had not only confessed to everything but was also willing to testify at the Game Master's trial in exchange for leniency.

"Of course, the boy doesn't know Reilly's identity, but I think he can be useful," Gaspard said, then cleared his throat. "You and your team have done a fine job, Detective. I'm ashamed we were unable to solve this case. If not for you, Sasha Leon's death would have gone unpunished."

"You didn't have all the facts," John replied diplomatically. "And you're right; anything the kid has to say might be another nail in Reilly's coffin."

"Coffin? You have the death penalty in Ireland?"

John couldn't stifle a short laugh. "No, it's just an expression. I meant it will be another piece of evidence against Gareth Reilly. All we can do is fight to get him behind bars for the rest of his life. I'm interviewing him this afternoon."

"Good luck. I would appreciate it if you kept me updated."

"Will do. Good job, Lieutenant Gaspard."

John rolled the car to a stop in the Garda parking lot. He wanted to check with the NYPD to see if they had any news about Amy Fielding, but that would have to wait for the moment. He walked into his office first. Finding it empty, he backtracked to Jenna's.

She and Aidan were huddled together in front of her computer, staring at the screen. John noticed both had red, bloodshot eyes. The desk was covered in papers, pencils, a couple of drained soda cans, some candy wrappers, and an empty donut box.

"Morning," he said, pushing the door closed behind him.

"More like lunch for us common folk." Aidan's grin was as cocky as ever, but it lacked its usual brightness. Both he and Jenna were worn out.

"I'm sorry I'm late. Have you got anything new?"

"Amy Fielding showed up," Jenna informed him, glancing up at him above her glasses. "We just got a call from NYPD. She returned home last night. Her mother told the police she was hungry and scared, but other than that, she's okay. The department will send a social worker over today, along with an officer to question the girl."

John pumped his fist in celebration of this small victory. For once, the morning had started off well. "That's great news. Would you please call Amber and tell her? Hayley was worried about her friend."

He didn't address the request to either of them in particular and ignored their raised eyebrows, as well as the meaningful side look they exchanged.

"Sure," Aidan said at last. "Don't you want to tell her yourself?"

John shook his head. "I have too much on my plate right now. I need to prepare for the interview and brief the chief. Jenna, please give me all the data you have on Gareth Reilly and everything Detective Coldwell sent you about the two kids they've found so far."

"I gathered more once I had their names," she said smugly.

"It's all in that file." She jerked her chin toward a corner of her desk, indicating a folder.

"Grand job, both of ya!" John said, reaching for the folder. "Once this is over, I'll personally rent a pub where we can get drunk and stay langered for three days."

"Hear, hear," Aidan and Jenna cheered in unison.

John grinned back at them. As he turned to go, he remembered something. "Oh, there's one more thing. I've sent the Gardaí back to Amber's house."

He explained about the media leak and Hayley's name being broadcasted on national television in the United States and anywhere else people listened to the American news. It was only a matter of time before the newswires here in Ireland and the rest of Europe got their hands on the story.

"Christ almighty!" Jenna exclaimed. "Who could be so irresponsible to do something like that?"

"I don't know. Detective Coldwell suspects Reilly's own lawyers may have done it. Unfortunately, there's a chance Maureen McKenna's killer might come after Hayley. A slim chance, but we're not taking any risks."

"I agree. Hopefully, we'll wrap this up by tomorrow," Aidan said.

"Yeah, hopefully. Thanks, guys. I'll be in the office."

He grabbed a coffee from the vending machine before heading to his desk, where he sat down and began to read.

Gareth James Reilly was thirty-three years old, born in Galway, the only son of Eleanore Reilly, who'd taught Psychology to NUI Galway students for more than three decades until she died at the age of fifty-nine after a long battle with breast cancer. Gareth's father was listed as unknown, but there were rumors that Eleanore had an affair with one of her students, an affair that resulted in the birth of her only child when she was forty years old. No one had claimed paternity, and since Eleanore had continued her teaching, it appeared the board hadn't paid attention to the unsubstantiated gossip.

After his mother's death, nineteen-year-old Gareth had sold their modest flat and bought a one-way ticket to the United States. He landed in Los Angeles, where he got work washing dishes at a restaurant. A few months later, he moved on to a gas station, then a few months after that, he moved to Las Vegas and landed a job in a casino.

The pattern was there. Reilly kept moving from place to place, from job to job, never settling. It was as if he was running from something.

"Or looking for something," John murmured, taking a sip of coffee.

Five years after he'd first arrived in the States, Reilly enrolled in Business Management classes, which he completed a year later. While he worked in an internet café, he took IT courses. Fast forward another two years, he moved to Chicago and got a job as a sales clerk in a gun shop. There, he seemed to have found his niche. He not only stuck to it, but he also worked his way up to managing the shop.

John rubbed his chin, vaguely realizing there was a spot he'd missed when shaving. So, working at the gun shop had been Reilly's launching pad. He probably started liking guns, met all sorts of people, from honest-to-God passionate target shooters to shady individuals willing to pay much more than the official price tag for a certain type of weapon. Being in control, albeit in this actually small world of dealing with deadly objects and dirty money, must have made Gareth Reilly realize he liked power. And he wanted more. More power, more money.

It was around that time he'd started his blog about being an entrepreneur, John noticed, making a note on his pad, which was already covered in scribbles only he could understand.

Reilly attended every crash course about computers and

coding that was available. The idea of The Game must have crossed his mind by then. It might not have been a definite plan, but it gave him a well-defined purpose, which he turned into reality after quitting his job at the gun shop in September last year.

John assumed it had taken him years to develop The Game and make the connections he needed to get it going. After that, his financial situation had magically improved. Not his official income, of course, but he couldn't have managed the rent on his penthouse and a new car just from his employee checks. Connelly had paid the equivalent of several hundred thousand dollars to have Maureen killed. Had some hits been costlier than others? Whatever the case, even after paying the game winners, murder was a profitable business for Gareth Reilly.

John checked his watch once more, wishing time wouldn't drag by so slowly. He had at least four more hours to kill before he would have Reilly in an interview room. He was tense, twitchy, anxious to start the battle. As dramatic as it sounded, that's what it was — a battle. John fought for all those who were dead, for their families, even for the stupid teenagers who'd been brainwashed into becoming murderers.

But when it came right down to it, the fight was between him and the creator of The Game. Instinctively, John knew Gareth Reilly was the most formidable opponent he'd ever had.

LATER THAT AFTERNOON, his nerves strung and taut, John stood behind the observation glass with Chelsea.

"So, what do you think? Is he really insane?" John asked as they watched Gareth Reilly and his two lawyers.

"No." Chelsea shook her head, shifting her weight from one foot to another. John had asked her to have a one-on-one session with Reilly before he interviewed the criminal, so he could have more ammunition. After almost an hour of talking with the man, she'd just exited the interview room.

"He dissembles well," she continued. "But in my professional opinion, there's no trace of pathological mental illness. He's extremely cold-blooded and knows exactly what he's doing. I'm sure they'll find a doctor to testify otherwise; however, we'll have him thoroughly tested, including CAT scans and psychological exams, and I can guarantee you his defense won't stand."

John nodded a few times, satisfied with her answers. He'd anticipated them, just as he anticipated the results of Jenna's search. She was digging through Reilly's computer and promised she'd inform John of any evidence she found, even if he were in the middle of the interview.

"Thanks so much, Chelsea. You've given me a lot to work with."

She smiled, squeezing his arm. "Are you going in to interview him now?"

"Yes."

"I'll stay here and watch the show. I can't wait to see you break him." Her eyes glinted like amethyst.

John felt steely determination harden his gaze as he opened the door and stepped into the interview room.

His blood ran faster through his veins while he faced his adversary across the square, cold, metal table. He'd seen photos of the man, but the reality was different somehow. Gareth Reilly was remarkable despite his average features. There was nothing unusual about his medium-cut dark hair, clean-shaven face, or mediocre built. One could take him for anything — a salesman, a teacher, a train conductor. Only his bright green eyes offered a glimpse into the man's mind as he sat in his chair and stared unblinkingly at John.

After he finished the formalities of reading the prisoner his rights, John propped his forearms casually on the table.

"So, Gareth, I hear you claim you're insane."

"Mr. Reilly suffers from a rare form of schizophrenia," began one of the spiffy lawyers sitting on each side of him.

"Save your defense for court, Counselor," John cut him off without a glance. "Our profiler says otherwise, and Mr. Reilly will be tested by doctors appointed accordingly. This is not a tribunal. Right now, I'm talking to your client, who's under arrest for four counts of first-degree murder. That we know of. Are there others, Gareth?"

Reilly kept silent.

"Ye might as well tell me now. As we speak, I have a cyber-crime unit taking apart your computers and servers, tracing the bitcoin to the winners/killers. We already have two of them in custody, and as the Yanks say, one is singing like a canary. To be honest, we have more evidence than we need to put you in jail for the rest of your life. Quite a snag in your plan, to actually pay them," he mused, then scrunched his face in an admiring expression. "But I respect you for that, for being a fair and honest businessman. All in all, your plan was brilliant. You know there are people out there who called you a genius after your story hit the news in America?"

More silence, but John saw a quick glint of satisfaction in the man's eyes. Even if Chelsea hadn't told him, he knew Ego was Gareth Reilly's middle name.

"Do you really want to put all you've accomplished down to madness, Gareth?" John lowered his voice to a confidential pitch. "Don't you want to take credit for your own brilliance? Do you really want to tell the world that this excellently thought-out plan of yours was only an accident caused by some strange chemical reaction in your brain, a genetic fluke?"

"I'm here, aren't I? I guess it wasn't so excellently thought-out after all," Reilly said bitterly. His voice sounded younger than his years.

John's heart gave a strong thud, just as the lawyers started speaking in unison, advising their client not to say another word. But Reilly lifted a hand in a short gesture that subdued them.

"It was, Gareth," John said, trying to keep his features earnest. "Your only mistake was trusting teenagers. They can be easily manipulated, true, but also they're too unpredictable, with their hormones and changes in personality." He spread his hands wide as though teenagers, in general, exasperated him. "Despite all the threats and rewards you used to keep them in line, one of them talked."

"Detective, we would like to know exactly what evidence you have against our client," one of the lawyers demanded, arrogantly leaning back in his chair.

John rubbed his chin thoughtfully. He was a huge Colombo fan, and playing the fool was a small perverse pleasure he wasn't able to enjoy often.

"Well ... Our cybercrime specialist, Detective Jenna Darcy, will explain more about that. I don't really understand all the computer terms, but I do know she has proof your client has been in direct contact with the teenagers who killed the four victims. All teenagers are in police custody, each in their respective countries, and their computers are being analyzed. As I said, we traced the bitcoin payments —"

"Which could have been made by anyone pretending to be our client, for any reason," the other lawyer interjected.

"And of course, we have Henry Connelly's testimony that he hired your client to kill Maureen McKenna. We also have the bitcoin transaction to prove it."

John's voice lost all semblance of uncertainty, just as Gareth's face had gone several shades paler. The lawyers fell silent. Clearly, neither of them had expected this turn of events.

It was all John could do to stop himself from grinning like a crocodile.

"We have you cold, Gareth. There's no way you're walking

away from this, no matter how many armies of lawyers you hire. Our psychologists will test you, and you can't fool them. You and I know very well you're a cold-blooded sociopath, but that's not enough to ensure you a comfy bed in a mental institution. Hell, I don't think you could stomach that treatment for the rest of your life."

"Then why do you need my confession?" Gareth asked, his cynicism back.

"I don't. The thing is, it's in your best interest to be tried and convicted here, and a confession would help. Otherwise, international law comes into effect, and a lot of judicial organizations want to get their hands on you. They want to tear you apart. Who can guarantee you won't have an *accident* in an American prison, for example?" John raised his eyebrows, curling his fingers to mimic quotation marks. "Or in a French one? That woman you had killed in Italy was very popular and loved by the public. You know how hot-blooded the Italians can get. Many of them may think jail is not bad enough for you. An eye for an eye used to be the law of the land. In Ireland, I can guarantee your protection. In another country, your arse is fair game — pun intended."

The silence in the room was as menacing as his punch line. John could smell fear and taste victory. As tension tightened Gareth Reilly's jaw — and his sphincter, no doubt — the same tension seeped out of John. The tension that had built from the moment he'd seen Maureen McKenna's body and the bloody playing card tossed carelessly over her. He knew he couldn't bring her back, but at least he'd kept his promise to Brian McKenna — he would make the killer pay. Not only the stupid teenager who'd shot her, not only Henry Connelly who'd paid for it to be done, but also Gareth James Reilly, the one who'd made it all possible, the one who'd instrumented all the murders, the man ultimately responsible for all the lives he'd destroyed.

John stared at him unflinching, knowing he'd defeated him. He wished Aidan were here, too, but he'd given his partner a task that was equally important. He was interviewing eighteen-year-old Alex Duncan, the boy who'd shot Maureen McKenna. The teenager had been brought in earlier to the police station by his own parents. The couple had been suspicious of their son's activities, especially when he'd bought himself a new computer, a sound system, and a few other luxuries they couldn't have afforded. And a gun. Mr. and Mrs. Duncan had found it in his room, and they had grilled their son until the truth came out. Devastated but determined to do the right thing, the boy's parents had forcefully brought him to the Garda. His mother, tears slipping down her cheeks, had asked what would happen to her son.

"I don't know," John had replied honestly. "That's something the judge will decide. Ballistics will analyze the gun to confirm it was the weapon used to kill Maureen McKenna. I'm sorry, but your son is old enough to be tried as an adult."

John had saved this piece of information up his sleeve, but as it turned out, he didn't have to use it.

Abruptly, Reilly planted his cuffed hands on the table, palms down.

"Alright. But I want to consult with my lawyers first, and I want a deal in writing before I say another word."

22

Amber had rarely been so anxious, so out of balance. Hoping to calm her nerves, she made herself more valerian tea. She was gulping it down like water these days.

It had been after twelve when she awoke. Hayley was still asleep. Amber hadn't slept in this late since before Hayley had started teething, a time she vividly remembered with both horror and tenderness. Being a parent was a hard job, but as a new mother, there had been times when she'd been so tired she was convinced she wouldn't wake up if she fell asleep. She'd had absolutely no help raising her daughter. Dean's parents were dead, and hers lived in a retirement home in Florida. Perhaps that was why she hadn't wanted a second child. Maybe she felt she simply couldn't handle it. She didn't regret it, though. Hayley was the light of her life, even if she had been a handful from the moment she was born.

Distracted, she tried to busy herself cleaning the house, doing laundry, taking care of chores, but concerns over what was going on at the Garda station were never far from her mind.

She'd called Amanda, her boss, to say she would be able to return to work tomorrow.

"Tomorrow is Saturday," Amanda reminded her a little dryly.

"Oh." Taken aback, Amber laughed nervously. "I'm so sorry, I've lost count of the days. On Monday, then. It will give me more time to recover."

"I hope you're feeling better. Work has piled up."

"I'll catch up, I promise. Thanks for understanding, Amanda. See you next week. Have a great weekend."

Putting the phone down, she kept her fingers around it for a few more moments. She was itching to call John, but she firmly pushed the thought away.

He was busy. That's why he'd asked Aidan to call to inform her Gareth Reilly was in their custody. He'd also told her Amy had returned home safe and would be questioned by the NYPD. She looked at the clock on the wall, ticking away even though it seemed its hands moved through honey. John was probably interviewing Reilly right now.

Her throat tightened in apprehension. What was it like to do John's job, deal with criminals, see the ugliest, most horrific side of people, of life, and of death? She considered herself to be a feminist, was adamant about the equality between the sexes, but whether it was that female sensitivity or simply her own nature as a person, she could never do his job.

Could she even cope with it, indirectly, day by day, knowing her man was exposed to all of it? Shanna must have been so much stronger than she was. The thought shamed and frustrated her because, since the divorce, she'd developed this annoying habit of putting herself down and underestimating her abilities.

She didn't have a dangerous job, but she was raising her daughter alone, and she must've done something right for Hayley to differentiate right from wrong when she'd had to, knowing where to draw the line. No matter what happened, she would stay the course throughout this whole ordeal. For better or worse, she would stand by her daughter and support her.

She pushed herself off the couch, then stood in the middle of the room, unsure of what to do next. She was wearing one of Hayley's shirts since all of hers were being washed. The white cotton left a good inch of midriff bare, and her boobs were probably more visible than they should be, but there was no one around to see her. Anyway, the washing machine had finished its second load, and the first was in the dryer.

Craving some fresh air, she went to the fridge, sliced some bacon, and went out on the porch. The cat — who had yet to be named — was in his place, perched on the railing, eyes closed, head tilted slightly upward. He resembled a meditating monk basking in the sunshine. She'd already fed him twice today, just for something to do, but the fat mass of fur never failed to meow whenever he saw her.

Seeing her kneel on the porch, he jumped down and started rubbing himself against her bare thigh, purring insistently. Loose threads from her washed-out, cut-off denim shorts tangled in the cat's gray fur. Amber laughed as she picked them out. He was completely oblivious to her actions, absorbed in chewing the bacon she'd placed in front of him.

By all appearances, he was here to stay. She'd have to take him to a vet, give him a bath, buy him a bed. At least Hayley would have a companion, and she was thrilled about it.

Amber sighed. Would she ever be able to trust her daughter again? Did she feel comfortable leaving her here alone while she was at work? Surprisingly, she felt she could. She was convinced Hayley had learned from this experience, as terrible as it had been, and in some ways, this thing had helped her daughter reach a new level of maturity. Last night's episode had brought the two of them closer — woman to woman — something that had never happened before.

In the light of day, each detail of that surreal nocturnal encounter took on a dreamlike quality. Her cheeks burned whenever she recalled how passionate she'd been in John's arms. What if he thought she was a slut, and that was why he'd asked Aidan to call her? Maybe he wanted to avoid any further contact with her. She'd been too loose, too uninhibited, too easy. Maybe she'd been too passive, or perhaps even too pushy?

"God, I'm never going to grow up," she muttered, absently stroking the cat, who'd finished eating and was licking his paws meticulously.

"Since when do you have a cat?"

Looking up at the sound of a voice she hadn't expected to hear again in person, her heart plummeted in her chest.

"Dean! What the hell are you doing here?"

How could she have been so lost in thought that she hadn't noticed the shadow creeping above her or heard his footsteps? She jumped to her feet, taking in his disheveled blond hair, wrinkled beige shirt, and jeans. The strap of a medium-sized travel bag dug into his shoulder.

"I came to see my daughter. And find out what the fuck is going on."

Anger and worry sparkled in his blue gaze. Just for a moment, Amber felt a twinge of ... something. She hadn't seen him for months, not since she'd confronted him about his affair and kicked him out of the house. Lawyers had handled the divorce because she hadn't wanted to have anything to do with him. It was strange to see him standing on her porch, barging into the new life she was trying so desperately to create. She'd known this man so well, that toned body and those fiery eyes, but if she were honest, all she wanted was for him to go away.

However, he was Hayley's father. She supposed she should be touched that he'd cared enough to fly across the ocean to make sure his daughter was safe. Suppressing a sigh, she motioned him into the house.

"Come in, but keep your voice down. Hayley's still sleeping. We had an eventful night," she added in response to his raised eyebrows. "I'll tell you all about it, just —"

She stopped, leaving the sentence unfinished. She would *not* tell him all about it, only the facts that pertained to their daughter. The rest was none of his damn business.

He left his travel bag in the hallway, then walked toward the living room. Amber motioned for him to sit down, but he shook his head, moving restlessly through the room, taking in the furniture, the walls, the fireplace. Judging by his critical expression, he clearly thought this house wasn't good enough for his offspring.

"Do you want some coffee?"

"I want some answers, Amber."

He turned to her, his gaze losing some of its edge when he measured her from head to toe. Self-consciously, she crossed her arms over her chest, remembering her skimpy attire. It was stupid to be modest in front of a man she'd been married to for seventeen years, but inexplicably, she was.

"I've already told you everything on the phone," she said, trying not to sound defensive. "I don't know what else I can tell you. I'm waiting for news from the police. I know they have that guy who created The Game in custody, and Joh — Detective O'Sullivan promised he would be in touch when they have more news."

Dean stood next to the mantelpiece, looking out of his element. He picked up a framed photo of Amber and Hayley, one she'd brought from New York. It was a snapshot taken at Hayley's seventh birthday party. She was blowing out the candles on a huge chocolate cake. Dean had taken the photo, so he wasn't in it, only a chubby-cheeked Hayley and Amber smiling broadly, her face shiny from cooking all day.

Dean studied the photo for a few moments. Amber noticed the lines on his face were more pronounced than they had been the last time she'd seen him. Although he was deeply tanned, as if he'd recently returned from some exotic vacation, he didn't look happy. She wondered if he and Lena were already having trouble in their adulterous paradise.

"How did she get involved in this game?"

His question interrupted her thoughts.

She shrugged wearily, already sick to death of discussing this subject.

"I told you, she had a friend we knew nothing about, a girl named Amy Fielding. Amy discovered The Game and urged Hayley to join in. It started out like any other typical dare game but turned out to be a contract-killing operation. That man, Gareth Reilly, accepted money to murder people, manipulated teenagers into killing the targeted victims, then collected the money from those who hired him and paid the teens who'd done the job."

Dean placed the photo back on the mantelpiece, his hand visibly shaking.

"I don't understand how this happened," he said, his voice low and gruff. "It's unthinkable to me that our daughter could be involved in something like this."

"She wasn't exactly involved," Amber emphasized, taking a step toward him. "She understood it was wrong, Dean. She didn't do anything terribly bad; that's the thing we need to focus on."

"Getting a tattoo and shoplifting isn't bad?"

"Of course they are, but it's not as disturbing as killing an animal. She refused to do that. She knew it was wrong, and she came to tell me about it."

Dean looked horrified, his lips parting in shock.

"Yes, killing an animal was one of the dares, but she *didn't* do it," Amber stressed out the words, clenching her fists to make her point. "She knows right from wrong. It was an unfortunate coincidence she got involved in this game, but she was the one who helped the police put an end to it. I know this might sound crazy right now, but we should be proud of her. Our daughter is a heroine."

His eyes held hers for a long moment before his mouth twisted into a shadow of a smile. Unexpectedly, he walked over and folded her into his arms, pressing his forehead against hers.

"Christ, Amber, it feels like we're living someone else's lives. How the hell did we end up like this?"

Amber's body went rigid the second he touched her. Rejection was her instantaneous reaction, and she was glad about it. She was over him. She sensed he regretted his question before he finished it, but she had to reply.

"You fell in love with someone else."

He drew away slowly but kept his hands on her shoulders. "Not in love. In lust, maybe." He exhaled slowly, moving his eyes over her face. "I don't know what came over me. I do know that I've made a huge mistake. I realize you can never forgive me, but ... Would you ever be willing to try?"

She couldn't believe her ears as she gaped at him. "Are you out of your freaking mind? You cheated on me with that inflatable doll, now you're engaged to her, and you're asking me to forgive —"

His fingers tightened on her skin. "I'm not engaged to her. I never asked Lena to marry me. She accessed my social media account and changed my status to *engaged*."

Amber was stunned. She'd dreamed of the moment when he would come crawling back, and she would feel vindicated, but she'd never thought it might actually happen. Now all she felt was outrage. "Oh, so she's good enough to fuck, but not good enough to marry?"

He glanced away. "I know it sounds —"

"Like the mentality of a class A jerk."

"Yes. I take full responsibility for that. But we all make

mistakes, Amber. I realized Lena isn't half the woman you are. You're smart, funny, strong ... Sexy as hell."

She couldn't believe the need, desire, even hunger she saw in his gaze as it cruised down over her body.

"I would do anything to make you forgive me, to get you and Hayley back, to be a family again. We were so good together, baby. Remember?"

Before she could react, he drew her toward him and crushed his mouth to hers, cupping her head in his palm, pressing her body to his. She let him deepen the kiss, let all the feelings flood her, amazed she could analyze them so objectively. And she was relieved that all she experienced was anger. Not desire, not love, just growing fury.

Planting her palms on his chest, she shoved him back hard.

"You really think I could ever let you touch me again?" she almost hissed the words. "After you wiped your feet on seventeen years of marriage? After you humiliated your daughter and me? You broke our hearts, Dean, nearly broke our lives because you couldn't control your dick. I told you once that cheating was the one thing I'd never forgive, and I meant it. No power in Heaven or Hell could make me love you again. Hayley and I have a new life now. If she wants you to be part of it, it's her choice, and I'll respect it. But to me, you are my past. It's over."

"Her ex-husband is in there."

"What?" John squinted at the uniformed young man in the patrol car, then back at Amber's house.

"Yes. He arrived about an hour ago. I stopped him and asked for his ID. All looked okay, so I let him in."

An unfamiliar, unpleasant sensation tightened John's gut.

Before the Garda could detect his change of mood, John told the young man he was relieved of his duties.

"Well done, lad."

"Thank you, sir. I'm happy it's over, and the lady and lass are safe. This was a messed-up case, Detective," the young man said, watching him with admiration. "You did a hatchet of a job."

John smiled briefly at the Garda's enthusiasm. Then he gave a short nod and watched the car as it rolled away, disappearing around the curb.

Turning toward the house, he hesitated for a few seconds before forcing his footsteps in its direction. A gray cat sat on one of the front steps. Bending, John gave him a friendly scratch between the ears. The cat was so surprised he didn't have time to react. Before he could decide if he liked it or not, John straightened.

The front door was ajar. He was still wondering whether to knock or not when he found himself walking into the living room. The sight that greeted him registered through a red haze, which he recognized as dangerous jealousy. He didn't know what would have happened had Amber not torn herself out of the arms of the man holding her.

Her posture radiated disgust as she spoke to her ex-husband. Each fierce word made John's heart swell with pride and joy.

"No power in Heaven or Hell could make me love you again. Hayley and I have a new life now. If she wants you to be part of it, it's her choice, and I'll respect it. But to me, you are my past. It's over."

She whirled around, turning her back on the man, but stopped short when she spotted John.

He reacted quickly. "Ms. Reed, I'm sorry I just walked in. The front door was open."

He hoped she could read through his formal tone and feel

his longing to touch her, to kiss her, but he didn't know if she was ready to let her ex-husband know she had a ... lover? A boyfriend? He didn't have time for semantics now.

He had to finish his official business before they got down to sorting out their personal relationship. God, how could he be professional when he couldn't take his eyes off her youthful breasts? He wanted to rip out Dean Jones's heart for having seen them, having touched them for all those years.

Amber looked as self-conscious and confused as he felt. From the other side of the room, her ex watched John with blatant animosity.

Giving them all a moment to collect themselves, John continued his explanation. "I came to dismiss the uniform on duty and to brief ye regarding the investigation. Oh, I also brought back Hayley's phone and laptop," he added, placing the devices on the coffee table.

Amber's face glowed since he'd entered the room. However, beyond the warmth that mirrored his own, John detected an overwhelming load of anxiety.

"I'm so grateful you came ... Detective," she said hesitantly. "This is Dean Jones, Hayley's father. He's here to learn about everything that's happened. Dean, this is Detective O'Sullivan, the officer in charge of the case."

The two men shook hands. Jones seemed to relax when he realized John was a cop, not just some guy who let himself into his ex-wife's house as if he owned it.

"I seemed to have arrived at an opportune time. Is there anything new in the investigation, Detective?" Dean asked.

"Aye, there is." John looked at both of them in turn. "You'll both be pleased to know the case is as good as closed. We have a full confession from Gareth Reilly, and all the teenagers who committed the murders are in police custody, as well as the people who paid Reilly to kill the victims." He reached into his back pocket for a sheet of paper, from which he read the basics.

"Alex Duncan, eighteen, from Dublin, guilty of the murder of Doctor Maureen McKenna, for which Reilly was contracted by Henry Connelly, who blamed Maureen for the death of his wife. Angela Craft, seventeen, from Boston, guilty of the murder of banker Frank Baxter. Reilly was contracted to kill Baxter by Dwayne LaRue, one of Baxter's business partners, who'd apparently done illegal business with the bank Baxter managed and was afraid of exposure."

As he read, he could hear his listeners' intakes of breath, especially when he specified the young killer's ages. It was indeed atrocious, but they all needed closure, so he cleared his throat and continued.

"Antoine Simon, eighteen, from Paris, guilty of the murder of truck driver Sasha Leon. Murder was requested and paid for by Amélie Alexandre, whose husband had died in a car accident Leon was involved in. And lastly, Chiara Lombardi, sixteen, from Milan, guilty of the murder of Paula Rossi, editor at a fashion magazine. The person who contracted Rossi's murder is Alessandra Moretti, an actress who Rossi had criticized in the magazine because of the dress she wore to a social event."

"She had a woman killed because she criticized her dress?"

John lowered the paper, then looked at his two spectators. Three now, as Hayley was standing at the base of the staircase, eyes puffy and wide with shock, waiting for an answer to her question.

"I'm afraid so, lass," John replied. "Sadly, life has so little meaning for some people that they think they can end it as thoughtlessly as you'd rip out a weed."

"So, are they in jail? What —" Hayley started to walk into the room but stopped cold when she saw Dean, who'd been hidden from her view until then.

"Dad! What are you doing here?"

John watched her closely to judge her reaction to seeing her father. She didn't jump into his arms; her face didn't light up with joy. Instead, she looked wary and confused. She took a few more steps forward but headed toward John, not Dean. The instinctive gesture made his heart melt. He reached out to stroke her hair reassuringly.

"It's okay, lass. Your dad was worried about you, so he came to see for himself what's going on."

"Really?" John couldn't see Hayley's eyes, but the frost in her voice was tangible as she addressed her father. "I thought you'd be too busy to care, with your wedding and all."

"There's no wedding, sweetheart. Lena and I aren't getting married; it was all a misunderstanding. I ... I'm sorry." He lifted his hand as though to reach out but let it drop when Hayley made no motion toward him. "Are you okay?"

"Yes. Mom and John made sure I was okay, day and night."

Dean's eyes connected with John's; his eyebrows arched up slowly as understanding dawned.

"I see," he said after a few moments, slowly bobbing his head. "Well, I don't suppose there's anything else I can say." He contemplated his shoes for a while, then looked back at John. "So, Detective." The bitter accent he put on the word was somewhere between insult and sarcasm. "Are you sure my daughter is safe now? It sounds as if this operation was very complex. Quite an undertaking for the police force of such a small country. Are all those people really in prison?"

"Yes, I'm sure Hayley and Amber are safe. Everyone involved in The Game is in police custody, awaiting trial. The minors won't go to prison until after they reach legal age; they'll be held in a juvenile facility until then. Frankly, I can't tell you exactly what will happen to them, that's something the judges in each country will decide. I am pretty sure Gareth Reilly will spend the rest of his life here in an Irish prison. The same will happen to those who paid for his services. Small country or not, Ireland has a very competent police force. I can promise you justice will be served, as much as it can be in any judicial system."

"I bet that line makes everything alright for the families of the victims," Dean remarked dryly.

"My job was to find the killers, which I did," John retorted. "I'm not the one who has to decide their punishment, but I believe in the system I serve."

"You have to, don't you?"

The tense confrontation between the two men was unseen, unheard, but John felt it deep into his core. There was a lot at stake here, much more than met the eye.

In the end, Dean gave a short nod and stepped back. He looked at Amber, spreading his hands lightly.

"I guess I'm going to go now. I thought you might need me. Turns out neither of you does. I shouldn't have come."

On his way out of the room, he stopped in front of Hayley. In spite of his loathing for this man who'd betrayed his family, John felt a twinge of compassion seeing how awkward Dean's hand moved to stroke his daughter's cheek.

"I'm sorry for everything, sweetheart. I made a lot of mistakes. Maybe one day, when you're older, you won't judge me so harshly. Until then, just know that I'm still your dad, and — just call me if you need anything, okay?"

Hayley nodded soberly, her eyes cast down. Dean's exit left a vacuum in the room. Soon, the tension dissipated. Amber and Hayley moved simultaneously, and John was ready to enfold them in his arms. He hoped he didn't crush them too badly as he lowered his face over their heads, laying gentle kisses over their soft hair. He closed his eyes, squeezing them in his arms, enjoying their tiny hands hugging him back. He would give his life for them — the woman he'd fallen in love with and the daughter he'd never had. His girls.

EPILOGUE

Amber's breath was fast and ragged as she collapsed onto John's chest, still trembling with the same aftershocks he was experiencing. He cupped her ass and drew her closer — if that was possible — making sure they both squeezed every drop of pleasure from their lovemaking.

It amazed John every time how hungry they were, how desperate they were to get their hands on each other. During the past months, they'd made love sparsely in the beginning, both mindful of Hayley. She was completely supportive of their relationship, but John still wasn't comfortable displaying his affection for Amber in her daughter's presence. Maybe he was too old-fashioned. They always went out together, the three of them, and he was thrilled. Except he'd rarely been alone with Amber. This was something new to all of them, and they were learning "on the job," as Amber had said once, laughing.

"Don't get me wrong, but I'm so glad Hayley's at school and has all those afterschool activities, like swimming and dancing, and ... The whole shebang," he said, lifting one hand off her bare back to gesture vaguely.

Her face was hidden against his chest, and he felt her smile.

"I understand. I feel the same way, too. She adores you, you know."

"And I adore her."

"I know. She wants to spend all of her time with you. I guess this is why whenever you spend the night, we end up watching movies together or playing games instead of ... This."

She rubbed her body against his suggestively.

Her image grew opaque through eyes gone glassy with renewed desire. John couldn't get enough of her, but it was much more than sex. Even when they never touched, he still loved spending time with her.

"There's one way to fix that, you know," he said.

"What?"

"Ye could marry me."

She was tracing lazy circles around his nipple, but at his words, her head snapped up, eyes wide. "What?"

He lifted his hand to stroke her soft cheek. "Sorry, I'd planned a better way to do this, but ... You know me, I'm a straight shooter. It seemed the perfect time to bring it up."

She moistened her lips, amber eyes searching his face. "You're serious?"

"Why wouldn't I be? I love you. I want to spend the rest of my life with you."

A small sparkle of tears shone in her eyes. "I love you, too. You already know I want to be with you all the time, day and night. I've begged you enough times to stay."

"It never felt right. I know it sounds stupid, but I felt it was disrespectful toward Hayley. And then, the simplest solution occurred to me."

"So marrying me is a solution?"

He spread his hands wide, beginning to enjoy the game. "Sure, look it. Ye know I'm a problem-solver by nature."

She propped herself on her elbows as she lay over him, eyes narrowing. "Oh, so now I'm a problem. You're not very romantic, Detective. You'll have to give me time to consider your offer."

"Sure. Take all the time you need," he said, then rolled her onto her back and crushed his mouth to hers.

"I guess ... I could marry you," she panted a bit later.

He grinned smugly, placing another lingering kiss over her lower abdomen, enjoying each small tremble of her body under his hands and lips.

"I thought you might see reason." Then an idea occurred to him that dimmed his haze of happiness. "Do you think Hayley would mind?"

Amber managed to lift her head and look down at him. "Are you kidding? She'll probably be happier than I am. Although that's impossible," she mused, stretching languorously. Grabbing his shoulders, she urged him up until they lay on their sides, face to face.

"What about Johnny?" he asked, referring to the cat all of them had adopted and spoiled rotten.

"You might have to use some fresh tuna to bribe him, but I think he'll cave. After all, he is your namesake."

"Aye, I can see why you named him Johnny. Just like me, he's old, gray-haired, and battle-scarred."

"You're not old." Amber reached out to run her fingers through his hair. "This is sexy as hell."

He scoffed, but she ignored him.

"There's a theory as to why women are attracted to men who are older than them," she said. "It has to do with gorillas."

"I thought men were pigs in women's minds, not apes."

"Shut up. Among gorillas, the silverbacks are the most powerful, the leaders, the wisest. Every female wants to mate with a silverback."

John raised a skeptical eyebrow. "Where do you read this stuff?"

"What can I say? I'm a walking fountain of trivia."

They grinned at each other. Then her smile relaxed, and she continued speaking.

"As for your battle-scars, as you figuratively called them, each one was earned honorably. I think this is what I love most about you — your integrity, your sense of justice, your dedication." She lowered her eyes for a brief second. "I know I said I wasn't sure if I could live with a man who has such a dangerous job, but ... It's part of who you are, and I accept that. I respect that. I can't say I was thrilled about being in the spotlight when Gareth Reilly's story hit the media, but at the same time, I was so proud of you I thought my heart would burst. All those huge international organizations must have shit bricks because you solved a case they couldn't, Mister Superstar."

Solving the case had brought John, Aidan, and Jenna the recognition each of them deserved, and Jenna had been promoted to Detective Inspector. John was secretly proud of himself, too, although he was grateful when the haymes generated by Reilly's conviction of life in prison began to fade. The press and television reporters had been a stink, following him everywhere for weeks, begging for interviews. Reilly wanted to tell his side of the story to the journalists, but he wasn't allowed to.

The killer-teenagers and the persons who'd paid for the murders had been tried differently, according to the legislation in each country. Neither of them had gotten less than twenty years in prison, though. That excluded the two minor teenagers, who were charged and tried as juveniles. John had to believe it was punishment enough. He'd dealt with his share of criminals, and in his heart, he didn't fully believe in rehabilitation. But his job was to find them, not decide what would happen to them. If he did, that would make him a vigilante, and that wasn't what he wanted to be. It was a constant struggle to keep from crossing that line.

In the past years, his work had been his only focus, which

was downright unhealthy. Then Amber and Hayley had appeared in his life, changing that — changing him. He still thought about Shanna every day and visited her grave once a month. The last time, Amber and Hayley had accompanied him. He'd seen tears in their eyes. These lovely, beautiful souls ached for him, wanted to protect him from pain. How lucky could a man be to be loved so much, twice in a lifetime?

He focused his gaze on Amber, feeling his eyes misty. Somehow, he knew she was sensing his thoughts. They had a level of communication that astounded him at times.

"I know we both have our reasons to be ... reluctant to love again," she began, choosing her words carefully. "We've both suffered tremendously, each in our own way. I want you to know I respect your love for Shanna, and I would never want to replace her. I love what she did for you, how happy she made you, and I know I have her to thank — at least partially — for the amazing man that you are."

He was so moved by her words he thought he might cry. He wanted to thank her, wanted to gush out love declarations, but instead, he pressed his cheek against her palm that lay on the pillow and listened.

"After Dean, I never thought I'd have any interest in men again. Marriage was something I could swear would never cross my mind. I associated it with routine, boredom, heartache, betrayal. Until I met you. I did my best to ignore the feelings you stirred inside me, but ..." She lifted one shoulder helplessly, a smile tugging at her mouth. "Anyway, what I mean to say — and I know this will sound cheesy as hell — is that I promise you I will devote myself to making you happy. Because you make me happy. I know we'll build a wonderful life together, happy-ever-after included. I just know it."

"Oh, hell." He drew her in his arms, not caring one bit when his eyes moistened. Tears of joy were never unmanly. "I know we will, *mo ghrá*. We've already started."

He took her hand and kissed her fingers, one by one. He wasn't good with words, but he remembered an Irish poem he particularly loved. He wanted to recite it to Amber.

"So if, my dear, there sometimes seems to be
Old bridges breaking between you and me
Never fear. We may let the scaffolds fall
Confident that we have built our wall."

Her eyes glistened as she looked up at him, smiling.

"Did you just make this up?"

He chuckled, chagrinned. "I wish I could say yes. But no, it's written by Seamus Heaney. I've never had a way with words. I'm more of a facts man."

Amber took his large protective hand in hers and lifted it to her lips. "That's all that matters to me," she said, closing her eyes.

Don't miss the next Irish Garda Squad novel!

JOHN HELPS an ex-FBI-agent-turned-Garda detective solve another complicated case. Find links to *Killer Score* and all the Irish Garda Squad books on www.MelindaColt.com!

THANK you so much for taking the time to read *Dare Game*. If you enjoyed it, please consider telling your friends about it and posting a short review wherever you buy your books, as word of mouth is an author's best friend and much appreciated.

ABOUT THE AUTHOR

Melinda Colt is a #1 bestselling author of crime fiction, romantic suspense, and mystery novels. She's a law graduate and professional target shooter, and worked as a journalist before deciding to become a full-time author. She also enjoys creating, and owns a graphic design business.

Melinda loves detective thrillers, chocolate, and her ideal date is to spend a rainy day cozied up with her husband and a classic movie. She loves to hear from readers, so if you have a question or want to learn more about her books, visit www.MelindaColt.com to connect with her.

To keep up with new releases and special deals, sign up for alerts on her website or www.BookBub.com/authors/melinda-colt.